Stranger Room

Books by Frederick Ramsay

The Ike Schwartz Series
Artscape
Secrets
Buffalo Mountain
Stranger Room

Other Novels
Impulse
Judas: The Gospel of Betrayal

Stranger Room

Frederick Ramsay

Poisoned Pen Press

Copyright © 2008 by Frederick Ramsay

First Edition 2008

10 9 8 7 6 5 4 3 2 1

Library of Congress Catalog Card Number: 2007942875

ISBN: 978-1-59058-535-1 Hardcover

Poisoned Pen Press
6962 E. First Ave., Ste. 103
Scottsdale, AZ 85251
www.poisonedpenpress.com
info@poisonedpenpress.com

Printed in the United States of America

To Susan, again.
She started it all.

Acknowledgments

I suppose I will get used to this writing business someday but so far, for me, having a book published is still as close as it gets to being six years old on Christmas morning. My heartfelt thanks to The Poisoned Pen Press staff, to Robert Rosenwald, my publisher, and to my editor, Barbara Peters, who makes me write far better than I ever thought I could. Special thanks to Glenda Sibley who took on the daunting task of proofing and correcting these pages. To Susan who scours every manuscript for hitches and glitches, and all the folks who contributed to the development of this story. Thanks too, to Dick and Betsy Anderson, who introduced me to stranger rooms, and to the folks at Brownsburg, Virginia, who were willing to share their homes, friendship, and town.

Author's Notes

The title of this novel refers to a phenomenon associated with stagecoach travel in the early centuries of this country's history. Because inns were frequently crowded and occasionally less than sanitary, by the standards of the day, wealthy or particular passengers would sometime lease rooms in adjoining homes for the night or short periods of time. As a rule, these rooms were not connected to the house proper, but had their own door to the outside which allowed the user to come and go without disturbing other occupants of the house. These travelers would be strangers to the homeowners, and thus, the term stranger room.

The home described in the book is modeled after one in Brownsburg, Virginia, probably built around 1820 and sited on the Brownsburg Pike. Because it is also built against a hillside, its basement is at grade with the road in front and the main floor is accessed by stairs to what appears to be a second-story porch. It, in turn, opens at grade in the rear. There is a building opposite that once functioned as a coach stop.

The Shenandoah Valley, in Virginia, had no railroads running north and south until 1870. Thus, prior to that date, the only commercial means of traversing its length from Winchester to Roanoke was by coach.

Finally, all the characters in this story are the invention of the author. Any resemblance to any persons, living or dead, is purely coincidental.

Chapter One

Though only an hour past dawn, the air was already hot and heavy with the aroma of wood smoke, frying fatback, and horses. Jonathan Lydell stepped through the front door onto his porch. He adjusted the brass buttons of his newly brushed and pressed gray uniform and took in the road below. Cato, the slave he rented by the day to Cartwright the innkeeper, had the coach horses in hand, leading them, snorting and stamping, from the barn at the rear of the inn across the road. The old man moved slowly, leading the wheel horses out first. The coachman held up his long coiled whip and saluted Lydell.

"Captain Lydell, your lodger up yet? We'll be pulling out 'soon's the boy gets us hitched up."

"I haven't heard a peep out of him all morning. I reckon he's a heavy sleeper."

"Well, pound on that door, if you please, sir. I'd hate to leave him behind. There's worrisome news on the wire."

"I'll see to it. And if that nigra doesn't move fast enough for you, why you just give him a touch with your coach whip. I reckon he'll jump to, then. You hear that, Cato?"

"Yessuh." The old man stepped a bit livelier at the threat. The coachman cracked his whip in Cato's general direction and laughed when it made him jump as predicted. Lydell turned and pounded on the door to the stranger room. "Say, you in there. Your coach is fixing to leave. You up?"

The wheel horses, now harnessed, stamped and snorted, tails flailing. August brings out the flies early. Cato held them close for a moment, cooing at them. The coachman set the long brake.

"Well, come along then, boy. Fetch out them other hosses."

"'Suh."

The coach, stage to be precise, had a team of four. They were not well matched. In the old days, before the war, there would have been six, matched and fresh. But the war had taken all but the scrags. The stage line had to make do while its manager, Col. Michael Harman, fought the damnyankees elsewhere. The two wheel horses, one gray and sway-backed, the other an ancient roan, its ribs clearly outlined through its shaggy, un-brushed pelt, stomped and nodded their massive heads impatiently.

Lydell pounded on the door again. "You there, your coach is about ready. It won't wait."

"You'd better open up that door," the coachman said, and fed a withered apple to each of the horses.

"Door's locked."

"Ain't you got a spare key?"

Lydell removed a key from his coat pocket and held it up for the coachman to see. He tried it in the lock.

"He's locked the door from the inside and left the key part the way turned. I can't turn her." He pounded on the door again.

"I've got that man's goods on the top here." The coachman pointed to the vehicle's roof. "I'll have to unload them." He didn't look happy. "Try that key again, if you would, sir."

Cato applied his shoulder to one of the wheel horse's rumps to straighten it out, adjusted its harness, and went for the leads.

Lydell wrenched the key back and forth. "No luck. Say, you don't suppose he's sick or something, do you? He seemed fine last evening when he retired."

"Can't say. Here, you boy, watch yourself, there." Cato led the lead horses to the coach. They'd drifted a bit turning the corner and pushed the coachman back a step. He laid the coiled whip on the old man's bent frame. Not hard, but still painful. Cato lowered his gaze.

"Yessuh. Sorry, Suh."

"Captain, there's no connection between your stranger room and the rest of your house...no window?"

"No sir. Didn't see the need of a window for travelers and I surely don't cotton to them imposing on my hospitality. If they wish to avoid the others in the inn, they may rent my room. If they feel the need of a window, well, there's other rooms and houses. That's all. If I know them, they may stay as my guest. But in these times...well, sir, there're deserters and Yankee spies aplenty. I don't take chances...Cato!"

"Yessuh?"

"You run fetch Big Henry and tell him to bring a log. I need this door broke down."

"Yes Suh, Captain Lydell."

"If he ain't dead or damned near it, that fellow is going to buy me a new door." Lydell applied his fist to the heavy pine door again.

Cato and an enormous black man, carrying a six foot log that had to weigh at least eighty pounds, climbed the steps from the road and shuffled on bare feet down the length of the porch. The slave handled the log with no more effort than if it had been a tooth pick.

"Henry, you just swing that there log at the lock and bust this door open."

Big Henry cradled the log and then took hold of its end. He took a deep breath, swung the length of it back and then forward at the door, which flew open with a crash and splintering of wood.

"Get in there and see what the fellow is up to," Lydell said to Cato.

A pair of legs, booted and still, were all they could see with the early morning light in the front portion of the room. The old man crept in the darkened room. "Oh Lordy, Lordy," he said and scurried back into the daylight. "That man, he dead, Cap'n Lydell."

"Dead? What do you mean, he's dead? He can't be dead. He's asleep or drunk, or both, you stupid nigger."

"No suh. He's a-lying there face up. They's blood everywhere, and his eyes…they dead man's eyes."

Lydell aimed a kick at the old man, but Big Henry stepped between them and took the blow instead. The look he gave Lydell would freeze a man's soul. Lydell started to say something, saw the look, and turned away. The coachman had climbed the stairs by that time and peered into the room. Lydell lighted a lamp and they studied the dead man.

"Well, I don't reckon he'll be riding with us today. You, boy, get that travel trunk with the brass fittings on it down off the coach roof."

"Yes Suh." Cato shuffled off the porch and across the road.

"I'll leave it with you, Captain Lydell. I reckon you'll be fetching the locals and they can figure this out. Key was stuck in the lock on the inside, you say?"

"More'n I say. You can see for yourself. Turn that door around and have a look."

The coachman did as he was told. "She's still in there alright. I'll have to write that in my paper work. Well, Captain, it looks like you got yourself a mystery on your hands. Who was that man, anyway?" The two men entered the room and studied the corpse.

"Don't know and don't care. Wished I'd never laid eyes on him. Cost me a very fine pine door, he did. Now I have to get some witnesses in here and make a determination as to the how of it. Though, for the life of me, I can't figure how someone could get in here, shoot that man dead, and get out with the door being locked on the inside and no other way in or out."

"Fireplace?"

"Only if our killer was thin as a snake. Franklin stove with a six inch flue."

"Maybe he killed himself."

"Doesn't seem likely. Appears he's been shot in the back, rolled over and maybe shot in the head to boot. I reckon there's easier ways to kill yourself than that."

"Well sir, as soon as that boy finishes harnessing them horses, I'm off. I'll be wishing you a good day, sir."

The coachman descended to the muddy thoroughfare, picked his way through the puddles that dappled the road, and began haranguing Cato. Thirty minutes later, one passenger short and a brass studded trunk lighter, the coach rattled south toward Roanoke. It would be the last trip on this coach road until after General Philip Sheridan had scorched the valley in "The Burning," after Appomattox, and after the venerable Robert E. Lee had taken up residency in Lexington.

THE STAUNTON SPECTATOR

August 23, 1864

Mysterious doings. *We are in receipt of correspondence from Bolton Township to the south of us that a great mystery has been visited on that fair city. Captain Jonathan Lydell, Commander of the Home Guard, reports that a traveler resting for the night in his stranger room was found robbed and foully murdered. The method of the deed remains a mystery at this time. The room had no access to the rest of the house and the door was locked from the inside. The traveler is reported to have been a Mister Franklin Brian of undetermined address. He had no baggage and no apparent reason to be in the Valley in these perilous times.*

Sad news. *Reports from Richmond describe the massacre of a company of General Jubal Early's cavalry, under the command of Captain Lane Duckett, on the Covington road last week. Details are sketchy but early reports suggest that a spy revealed the troop's bivouac position to a detachment of Sheridan's cavalry operating in the valley. In a surprise attack at dawn, the entire company of fifty-six good and loyal men was set upon and all killed, except for one brave bugler, Harry*

Percival, aged 14, of Bristol, Tennessee. We sincerely hope the Yankees involved in this dastardly display of cowardice will soon suffer some of the same. Our brave General Early most recently viewed the sights of Washington in his last foray north. We await in anticipation his return to that dismal city and a proper lesson meted out.

ℤ ℤ ℤ

A later bulletin from Bolton reports that a slave, Big Henry, a buck Negro known to be a hard case, was found with twenty Yankee greenback dollars and a map to Pennsylvania on his person shortly thereafter. The Home Guard took him into custody and promptly hung him for a traitor and an enemy collaborator. It should be a warning to any slave contemplating dealings with the Yankees. Slaves should be kept close at night and reminded that any contact with the enemy will not be tolerated.

Chapter Two

Jonathan Lydell IV stood on his front porch and watched as the sun lumbered upward into the eastern sky, red and blurred. He gathered his coat around his shoulders against the early morning chill. He rubbed his eyes and extricated his glasses from his waistcoat pocket. A gold, and obviously new, Cadillac with Michigan license plates pulled around from the parking lot at the rear of the building across the street. Someone had been calling his name. The car turned north toward Brownsburg. He peered across the street. Mrs. Antonelli waved to him. Antonelli, now there was a name that resonated oddly in the depths of Old Virginia. She and her husband had moved to Bolton two years previously from New Jersey, or some such place, and started a bed and breakfast in the old Cartwright House. That building began its life in the late eighteenth century as an inn on the coach road and now, after more than two centuries, had returned to that usage.

"Jonathan? Can you hear me?"

He did not like being addressed by his Christian name. He considered informality an unwelcome intrusion into the culture, but something to which the valley's newcomers seemed addicted. There were forms of address that were correct, he believed, and modern casualness irritated him immensely. At least Mrs. Antonelli refrained from calling him Jon like that odious Wilson woman down the street.

"Yes, Mrs. Antonelli, I can hear you."

"Well, you might try to wake your lodger. He asked me specifically to call him before six. His breakfast is ready."

"I will knock on his door, Mrs. Antonelli." Lydell tapped on the door. No response. He knocked harder. "You awake in there?" Still no response. "I'm afraid I cannot rouse him, Mrs. Antonelli. Perhaps you should defer his breakfast until later."

Rose Antonelli frowned, and sighed. "I will see to my other guests. Will you try again, soon, Jonathan?"

Lydell nodded, and reentered his house.

◇◇◇

By ten, at Rose Antonelli's worried insistence, Jonathan Lydell had tried several times to rouse Anton Grotz. She began to pound on the door as well.

"Jonathan, I think we should open this door and see what the trouble is."

"Door's locked, Mrs. Antonelli."

"Call me Rose. Don't you have a spare key?"

"I do." He went into the house and returned with a large iron key that had to be at least two hundred years old.

"My word, that must be the original."

"When I restored the house and the stranger room, I retrieved many of the original locks and keys." He attempted to insert the key in the lock. "It's locked from the inside and that key's still in there. I cannot unlock the door."

"There's no access to the room from your house?"

"No. When I set out to restore the house, I sealed this room off from the remainder—part of the whole project to qualify for my historical plaque." He nodded toward the signage on the front of the house.

Rose pounded on the door with her fist. "Mr. Grotz, are you all right? Mr. Grotz?"

Lydell stood back and scratched his head. "You know, this is very odd."

"Mr. Grotz, are you in there?"

"Of course he's in there. The key is in the lock on the inside. I'll have to have this door broken down." He walked to the end of the porch and leaned over the rail. "Henry? You there?"

A wiry twenty-something with a long, spiked Mohawk haircut and goatee, both dyed scarlet, strolled to the street. "Yo. Wassup?"

"Henry, get a log or something and come on up here. We have to break into the stranger room."

Henry climbed the steps with what appeared to be a log, a leftover from a cabin.

"How do you want me to do this?"

"Henry, I don't want to splinter that door so just aim at the lock, there, and bang it open."

"What? At the lock, not the panel?"

"Yes, yes. That lock isn't mortised in and the receiver—the place where the bolt goes isn't either so…"

"I got it. Step back, Mrs. Antonelli."

Henry swung the log back and then forward. On the second try the door smacked open.

Rose pushed into the room. "Oh, my God, Jonathan, call 9-1-1. This man is hurt." Anton Grotz lay face down on a frayed prayer rug, the back of his head a bloody mess. Henry knelt next to the body and felt for a pulse.

"You need to call the sheriff, Mister Lydell. This dude's dead. He's been shot."

"Suicide?" Rose asked. Her knees began to buckle. "Oh my God."

"That's for the sheriff to say, but he's been shot in the back three times, it appears, and it don't seem likely he'd practice on his back before putting the gun to his head." Henry, bright red hair notwithstanding, seemed to have a fundamental grasp of forensics.

Rose Antonelli collapsed onto a damask settee.

"Where're we headed?" Karl Hedrick held the wheel of the cruiser lightly and kept his eyes on the road.

"Turn here," Ike directed. "This is Old Coach Road. It used to be the main drag north and south for commercial travelers. The valley was connected by stage coaches up through the War Between the States. We didn't get a railroad in these parts until about 1870. Col. Harmon assembled the financing to build the Valley Railroad. When it came, it ran closer to the valley pike—that's old route 11—and through Picketsville, not Bolton. The coach stop fell into disuse then. Picketsville gained enough prominence to outrank it and finally incorporate Bolton as a suburb."

"Suburb?" Karl said with a smile. "Ike, with respect, Picketsville is hardly an 'urb.' Having a *sub*urb is a stretch."

"Nevertheless. Bolton is an old section, with homes dating to the early nineteenth century, and the house we are going to belongs to Jonathan Lydell. He is Old Valley."

"Meaning what?"

"His family has been in the valley for God only knows how many generations, living in the same house, even. He is FFV, DAR, the Society of the Cincinnati, and on and on."

"FFV means what, exactly?"

"Where do you come from, Karl?"

"Originally or lately?"

"Originally."

"Chicago, south side, down near the University."

"Okay. Well, FFV means First Families of Virginia. That is, people who can claim descent from the earliest settlers, colonial families at least."

"Are you FFV, Ike?"

"You're kidding, right? With a name like Schwartz, what's the likelihood?"

"No Jewish tailors on the…what was the name of the boat? Not the Mayflower."

"Not one. Three at first, the Susan Constant, the Godspeed, and the Discovery," Ike recited drawing from his sixth grade memory bank. "And then a succession of others. And no, they had enough trouble without that."

"My grandma used to say our family was related to Thomas Jefferson. Could I be an FFV?"

"A word of advice. I wouldn't bring that up, especially around Mr. Lydell. He's among those who find the concept of Sally Hemings and her offline Jeffersonian descendents extremely upsetting. As I said, he's Old Valley."

"I take it he's going to have a problem when he sees the two of us—the Jewish sheriff and his African-American sidekick. Kosher Salt and Peppah, that's us."

Ike smiled. "How long are you going to be with us, Karl? I don't mean to push, but you've been on loan from the Bureau for months now."

"Can't say, Ike. My hearing was set for January. Then my boss went one step too far and now he's under review, and that leaves me in limbo, you might say."

Karl had crossed his boss once too often the previous winter and had been put on suspension. As a face saving device, that designation had been changed to inactive duty and finally to Agent in Place for Picketsville, even though there was no perceived need to have someone stationed there. So, Karl, like a latter-day McCloud, worked as a deputy sheriff in Picketsville while he waited for the wonks in Washington to work out his status with the Bureau.

Ike pointed to the house in the middle of a cluster of brick two-story buildings lining the road. "Pull up here. That's it. The one with what looks like a porch on the second floor."

The row of three 1820s era houses, each separated by fifty feet or so, was set back into a hillside. Time and nature had weathered them so that they seemed to blend into the landscape, their salmon bricks softened by the purple of the newly blooming Judas trees clustered between them. As they were positioned on the hillside, their basements were at ground level in the front. Their main floors, one story above, were accessed by stairs leading to broad porches across their façade, but were at grade to the rear. Lydell's house had what appeared to be two front doors and looked like a modern duplex. One of the doors hung open.

"Two doors?" Karl said, and retrieved a roll of crime scene tape from the cruiser.

"Yeah. These old houses used to have rooms available if the inn was too crowded or a traveler wanted more privacy. The home owners would build a room separate from the rest of the house and rent it out to strangers—the stranger room."

The two climbed the steps to the porch. Jonathan Lydell, Henry Sutherlin, and a plump woman with her hair in a bun, clustered together in a ragged group, waiting.

"You can tell your driver I won't have that hideous yellow tape on my house," Lydell said.

"Good morning, Mr. Lydell, Henry…and, excuse me, you are?" Ike turned to the woman.

"Rose Antonelli, Sheriff. Thank God you're here."

"This is Karl Hedrick, Mr. Lydell. He is not my driver, he is a Deputy Sheriff and he will be conducting most of the investigation. As for the tape…it's not an option. Until we've exhausted all the possibilities and the evidence technicians are done here, it goes up and stays up. You do have another entrance to your house around back, I assume."

Lydell, the product of another time and culture, at seventy-eight was used to having his own way, and certainly not open to taking orders from people like Ike Schwartz. As with most self-styled aristocrats, he despaired for a future when people with little or no family history assumed control. His face turned crimson and the blood vessels that wreathed his nose stood out like dark spider webs. Before he could answer, Ike stepped into the room, inspected the shattered door and the floor from the door sill to the body. He frowned.

"The door was locked from the inside, you say?"

"See for yourself, Sheriff."

Ike stepped back to the door. He slipped on latex gloves and removed the key.

"There are other keys?"

"Just this one." Lydell produced a second key from his pocket and handed it to Ike.

"They look different."

"Different locksmith, I expect. The one you have in your hand is probably the original and would date to the 1800s or 1820s. The one in the door, I would guess, was fashioned in the sixties—that would be the 1860s."

"I'm impressed. Karl, bag these two separately. I'll want prints—the usual. No other keys? How did you manage to hang on to these so long?"

"My ancestors were, among other things, packrats, Sheriff. I found a box of old keys, locks, and fasteners in a back room in the basement, under a hundred years of mouse droppings. Those two fit the lock that matched the original so I pulled them."

"Just these two?"

"Just those two."

Ike stepped into the room. It smelled of recently applied latex paint. Without a window, only the lamp on the side table cut the gloom. He made a mental inventory of its furnishings. A small settee stood just beside the door. A large four-poster bed dominated the center of the room. It had not been slept in. There were several heavy pieces of furniture, a walnut bureau and matching chifferobe. Two bedside tables and a delicate antebellum desk completed the décor. An open suitcase had been placed atop an old brass studded campaign trunk at the foot of the bed. The trunk had obviously been recently restored. He could just make out a set of elaborate initials engraved on a brass plate on its front. Several notebooks were scattered on the desk, one on the floor. The rug, on which the body lay sprawled, seemed out of place for a bedroom. Ike studied the body for a moment and returned to the door.

"There's no window in the room. Were the lamps on or off when you broke in?"

Lydell hesitated and scratched his head. "On."

"Could I see that box?"

"Box?"

"Where you found the keys. That one."

Lydell seemed perplexed. "Now?"

"Now would be good."

While they had been speaking, the evidence techs had arrived with a county ambulance. Ike set them to work and asked Karl to take statements from Henry Sutherlin and Rose Antonelli. He followed Lydell to the basement level.

"Is your daughter home?"

"Yes, but she is, ah…indisposed at the moment. If you wish to speak to her, later would be better."

Ike nodded. Lydell's daughter drank, the gossips said. "The stranger room is directly above us, is that right?"

"Yes."

"I suppose it would be asking too much for there to be a trapdoor."

"No trapdoor—no."

"No other access to the room from the outside?"

"None."

An old memory—a childhood memory nagged at him—a locked room with a murder—something to do with the area's history. He shook his head and sighed. Nothing ever came easy.

Chapter Three

As Ike and Lydell disappeared down the steps and into the basement, Karl finished attaching the yellow crime scene tape to the balusters on the porch and turned to Henry Sutherlin.

"You're Billy's brother, aren't you?"

"That's me…the black sheep of the family." Then, glancing at Karl's café au lait complexion added, "No offense."

"None taken. Why black sheep?"

"Well, now you just lookit me, Mr. Deputy. Do I appear to you to be a law abiding, God fearing citizen, or do I look like someone you'd rather not introduce to your dear old momma?"

Henry had converted his body into something approaching a billboard. In addition to his bright red Mohawk, which must have required a quart of mousse to hold it upright, he had acquired a panorama of colorful tattoos. In addition, he'd had a succession of tunnels inserted in his earlobes, so that now he had metal-rimmed, three-quarter inch holes in both of them. The stems of his sunglasses were slipped through each and the lenses rested on the nape of his neck. With his red hair spiked up, skimpy matching goatee, prominent hooked nose, and those wattle shaped earlobes, Henry looked more like barn fowl than one of the Sutherlin boys.

"You sure you want me to answer that?"

"Yep, why not?"

"Well, Henry, I come from a part of society that regularly gets judged by the way we look. Profiling, they call it, so I'm not so quick to jump to the conclusions you just proposed."

"And..."

"I will say this, if you look like anything, it's a rooster, and no, I don't think I'd take a chicken home to momma except she's going to fry it up."

Henry gave Karl an appraising look and smiled. "It's a pistol, don't you think...my hair?"

"Oh yeah."

"So, you're the new deputy."

"Nope. Just an out-to-pasture FBI agent on loan. I heard your brother hoped Ike would give you a shot at the job."

"Billy? Well, I reckon he might have done, but it ain't never going to happen. I gave the Police Academy a go once and busted out. Ike, there, he ain't likely to wait and see if I could make it through a second time."

"But you'd like to do police work?"

"I don't know, maybe. I'd have to lose all this, you know—all my hair and such, so I ain't all that keen."

The two leaned on the porch railing and stared across the street where Mrs. Antonelli, pointing periodically at the house, was in animated conversation with one of her lodgers. Henry pulled out a rumpled package of Marlboros and shook one out.

"Lydell, he don't like us smoking around the house." Henry lit up and exhaled a plume of smoke in the general direction of Mrs. Antonelli.

"Tell me about Lydell, your boss."

"Well he isn't rightly my boss. I work for Mr. Wainwright. He has a dairy farm about a quarter mile up the road from here. Lydell sort of rents me from time to time, you might say."

"What's he like, Lydell, I mean, to work for?"

"He's okay, I guess. Sort of snooty and stuck up, like. He's old and creaky so he can't do much of the heavy lifting, see, so he gets me to come down couple times a week to catch up on the work he can't do."

"Pay good?"

"Nah. He's a tightwad, he is."

"But you need the money."

Henry spread his arms wide exposing more skin art. "Hey, how else you think I pay for all this?"

"Right."

They continued their inspection of the bed and breakfast across the street. A small breeze chased a scrap of paper across the road and plastered it against a fence post. Mrs. Antonelli had retreated into the relative gloom of her building. Henry flipped his cigarette into the street, and watched as it hit the macadam, and exploded into a cloud of sparks.

"He's a author, you know."

"Who, Lydell?"

"Yeah, he's wrote a half dozen books. Maybe more."

"What about?"

"Oh, boring stuff. About his family and how important they are. Historical stuff. Only I call it hysterical stuff."

"Family history, like that?"

"Yeah. He's one of them guys, wished he was a big shot, like a Duke or a Earl. Always thinks because his granddaddy fought in this war, and his great granddaddy fought in that'n, he's more important than people."

"Ike says he's FFV. That so?"

"FFV? Oh yeah, First Fools of Virginia. Yep he's pretty proud of that. He has a DAR certificate up on the wall, too, just in case you need to know how far back him and his family goes. And if that ain't enough, there's them books."

"You read any of them?"

"Me? You got to be kidding. Who wants to spend hours reading about the Lydells, then and now?"

"I don't know. Somebody must, because he's published the books."

"He paid to get them books printed up. See that shed up there?" Henry gestured over his shoulder with his thumb. "It's loaded with cases of his books. He's sent copies to all his buddies and the local libraries and he still has himself a passel of them tucked away in there."

Karl hitched himself around to look at the house wall. "This house is old, Ike says."

"Old and creepy. I don't get what people see in these old dumps. Folks from up north pile into the valley and pay big bucks for them. Me? I wouldn't give you a dollar and a half for any of them. They're all broke down and need somebody working on them twenty-four seven."

"Lydell's family has owned this house for a long time, that right?"

"Yeah, that's what he says. He's taken to restoring it like it was back in the day."

"How so?"

"Oh, you know, like, putting those old-time doors and locks on things. He's rebuilding the slave quarters out back. Do you believe that? Buys old log cabins in Tennessee and ships them up here. He's got three of them out back."

"Slave quarters?"

"Yep."

"You did say *slave*?"

"Yeah, come on, I'll show you."

Ike expected the basement to be draped in cobwebs. It was remarkably clean and tidy with only the faintest hint of antique basement damp. He supposed Lydell's reference to mouse droppings was a bit of hyperbole. The two of them made their way to the rear. A small window set high on the wall allowed sunlight to filter in from the back garden. Its slanted rays lighted a workbench covered with tools in various states of disrepair. Miscellaneous hardware, some rusted, some relatively new, sat on shelves and cabinets, in old mayonnaise jars filled with an olio of screws and bolts, in boxes, and piles. In the center of the bench sat a wooden container filled, as Lydell had predicted, with lock parts and keys.

"You have quite a collection here, sir."

"We Lydell's have always been packrats, I'm afraid. Family trait. There are the items you wanted to inspect." Lydell waved in the direction of the box. "I must say, it would be convenient if you would complete your inspection of my keys as soon as possible. When I can, I want to repair my door and I will need a key."

"We'll do what we can. How is your daughter taking this? We'll need her statement."

"She may not be aware of the circumstances. She is as I said, indisposed. I will inform her of your request. Perhaps this afternoon would do."

Ike picked a few rusty keys and tarnished lock parts from the box and inspected them. "I'd say you had enough bits and pieces here to make half a dozen locks if you wanted to."

"Yes, well, perhaps. I am not particularly mechanical, but I expect a locksmith could. I was looking for a key to that old trunk up in the stranger room."

"It's a family heirloom?"

Lydell hesitated, frowned, and scratched his temple. "I've no idea. As I said, we are a family of packrats."

Ike turned his attention back to the box and rummaged some more. Lydell shuffled his feet, from annoyance or anxiety, Ike couldn't be sure. Agitated is what Ike guessed, but agitated about what? He gathered up the odd bits he'd placed on the table and stopped. "What's this thing?" He held up a device that looked like a small crank.

"Oh, if I'm not mistaken, that is a very old clock winder. It works like a clock key only it's constructed like a crank, instead. That configuration allows it to create enough mechanical advantage so winding a heavy spring or lifting weights could be done easily."

Ike dropped it back in the box. *Not mechanically inclined my foot!* "A clock winder. Odd place for it—mixed up with all these keys and locks."

"Yes, well, I haven't had a chance to sort through all this yet. I will take that and put it in a separate container with the other clock paraphernalia." Lydell retrieved the device and dropped it in his pocket.

"Tell me about the door. You said it was locked and the key was still in on the inside?"

"Yes. It had been turned enough to throw the bolt but not enough to be free in the slot. Otherwise, I could have pushed it through, and then unlocked the door with the spare key."

"Why is the key, the one you were using, so long?"

Lydell withdrew a linen handkerchief from his pocket and noisily blew his nose. "You see, the locks in these old houses were attached to the door proper, not set into the door. You needed a long shafted key to cover the distance from the outside key plate through the door and then into the lock. That door is pretty thick."

"And the key on the inside—"

"That one could be shorter. It only had to be inserted into the lock proper."

"So, even if you wanted to, you couldn't have inserted a pair of pliers, like these," Ike picked up a pair of rusted needle nosed pliers, "and turned the key?"

"Unfortunately, no. The distance to the tip of the key, which is what you would have to grab onto, is too great. You might be able to reach it, but not open the jaws and grasp the end and then turn it, you see."

Ike shook his head. "Nothing is ever easy, is it? Tell me about the murdered man."

"Tell? There's nothing to tell. I never met the man before, had nothing to say to him. He collected his key and went to his room."

"That's it?"

"He was from up north somewhere I think he said."

Ike didn't know why he'd dragged Lydell down into the basement, except to give Karl some private time with Henry Sutherlin. And then there were some things about locks and keys he wanted to remember and he thought if he looked at a few they might surface.

"No trapdoor," he repeated.

"No trapdoor, no secret passages, no 'priest's hole,' nothing, sorry. Are we finished here?"

"For now, but don't remove anything."

Chapter Four

Ruth Harris stared through her office window at newly mown grass. Her freshly polished nails tapped out the hesitant beat to *Memories* as she contemplated time—the passage of time to be precise. Outside, spring tiptoed into the Shenandoah Valley. New growth pushed out from early buds, birds sang their courting songs, and gray squirrels cavorted across the lawn. Soon Callend College's signature wisteria with its lavender panicles would be in full bloom and the postcard appearance of the campus would be complete. Greenup time. A time for new beginnings, new...new what?

Agnes Ewalt, her secretary, stood across the desk and shifted her weight from one foot to the other. Finally, her patience apparently exhausted, she snapped open her dictation book, poised a freshly sharpened pencil and said, "Dr. Harris, you wanted me?"

Ruth surfaced from her reverie. Agnes, dictation pad, work.

"Yes, and you won't need that, Agnes. I just want you to go down to the library, please, and find out whatever you can on Jonathan Lydell—the current one who lives over in Bolton. I believe there may be multiple Jonathan Lydells, certainly there were in the past because he's a 'fourth.' At any rate, I want the one who wrote this." She pushed a letter across the desk to Agnes who picked it up and glanced at its contents.

Agnes had already read it and her expression confirmed it to be one she'd seen, and not one that might have slipped by her or Ruth had received at home. She refolded it and slipped it into her dictation book.

"Are you sure the college library will have something on Mr. Lydell?"

"I think maybe...no, certainly. He donated half a dozen books recently and if I remember correctly, they were Lydell family history, things like that. I think he must want to teach or something. I can't be sure."

Callend College, in spite of persistent and quite inaccurate rumors about an industrial park to be built in the vicinity, endured as Picketsville's primary claim to fame and major industry. Its library, while heavily academic in nature, was better than the county's down on Main Street. If anything was to be found on a subject, it would be down the hall from the president's office, Ruth's office, or would require a trip to Richmond.

"Are you all right?" Agnes said.

"What? Yes, I'm fine. Why do you ask?"

"You look distracted. Is something bothering you?"

The clock on the mantelpiece dinged ten. It had been a present from Ruth's former department members when she left them to lead Callend College into the twentieth-first century. It was a modern clock set in lexan or some clear acrylic material and seemed wholly out of place on her neo-Georgian mantel. In truth she was not fine. The notion that time had crept up on her nagged at her lately. Her biological clock ticked away in sync with the one over the fireplace and furthermore, Sheriff Ike Schwartz intruded into her thoughts far more than she cared to admit. She sighed.

"I'm fine," she repeated and pivoted her chair around, away from the window. She attacked the pile of papers in her in-box and, glancing up, realized that Agnes was still planted in front of her. "That's it, Agnes, thank you."

"May I speak plainly?"

"What? Certainly. What's on your mind?"

"It's about your...about you and the sheriff."

Ruth let her eyelids drop for a moment. "Sheriff Schwartz, you mean?"

"Yes. I…that is we…well the truth is, we were wondering what you intended to do about that…situation."

That situation meant the faculty, for their part, was less than pleased that Ruth and Ike had become, not to put too fine a point on it, lovers. Certainly, they would not admit to anything approaching intellectual snobbery, but in truth, they felt Ruth had become involved in a relationship with someone far beneath her. Curiously, the good people of Picketsville, in turn, agreed with them but not for the same reason. They felt that Ike should stick with his own kind—folks like themselves, folks whom they viewed as akin to the Biblical salt of the earth.

"Agnes, you are a superb secretary and a very loyal friend, so I believe I can speak frankly."

"You would anyway."

"Yes, well. You and the faculty cabal that put you up to this should know that what I do with my private life is my business. So to you and to them—butt out."

"I didn't mean—"

"And furthermore, whether you or they are willing to admit it or not, Isaac Schwartz is as qualified to be a member of this faculty, in the unlikely event that he would ever want to, as well over half the people on our payroll, and some of them in tenured positions at that. So please…no more town-gown crap, okay?"

Agnes' face flushed a bright red. "Yes Ma'am." She turned and left the office.

Ruth sighed again and turned her attention to the papers on her desk.

The clock sounded the quarter hour.

Ike had Karl drive back to the sheriff's office while he leaned back and closed his eyes. He had a murder on his hands and it was going to be a dilly.

"Sometime this afternoon, get back to Lydell's and interview his daughter."

"Daughter?"

"Yes. She lives with him. People tell me she drinks. I don't know. Whenever I've talked with her she seemed pretty normal, but you can never tell with drinkers. Anyway, she was 'indisposed' as Lydell put it, so see what you can find out from her later today."

"I got it. Now, explain that lock thing to me again. I don't get it. The lock is screwed to the door, not set in it?"

"Right. In the past, locks, like the one Henry knocked open, were as much a part of the décor as the door. The casings were usually brass and polished every day. They were attached to the door, not inserted into it. The bolt fit into a keeper, also brass, polished, and attached to the jamb. Some developers of new houses are installing reproductions on colonial style mansions here in the valley and there is a big market for reproductions."

"No kidding."

"No kidding. Anyway, from the outside—or the exterior, you need a fairly long stemmed key to engage the lock on the backside of the door. The point is…" Ike frowned and thought through his discussion with Lydell earlier, "…if the key is wedged in the lock on the inside, you can't really get at it from the outside. So, Henry had to break down the door."

They drove in silence for a few moments.

"Karl, speaking of Henry, what did you learn from that elegant display of body art while I was in the basement?"

"Well, for one thing, and for what it's worth, he is not angry you passed him over for the deputy's job. He thinks you hired me. I told him you haven't hired anyone, yet. Second, Lydell, he says, is cheap, arrogant, and has a high opinion of himself based on his membership in all that alphabet soup you told me about when we arrived."

"Soup?"

"DAR, FFV, that soup."

"Oh. And…?"

"Lydell writes books and is thinking of turning his home into a reenactment tourist stop."

"A what?"

"You know, like Williamsburg—people in costumes showing folks around 'de ole plantation.' He's restoring three slave quarter cabins out back. I don't know where he's going to find any black folks to play slaves, but that's what Henry says he has in mind."

"Maybe you could volunteer. Is he paying?"

"No way, Boss…oh, and I had a chance to talk with Mrs. Antonelli. She's from New Jersey. She made a point of telling me her niece was dating an African American."

"What?"

"Northern liberal angst. She wants me to know she's not a racist."

"But when she says something like that—"

"It tells me that she is, in the upside down way…'Some of my best friends…' and all that."

They'd turned the corner and left the shady two-hundred-year-old trees that lined the Old Coach Road to Bolton. Ike put on his sun glasses. Karl had never taken his off.

"Anything else?"

"Yeah. This might be important. Mrs. Antonelli says that Grotz booked the room in her place, but was more than happy to swap with another guest who had been placed across the street. Apparently her brochure states that in the event too many guests arrive and the room configuration can not accommodate the various combinations of guests—"

"I get it."

"—and Lydell gets paid for the inconvenience. Anyway, this one guy was disappointed. He'd wanted to stay in the two-century old inn. So Grotz said, 'No problem,' and he offered to change places, even seemed eager to do it. Very nice of him she thought."

"Why would that be important?"

"I don't know, but in my experience, such as it is, small things, even inconsequential stuff like this, can come back on you later, like…"

"Like?"

"Like chili peppers."

"Or door keys."

Chapter Five

Henry Sutherlin watched the police car disappear down Old Coach Road and turned back toward Lydell's house. He gazed at the door and its lock, its screws nearly pulled free, and the receiver lying on the floor. He frowned and scratched his head. Henry and his six brothers grew up in Picketsville and had been raised in its history and folklore. So, he figured Ike must know about the first Lydell house murder. Of course, the new guy, the Black Stork, they called him around town, he wouldn't, and so he didn't ask. But you'd have thought Ike would have. He bent over and was about to pick up the receiver when a big guy in a pair of blue overalls and latex gloves yelled, "Don't touch that."

The evidence technicians were working the scene. Henry jerked back and apologized. He spent the next two hours watching them work. One of them, a short thin guy Henry thought he remembered from high school, but whose name he couldn't recall, had a set of tattoos that must have cost a bundle. The same guy had a lip ring and a nose stud. At that moment Henry thought he knew where his future lay. He might be too weird for the police and too stubborn to give up his singular appearance, but the ET's—they understood this new world of self-expression. He decided he would resubmit his application for the police academy and this time he would actually do the work. Then he'd study up and be an ET.

"Great work, there," he said to the short guy, and pointed to a particularly garish orange and green beach scene on the guy's upper arm. "Say, I remember your face but can't place the name."

"Bob DeGraaf," the guy said, "I was two years behind you in school."

"Now I got you. You used to pole vault."

"That's me."

Henry stuck out his hand. "Henry Sutherlin, Bob. So, how'd you get into the ET business?"

"Funny about that. I liked science and the idea came to me I could be a healthcare provider of some sort. Since my old man was a corpsman in the marines, I took some pre-nursing courses down at the Community College. I did pretty good in biology and chemistry, but I pulled a C in A and P, and that slammed that door shut. I liked the science stuff, so I read about openings in this line and did the academy, took the ET course, and here I am."

"A and P? Like the grocery store, A and P?"

"Anatomy and Physiology. It's a course you have to pass with a B to get into the Nursing track."

"Oh. What's it about?"

"It's how your body is put together and how it works."

"Hey, DeGraaf," the big guy yelled, "we don't have all day."

"I have to get back to work, Henry. I can send you something if you want."

"Super. Send me whatever you have. You know where I live?"

"I can get your address from your brother, Billy."

"Great tats, by the way."

"Thanks. Back at you."

The coroner arrived, wrote his notes, and released the dead man to the morgue. Henry watched the men bag the victim's clothes, luggage, and books. They didn't miss anything, Henry thought.

Afternoon sun glinted off the silver of the painted tin roof on the B & B across the street. He retreated to the shade in the back yard where the partially assembled "slave quarters" stood and wandered over to the stack of logs and lumber waiting to be incorporated into the structures. Lydell had stacked a few weathered, rough-cut pine doors as well. Henry pushed at them with his toe and one fell forward. He managed to stop its fall and its lock, its screws long since released from their tight set in the dried out pine, fell out and landed at his feet. He reset the door and stared at the lock.

"Okay," he said, "Let's say I'm the ET on this case, so what do I look for here?" He scrutinized the lock and mentally took a picture of it *in situ*. He picked it up and studied it for any indication it had been tampered with. He knew it would have been dusted for prints first, but…He replaced it on the door, reset the screws in their holes, lifted the door, and watched as the lock fell away again. He smiled and then frowned, and shook his head. Just for a minute, he thought he had it…But then he'd remembered he had to hit the door twice before it gave way…still. He tossed the lock on the ground and strolled toward the street. He'd have to mull it over some more.

Wouldn't it be a hoot, he thought, if he figured out how the door thing worked before Ike or the Black Stork did? Yeah, he sure would mull it over, there had to be an answer.

"Henry, Billy," Dorothy Sutherlin bellowed, "you wash up and get in here for your lunch. Land sakes, I been fixing this meal for hours and you boys just a shilly-shallying around is enough to send me to the institute."

Henry and his brother Billy were the only boys at home, but their mother called to them as though the other five were still in the house—at the top of her lungs. She had done so for over three decades. Dorothy Sutherlin raised seven sons, most of the time as a single mother, back in a time when that appellation did not carry the quasi-heroic quality it does now. Except for her youngest, all of her boys had chosen professions that placed them in harm's way. Billy worked with Ike as a deputy. Frank joined the highway patrol right out of high school. Michael, the twins, Jack and Johnny, chose the army. Danny joined the Navy SEALs and was stationed over in Little Creek, but she never knew where he would be on any given day. The last time she'd seen him he had a Purple Heart and a limp, but he wouldn't say how or where he'd earned them. Jack had been killed by a roadside bomb in Iraq. Every night Dorothy knelt by her bed on arthritic knees and prayed for her boys, that they would stay safe wherever their country sent them, and even though she sometimes despaired for her tattooed youngest, she secretly hoped he'd remain an oddball and safely home.

Billy, still in uniform, punched his younger brother on the arm. "Where you been, Sunshine?"

"Had some hours out at Lydell's. You probably heard about the murder."

"You were there?"

Dorothy Sutherlin beat on the backside of a skillet and shouted at her boys a second time. Ham, sweet potatoes, and fresh picked asparagus filled bowls and platters on the table. Billy and Henry sat and tucked in.

"I was the one that busted down the door. Didn't Ike or the new guy say anything?"

"No, I was leaving when they came in. Just got the gist. So, what happened?"

Their mother gave them a look. "Grace first," she said, and the three bowed their heads while she thanked the Almighty for the day, the food, and keeping them all safe. Henry filled them in on the details, laying heavy emphasis on his role in breaking down the door. He described the scene and what he'd learned from the ET's.

"I reckon, that's what I'll do, Billy. I'm going to give the academy another try and see about being an evidence tech."

Billy stared at his brother's amazing red hair and raised an eyebrow.

"Hey, there was this guy, DeGraaf, you know? He used to go to the high school, and he had all kinds of tattoos on him and they hired him. So, okay, I'll have to take care of the hair for a while…

and um, maybe the ears, I'm not sure about that…and yeah, I'll have to study…and…you don't think I can do it, do you?"

"I ain't said anything."

"It's all over your face…you just wait and see."

"I have enough sons in danger. Don't you go joining them, Henry, you hear?"

"Being an ET ain't the same thing, Ma. Anyway, I thought I had the solution to the locked door thing this afternoon but it didn't work."

"What did you think?"

"See, I was poking around an old door and noticed that the lock…it was set like the one we busted, you know, on the back of the door…I see this old lock just fall off the door and I think, what if the lock was busted before we got there, see?"

"See what?"

"Come on Billy, you're the cop, if the door was already broke and Lydell just pretended it was locked up tight, who'd know? Then when the door's busted open, you just see screws lying around and you don't ask if maybe they were pulled out before."

Billy nodded, impressed. "So why doesn't it work?"

"I banged the door down and I'm here to tell you that lock was set in solid. I had to whack it twice before she gave way."

"Lydell ain't your candidate?"

"Nah, he might bore you to death, or talk you to death but…no, shooting a stranger don't seem likely."

"So what's your theory now, Mr. ET?"

"Don't have one. Wait, how about this? You and me have a contest. The one that figures it out first wins and the loser has to buy dinner somewhere nice."

Billy grinned. "You're on, only we add that Ma gets in on the dinner."

"Done. I'm thinking mistaken identity, now. What's your guess?"

Billy narrowed his eyes and said nothing.

Chapter Six

Karl parked the cruiser in front of the Sheriff's Department and waited for Ike to get out. "How about mistaken identity?" he asked.

"What?"

"Suppose the real victim was the guy who switched places with Grotz? If we track down that man, we may get a lead."

"It's a possibility, I guess. Of course, the killer would have to know he was registered at Mrs. Antonelli's. That's a lot of information for one person to know. Who would?"

"Mrs. Antonelli and anyone with access to her books."

"Yes, and that would rule her out as well because she would know about the change—the killer wouldn't. We need to find out how she tracked her guests. If they were in a computer, for example, then they'd be available to anyone who could access it and the change might not show. But there is a more important question we need to answer first."

"What's that?"

Ike slid out of the door, stood and stretched. He bent over and peered back into the car. "*Cui bono?*"

"Kwee what?"

"Latin. *Cui bono*—who benefits? In books, mystery stories, the fascination for readers lies in the locked room. They rarely ask why in the world the corpse is in a locked room in the first place. But we should. What is the point of a locked room killing? Who benefits from all that manipulation? If you were going to kill Grotz or the other man, wouldn't you just slip in and pop him? Why go to all the trouble to set up the locked room business?"

"Kooey bono. Right, I got it. Okay, my first thought is, the killer benefits."

"Of course he does, but how? That's the question. In what way does he benefit? If we knew the answer to that, we'd be at least halfway home."

"Well, suppose the motive to kill him was obvious or easy to figure out, wouldn't that finger the perp right away? And then he'd be an easy arrest. But before we could bust him we'd have to be able to prove he did it and—"

"He or she. We don't know it was a he."

"Whatever. Even if we were positive we had him or her—if we can't put him in the room—we have nothing. No matter how carefully we construct the case, it's circumstantial. Unless we can show how it got done, he…she walks."

Ike straightened up. "So, that would mean that the killer believes he could be fingered and needs to set up the situation so that he can't be convicted because we can't prove he did it, even if we're sure."

"Short of a confession, that's right. Clever isn't it."

"Yes, and then again," Ike stared off in space for a moment, "it might involve something else entirely."

"Like what?"

Ike shook his head. "I need to talk to Leon Weitz."

"Who's he?"

"Local historian."

"Is she in?"

Agnes Ewalt took her duties as the personal secretary to the President of Callend College seriously. She looked up, started a smile, but seeing Ike in the doorway, let it fade.

"I'll see," she mumbled, and pushed a button on the desk phone that served as an intercom. "Dr. Harris, there's a man here to see you."

Ike could barely make out her reply.

"Sorry, she's busy right now. Perhaps you could come back later or make an appointment."

Agnes had never really taken to Ike and over the eleven months they had known each other, their relationship had worsened, just as the relationship between Ike and Ruth had bloomed. He never understood why. Today it seemed she had ramped up the enmity ten-fold. He sighed and strode across the room and pushed into Ruth's office. Agnes started to protest and then looked away.

"Hi there, Sheriff. What can I do for you? Make it quick, I have a meeting in a few minutes and there's someone out there who wants to see me."

"Agnes said a man."

"Yes. I asked her to have him come back later."

"I'm the man."

"You? Why didn't she…? Oh dear. I'm sorry Ike, she has a bee in her bonnet about you and—"

"It's not in her bonnet."

"What? Oh, I see. Well, time heals all wounds or something like that."

"In her case, I think Groucho Marx had it right, 'time wounds all heels.'"

"Look, I'll talk to her, okay? Let it go. Now, why are you here?"

"I came to see Leon Weitz and while I was on the premises, I thought I'd drop by and see how the college's beleaguered President was doing…" The clock on the mantle started its strike cycle and pinged away. "You should get a better clock."

"What's wrong with my clock? It was a going away present."

"I know, but it looks silly on that shelf. You have this beautiful fake Georgian office and then you put a piece of abstract clock art on the mantle."

"Well, it's the only clock I had that belonged in an office, so there it is. When did you take up interior decorating, anyway?"

Ike put his hand on his hip, bent one knee, lifted an eyebrow, and looked over his shoulder at her. Her eyebrows, in turn, descended into a sharp V. "Don't you dare, Schwartz, you know how I feel about stereotyping."

He straightened up and grinned. "You are so easy."

"Smart ass. You have thirty seconds to finish whatever you came to say and then I'm calling Agnes in here to escort you to the door and out of the building."

"Dinner and a movie?"

"What time? Wait a minute, what movie?"

"Your choice. I'll pick one up at the rental store, grab some Chinese take-out and meet you at your place at...six thirty?"

"You pick it, but no macho war-is-beautiful flick. I'm not in the mood to see *The Dirty Dozen* again. And why is it always my place? What are you hiding in that apartment of yours?"

"It's too small to hide anything. We could go to the A-frame. That suit?"

"Much better. My faculty has enough trouble without you chowing down in the president's house every whipstitch."

"Not chowing down, I think. Chowing down is not the problem."

"No, I guess not, unless that's a euphemism for—"

"It isn't, at least as far as I know. So, you have other problems in the halls of academe?"

"Maybe. I have a meeting tonight to discuss a rumor making the rounds that the Board of Trustees is going to move we go coed, maybe by merging with some well endowed, but land poor college up the road somewhere."

"It was bound to happen sooner or later."

"I know, but later would be better. If you're going to change the whole personality of a place, it needs to be thought through. Otherwise you get...what's the academic equivalent to oatmeal?"

"I dare not say. You may have taught there at one time or another. A degree mill that grinds out academic oatmeal. Nice metaphor. And you're right. Some thought ought to be given to where the board wants this new entity to go, before they just throw open the gates and assume that what works in a single sex institution will work in a coed one."

"Well, at least we agree on that. But you are not on the board and so that message may not be heard." She sighed and frowned. "I don't know how long the meeting will last. How about I just meet you at your A-frame and we skip the dinner?"

"You remember how to get there?"

"I remember. And I'll bring an overnight, in case it snows."

"It doesn't snow in the Shenandoah Valley in April."

"Well, it may just snow somewhere, Wyoming maybe, you never know. Now, go away before I call Agnes."

Ike left the college's main building and walked to his car. Two students passed by and smiled a greeting that barely disguised a knowing look and a glance at the President's office window. His police car had become a fixture on the campus and, Ike guessed, exacerbated Ruth's problem relationship with him. The townsfolk would have the same feelings if her Volvo were seen parked on the street near his apartment.

They could not ignore it any longer. They'd decided to wait, to be patient. She needed time, she'd said. She had a career to consider. And now, Ruth's future at Callend College might be protracted or curtailed. Who knew? She had offers—some very good ones and the rumored winds of change to a coed campus might be just the thing to blow her right out of town. As for his career, he was the sheriff and he was comfortable with that, but he thought of it only as something he did, something he enjoyed, but not something he needed, not a career, not a future. He didn't need the money or the aggravation, either. Wait and see, he thought. He imagined he heard Ruth's clock strike the quarter. The clock tower atop the main building began to bong at the same time and drowned out any possibility of hearing anything at all.

He always parked the cruiser near a clump of old azaleas at the end of the driveway, but there was no mistaking the obvious. The black and white paint scheme and shield on the door screamed for attention. The department was due to trade two of its oldest vehicles and he decided then that he would have one of them delivered unmarked. It wouldn't fool everybody but it might take some of the heat off. Besides, every sheriff's department needed at least one unmarked car.

Chapter Seven

Ruth dug her heels into the carpet and propelled her swivel chair backward onto the oak flooring and over to the window. She watched Ike stroll down the walkway toward the clump of azaleas where he parked his patrol car. Somehow, he'd arrived at the bizarre notion that if he parked it there it would be less noticeable. She sighed and rolled the chair back to her desk. Papers were strewn across its surface. She really needed to get to work. God only knew if the rumors about accepting men at Callend were true, but her faculty needed to be calmed down. What they did not know, but she'd been told, was the rumors included a possible merger with Carter Union College—an all male school short on space and long on endowments. It would be a perfect fit. Callend's enrollment dropped dangerously after the removal of the Dillon Art collection, previously stored on the campus. As it formed the backbone of the school's art department, students who might have enrolled at Callend drifted elsewhere. CU needed facilities; Callend needed financial security. There could be only one president of the combination. And if all the rumors were true, she might soon find herself in the job market. She kept a file of offers from other institutions in her lower right-hand drawer. One or two of them might still be available. Who knew?

Ike hadn't said a word about their long weekend in Toronto in January. Then, neither had she. Was all his talk about clocks just a subtle way to remind her, or maybe just a Freudian thing?

Perhaps she'd read way too much into a simple conversation. She closed her eyes briefly—a long blink. He'd told her in Canada that he'd wait as long as needed and that was his last word on it. Maybe at the A-frame tonight, at his hideaway in the mountains, maybe then they could talk and…She squeezed her eyes shut, hard this time, to hold back the tears. In frustration, she hammered the desktop with her hand. In doing so, one of Agnes' newly sharpened pencils somehow managed to stab the fat part of her palm.

"Ow! Agnes," she yelled, ignoring the intercom, "do we have any band-aids?"

Now, at least, the tears wouldn't provoke questions.

Five miles away, Jonathan Lydell stood motionless at his desk. He pulled the clock winder from his pocket and looked at it as if for the first time. He let it fall to the desk top, then, a frown on his face, swept it into an open drawer. Had the sheriff seen anything out of the ordinary? It would take a fair intelligence to unravel a locked room murder and he doubted that the sheriff, the son of a hack Jewish politician, possessed that capacity. He hoped not. Once he established Bellmore as a tourist attraction, a second unsolved murder would add a real incentive for people to come and that could ensure its success. He'd put a sign on the highway:

VISIT HISTORIC BELLMORE!
COME AND SEE THE ROOM WHERE
TWO UNSOLVED MURDERS TOOK PLACE!

How very convenient. Almost as if he'd planned it. He slammed the drawer shut and smiled. No, they'd never figure it out. He would add a bookstore in the third slave cabin. A knock at the door brought him back into the present.

"Yes?"

"Daddy?" His daughter, Martha Marie, fifty-something and fading, slipped into the room looking, he thought, a little worse for wear.

"Well, I see you're finally up."

"What was all the commotion about? I thought I heard sirens and men clumping about."

"Well yes, Em, we had a murder last night."

"What? Someone was killed? Where?"

"Here. You recall your friend Grotz, who stayed in the stranger room last night?"

"I would hardly call him my friend. My God, he's dead?"

"You spent almost an hour *tête à tête* with him last night. Seemed pretty friendly to me. Yes, shot to death."

"My God. We just had a drink together, that's all."

"Just a drink? You were as thick as thieves last night and I don't want to know what you were proposing, thank you."

"Daddy, I never…he's really dead?"

"As I said…How would you know what you said or did?" His daughter lowered her eyes and clasped her hands tightly together, presumably to reduce their shaking.

"At any rate, someone put a couple of bullets in him," Lydell continued. "We had to break down the door to find him. Seems the room was locked from the inside."

"No."

"Yes. You didn't hear anything last night? No, of course you didn't. You were too far gone to hear anything—as usual."

"Daddy, that's not fair. I only had—"

"Your usual. And God only knows how many pills you added to the mix."

"I didn't…I don't think…"

"It doesn't matter. I told the police you were indisposed, but they will be back later today and want to question you."

"Yes, thank you. Did you hear from Benji, yet?"

"Your son is still in Richmond, plotting how to get rich without expending any energy. He told me, in great detail, that he and his partners were looking into class action suits for victims of salicylic acid overdose, whatever that is."

"It's aspirin."

"Drugs. You would know. At any rate, they hope to get a mul-timillion dollar settlement from some pharmaceutical companies and, of course, keep forty percent for their effort."

Martha Marie's face brightened. "Is that possible?"

"What? Cheat companies out of money because they have deep pockets and insurance. Of course it is. We have a completely new class of millionaire lawyers who've developed the technique, and a legion of imitators, like my grandson, who hope to mine the same lode. It's shameful."

"But it might work."

"Might—will, I think. Judges are not what they used to be. And juries…well. All these new people…no sense of history or values moving into power…the aftershock of the sixties, if you ask me."

Jonathan was on a rant. His daughter drifted out of the room and into the study where a whiskey decanter and glasses were arranged on a silver tray atop a mahogany credenza. Lydell finished his speech to the now empty room. His daughter, no doubt, had filled her head with hopes of a newly wealthy son, who could return her to the lost lifestyle of country clubs and parties. A lifestyle forfeited by her divorce from Franklin Pierce Winslow, heir to the Winslow Sugar fortune. The divorce had been messy with accusations of infidelity, drug abuse, and public drunkenness—all attributed to his daughter. The upshot—she received a very modest alimony settlement and would not have even been entitled to that had certain tapes been played in court. To spare her that, and at the insistence of her father who had been forced to view them, she accepted the proverbial "offer she couldn't refuse." Now she lived at Bellmore in an apparent alcoholic haze, taking up space and contributing nothing.

Jonathan Lydell contemplated his family's noble past, its heroes, statesmen, soldiers, and patriots, the vast panorama of Lydells in Virginia's history, and wondered how it had come down to this pathetic woman and her equally disreputable son. He did not know much about genetics. He'd studied the classics. Science, he deemed a suitable study for lesser lights. But still, all that breeding for so many generations and then to devolve to sad, sad, Martha Marie and Benjamin, the shyster. Lydell had a heavy burden to bear. Thank goodness his wife had not lived to see it.

Chapter Eight

Betsy Blessing's Antique store reeked of dust, old paper, and furniture polish. Ike intended to correct the anachronism perched on Ruth's mantle, a surprise he would spring that night.

"Well, good afternoon, Sheriff. Is this a social call or did my husband, the lawyer, rat me out for running a numbers racket in my back room?"

"I need a clock."

"What sort of clock?"

"Something suitable for display in a neo-Georgian office."

"I have some very nice shelf clocks, two cabinet clocks—one grandfather and one grandmother, a—"

"Show me a shelf clock. It has to sit on a mantelpiece."

Betsy led him through a circuitous path around tables, wardrobes, and cabinets filled with chinaware and miscellaneous bric-a-brac, to a small space where several clocks of various sizes and shapes competed for space on a drop-leaf walnut dining table. She pointed to a clock in the middle.

"That one is a Chauncey Jerome, I think. At least that's what it says on the inside of the case, but I can't be sure. The works might have been swapped out. These are brass and the early Jeromes had wooden movements."

Ike inspected the clock. It stood not quite two feet tall and had what he guessed were rosewood veneered columns. There were two round holes in the face designed to take a clock key, one to wind the striker, the other to wind the works. He whistled when she told him the price.

"I could buy a pretty good used car for that."

"Not quite, but even if you could, how would you get it on the mantelpiece?"

Betsy offered him a ten percent discount. "For friendship," she said, and Ike had her secure it in bubble wrap.

"The key?"

"Inside the clock," she replied.

He carried the parcel to the car, locked it in the trunk with his police paraphernalia, duty belt, gun, and hat, and headed to the cemetery. He needed to think.

Jonathan Lydell fiddled with the top button of his waistcoat. This afternoon he wore a forest green one, a pair of khaki jodhpurs, hunt boots, and a plain white shirt, open at the neck. He'd discarded his tweed jacket earlier. Lydell did not ride, although he knew how. He'd discovered early in life that horses know instinctively when a rider is intimidated and usually react in unpredictable and often embarrassing ways. And horses knew Jonathan. He did think, however, that the riding habit he affected made him look dashing. His ordinary dress, that is, when not posturing as a country squire, would be the tweed jacket or one of its several brothers, dark gray flannel slacks, an oxford shirt, and rep tie. In the summer, he donned a white suit, a foulard tie, and a Panama hat. He realized his acquaintances thought his mode of dress an affectation and, in fact, he supposed they were right. He had worn waistcoats—he refused to refer to them as vests—since his college days—and remained steadfast in their continued use. He owned an even dozen of them.

He lifted his watch from the pocket, allowing its gold chain to slip through his fingers. A practiced flick of his thumb snapped its case open and he glanced at the time. It was well past noon, and he reckoned that Martha Marie would be well into her third or fourth bourbon by now, and useless. He'd required her to be his *pro forma* secretary as recompense for her room and board. She rarely, if ever, earned out. So, as it stood, he'd have to make the calls himself. He closed the watch case, replaced it in his pocket, and sat at his desk, a recently acquired walnut reproduction, which had set him back nearly two thousand dollars. He'd need to address his cash flow problems, and soon. Banks did not have the same respect for his kind as they once did. Years ago, the Picketsville bank would extend his credit for months, years even. But now it was just another branch of a large international bank with headquarters in New York and London. A young woman, with what he took to be a Boston accent, dunned him monthly, as if he were one of the local farmers. He snorted at the thought. His boots creaked a bit and the cracks at the folds opened as he gathered his feet under his chair. No matter, soon all would be set to rights again. He just needed some time and a little luck. The murder could have been a disaster, but a locked room…well, that just might turn the trick. He lifted the paper on which he'd scrawled his proposed signage earlier. He picked up a pencil stub and traced over the letters, adding an occasional seraph to his block printing

VISIT HISTORIC BELLMORE!
COME AND SEE THE ROOM WHERE TWO
UNSOLVED MURDERS TOOK PLACE!

There was his luck.

The phone had an unreliable keypad and he had to punch the two repeatedly before he managed to elicit a dial tone from it.

"Dr. Harris?" Agnes' voice sounded tinny. Ruth pressed the intercom button on her phone.

"Yes?"

"Can you take a call from Jonathan Lydell? He says it's important."

"For him, I'm sure it is. I don't know. Did he say what he wanted?"

"Sorry, no, but I told him you were in a meeting and I didn't know if it had ended yet."

"Thank you, Agnes. That was very inventive. Hold on a second."

Ruth hesitated. She did not want a confrontation. She had just spent the previous half hour with Dr. Antoine Baxter who ranted on for twenty of those minutes about being accosted by an old honkey named Lydell, in the street, who wanted to know if he'd play a slave at his mansion on weekends. "He wanted me to say 'yassuh' and 'nosuh' I expect. I almost hit him. Then, while I was counting to ten for the umpteenth time, he wanted to know if I could direct him to some other boys…*boys* he said…who might be interested in earning a little drinking money. Who is this cretin?"

"What did you say?"

"You don't want to know, but after I told him, among other more trenchant things, who I was, he said he'd call the college and stormed off."

Ruth drummed her fingers and stared at the phone. "Okay, Agnes. Let's get this over with. Put him through."

"Dr. Harris…or should I call you Madam President? I am calling…you know I was very close to your predecessor, Dr. Daniel Clough, you know. Fine gentleman…a scholar, who, I might add, had a genuine sense of history."

"Yes, I'm sure he was."

"I won't keep you…right to the point…As you know I am the owner of, and resident in Bellmore. It is an authentic antebellum mansion out here in Bolton."

"Yes, I've heard of it." Here it comes, Ruth thought.

"Yes, and I've authored several books on local history, as you no doubt know."

"We have them in our library, yes. And thank you for donating them."

"As I wrote in my letter to you…you did receive my letter?"

"Yes, I did. I have not had a chance to study it carefully but—"

"Yes, I quite understand. You are a busy woman these days. Well, as I wrote to you, I am distressed by the revisionist tendencies of today's historians. I believe there is a need to recast much of modern curricula."

"I'm not sure I follow you, Mr. Lydell. What, exactly, are you suggesting?"

Ruth swiveled back and forth in her chair, looking alternatively out her window and at the fireplace mantle and the clock that Ike couldn't stand.

"I think I can rectify that situation at Callend. Dr. Clough often suggested I do so, but my time was precious, you understand. Well, my proposal is that you employ me as an adjunct member of your faculty. I would be more than agreeable to teaching several seminars in history."

"By history, am I to assume you mean Civil War history?"

"The War of Southern Independence, yes, I am an expert on that subject, as my books clearly demonstrate, and I am distressed at the current treatment the southern cause receives nowadays."

"I see. As you know, Mr. Lydell, Callend is a woman's college and, quite frankly, we do not spend much time on war in general and that one in particular."

"I find that quite remarkable."

"Now, if you were to structure a seminar on the role women played in that tragedy, I might be able to work something out next semester."

"Women? Tragedy? Dr. Harris, I am dismayed. The war was—"

"A terrible time, filled with wholly unnecessary death and suffering, because the politicians in the south and the politicians in the north could not bring themselves to sit down and work out a sensible compromise. All of them were men, naturally. Even your venerated Robert E. Lee knew that slavery must end. Only his loyalty to the Commonwealth, rather than to his country, prevented him from commanding the union forces. But, of course, you already knew that." Ruth thought she heard Lydell sputtering on the other end. "Mr. Lydell, are you there?"

"I will have a word with Dr. Clough and some of my friends on the Board of Trustees."

"Yes, do that. And if you change your mind about the women in the war seminar, do call. Oh, and Mr. Lydell?"

"Yes?"

"My faculty, whether black or white or in between, are not available to play at servants, yeomen, or whatever you have in mind, on your plantation, and certainly not for profit or the amusement of tourists."

The line clicked dead.

There, she thought, that ought to be the end of that.

Chapter Nine

Ike looked at his watch. Ten minutes had passed since he'd last checked. If Ruth didn't appear in another twenty, he'd call it a night. Her faculty meeting may have run over—as if she didn't have enough on her plate. Real or not, the concept that Callend College might admit men, after a century or more as an all-woman's college, would agitate even the coolest faculty member. He stood, paced, and looked at his watch again. It would take her an hour to drive from town. He glanced once more through the glass slider that faced the driveway. She hadn't been out to the A-frame that often. She had her cell phone. She would call. Though he did not really want any, he made a pot of coffee. While the coffee maker hissed and clunked, he turned to consider Ruth's clock.

He removed the bubble wrap, checked that the key was inside the case, and placed it on the breakfast table. He stepped back. He had second thoughts about winding it. What if it bonged away all night? He didn't know how he would manage that. If you are not used to a noise in the night, it could keep you from sleep for hours. He'd had that problem with a dripping faucet once, and a ticking, chiming clock, he reckoned would be at least as distracting. As he busied himself gathering up the wrappings, he heard a car approach and saw the sweep of headlights against the kitchen wall. Ruth. He strolled to the door and slid it open to greet her.

"Hi," she said as she pushed past him. "You have booze, I assume."

"Yes ma'am, I do. I take it that means you would like a drink, wine, beer, or the hard stuff?"

"Stiff one, that's all I care about."

"I have some moonshine, a little local white lightning, if you want a real jolt. I don't recommend it, though. Knock you on your rear if you're not careful."

"Sounds good to me, but it might get in the way of the evening's agenda. Better make it a light scotch."

Ike dropped ice cubes in two glasses and poured two fingers of scotch in one, added a splash of water, and fixed himself a gin and tonic in the other. "What happened to your hand?"

"I stabbed it with a pencil."

"Suicide attempt gone wrong?"

"Don't be smart, Schwartz. It hurt like hell."

"You'll have a little tattoo when that heals."

"What do you mean, I'll have a tattoo?"

"Well, usually when you push a pencil into your skin like that, some of the graphite is left behind and it shows up as a blue dot, a tattoo."

"Great. I'll have something in common with my students at last."

"Your students have tattoos?"

"'You wouldn't believe."

"Where?"

"As I said, you wouldn't believe. The school's nurse tells me there isn't a single spot on a woman's anatomy where she hasn't seen one or more."

"You don't have one?"

"Is there any part of me you haven't seen?"

"Well…"

"You see any tattoos?"

"No, but it's been nearly a week."

"That can be corrected. But first, I need this drink and we need to talk."

Ruth hoisted her glass, drank, and absently started popping the bubble wrap next to the clock. The aroma of freshly brewed coffee filled the room.

"You made coffee?"

"Trying to stay busy. How'd your meeting go? Any substance to the rumors?"

Ruth took a long sip of her drink, swirled the ice cubes around, and shook her head.

"Who knows? I mean where there is smoke there's fire, right? I don't believe I said that. Any cliché in a storm, I guess. Actually, the head of the chemistry department said that at least forty times. It must have stuck in my head like a tune will, if you hear it often enough."

"I got stuck on *A Pretty Girl is like a Melody* one year and it took three months to get it out."

"How'd you do it?"

"Cher."

"You replaced it with one of her songs?"

"No, she appeared in a fantasy which stuck in my mind just as long, but I didn't mind that so much. Speaking of tattoos…see, she would come into the room wearing this diaphanous…"

"I don't think I want to share that one, thanks. Anyway, since the rumors are coming from several sources, the guessing is this time they're for real."

"If they are, what happens to you, Madam President?"

"Good question." She handed him her now empty glass. "Refill?"

Ike fixed them each a second drink, being careful to go light on the liquor. They had some ground to cover first, and Callend going coed, might or might not be a part of it. He put the new drink in front of her. She snapped another row of blisters on the wrap.

"I won't know for another month, I don't think. Board meeting is in May and I should have some sort of action before then. Lord, was it only last year that bunch shut down the art storage facility and we lost the Dillon Art Collection?"

"Yes. The end of an era for the college, and the beginning of one for us. Am I sounding like Sixty Minutes?"

"Not that good."

"Sorry. But it's a fact. If we hadn't had to work together on that who knows…"

"I know. Okay. So, is that new?" She waved her hand in the direction of the clock.

"It's for you, for your office."

"It's very nice, but I already have a clock in my office."

"I know, that plastic thing, it needs to be moved to a different venue. This one will look much better on the mantle of that fireplace you have."

She stood and bent forward to contemplate the clock. "It's a present?"

"Yes. For your office."

She studied the clock for a moment more, straightened up, and a half smile lit her face. "But a present for me?"

"Yes, of course."

"You realize this is the first present you've ever given me?"

"No, that's not right. I bought you a Christmas present."

"That doesn't count. Christmas and birthday presents are obligatory. This is the first time you bought me something as just a present. I'm touched."

"Down here, we would say 'teched' as in—she's a little teched in the head."

"Can the rustic comedy. I mean it. I am. Thank you." She leaned over and kissed him on the cheek. Ike saw what might have been tears in her eyes. She'd turned her head away too quickly to be sure.

"You're welcome," he said, and waited. "Are you crying?"

She shook her head. "I don't know what's wrong with me lately. Ever since your mother died, I get these mopey moments. I start thinking about her, and us, and the gates just open. What's wrong with me, Ike?"

Ike's mother had been only a short interlude in Ruth's life. Close to death when they met, the force of her personality, and her fierce love for her son, had moved Ruth far more than she'd expected. She took the death hard—perhaps harder than Ike. He pushed a box of paper napkins toward her, the nearest thing he had to tissues. She took one, gave him a weak smile, and blew her nose. Ike started at the noise. She honked like a man.

"It's the pressure, I guess," he said. He didn't know what he meant by that but it seemed to be the thing to say. It wasn't.

"Pressure," she snapped. "I live with that twenty-four seven. Not pressure." She helped herself to another napkin and wiped her eyes.

"Sorry," he said. "It occurred to me that the merger, or coed, or whatever, business has put an extra strain on your system which is, as everyone knows, already at capacity. Sometimes that's all it takes."

"You know about those things? You aren't going to do a recitation on PMS next, are you?"

Ike raised his hands in surrender. He knew he was right but he also knew enough not to press it. "I went to the cemetery this afternoon."

"To visit your mom?"

"To visit them all. Eloise, for a moment."

"She's not still…?"

"No, I just like to stop by, you know. Eloise and I weren't married that long before she was killed and ever since you…well, memories fade. No, I went to put some flowers on my mother's grave. It will be another ten months before we can place a headstone. I just figured I needed to get connected to what happened in Toronto, and since she started all that, in a way, I figured I'd…I don't know, check in or something."

In January, Ruth and Ike spent part of a week in Toronto. She to give a speech, he to take a break, a short vacation, after the upheaval in his department that left his main deputy dead, and a vacancy yet to be filled. They'd used the time to talk—about themselves and their future, or, more precisely, their apparent lack of one.

"You told me, however it went, you'd be okay," she said, eyes averted. "That put it all on me."

"Not all on you. It's just that I don't want to be the one to put a crimp in your career, Ruth."

"What about your career?"

"I don't have a career, I have a job. I like it, but I can walk away anytime."

"Walk away…you're sure of that?"

"Yes…No…I don't know. But I would if I needed to."

"Excuse me?"

"I would not let being sheriff of Picketsville keep us apart, not for any length of time, anyway."

"Wow. So, if I accepted an offer in Berkeley, or Chicago, or…somewhere, you'd be okay with that?"

Would he? For the first time in his adult life, Ike felt he was making a positive contribution to something. True, Picketsville was not the "Big Apple," and rural law enforcement hardly rated as glamorous, but he liked the people, the town, and he did not want to leave. He routinely trashed any feelers he received, for jobs elsewhere, and ignored his father's chronic nagging that he should run for Attorney General.

"Yes," he said, and having said it, hoped he meant it.

She stared into his eyes. Then, voice barely audible, "You'd follow me?"

"Yes," he repeated and then, before he could stop, added, "I love you."

She snatched the whole box of napkins from him and tore out a handful.

"That's another first, Ike." He started to say something, but she put her fingers over his lips. "No more, not now."

They sat in silence a moment, mentally regrouping. He cleared his throat. Time to change the subject. "The clock," he said, "is a sort of reminder. You wanted time, and I thought I'd give you some…literally." She nodded her head and blew her nose.

"Don't mind me." She wiped her eyes and balled up the napkin.

Ike opened the case and withdrew the key. "You wind it with this," he said, and then felt like a fool. Of course you wind it with the key.

"Show me."

He attempted to insert the key in a hole in the clock's face. It didn't fit. He tried the second with the same results.

"Betsy must have given me the wrong key."

"I guess you just bought yourself a little more time."

"Don't need it." He replaced the key, closed the front panel and turned back to her. "Will you mar—" She threw up her hands and silenced him.

"Not yet. Not tonight, Ike, please."

"When?"

"It's enough that I know."

Ike stood, and dimmed the lights, letting the full panorama of the down slope at the back of the house come into view. A half moon lighted the hillside. Three miles away and a thousand feet down, headlights sliced through the night on I-81, people heading north-east or south-west late at night. Good people and bad, lost in the darkness. Judas trees, which in the daylight would have provided a splash of magenta against the white of the adjacent dogwoods, were muted to shades of gray. They stood, side-by-side staring into the distance.

"Movie time?" he asked.

"What did you get?"

"*For whom the Bell Tolls,* Gary Cooper, Ingrid Bergman—"

"You rented *For Whom the Bell Tolls?*"

"It's one of my collection. An old VCR."

"You collect old movies?"

"A few classics."

"You are a many faceted gem, Schwartz. Who'd a thought? The movie has a sad ending, doesn't it?"

"Roberto waits at the machine gun while Pilar, Maria, and the others flee, yes."

"I'm not up for sad, can we take a pass on that?"

"Sure."

"Are you ready?" she murmured.

Ike thought a moment. Were they still in the tag end of their earlier conversation or something new? "Ready for what?"

"Ready to check me for tattoos."

Chapter Ten

Sam toyed with the food on her plate. She didn't eat much ever, and tonight, not at all. Karl, oblivious of her silence and lack of appetite, attacked his crêpes as if he hadn't eaten in a week. In truth, Sam did not care for French cuisine, real, or the genre offered at *Chez François*, Picketsville's "other restaurant." Most of the townspeople ate at the Crossroads Diner, if they ate out at a restaurant. Fast food, out on the highway, had replaced most of the townsfolk's culinary needs beyond the Crossroads. The nearest alternative eateries were north to Lexington or south to Roanoke. *Le Chateau*, a pricy tax write-off for a local orthodontist, did serve excellent food in a location up in the mountains, but it was not well known nor often frequented by anyone from the town.

The faculty from the college rarely, if ever, patronized the diner, could not find or afford *Le Chateau,* and contented themselves with trips north or south. They considered it to be one of many sacrifices they made in their efforts to bring a measure of culture to the area. The townspeople, for their part, thought the college folks were jerks. Too stupid to realize what an easy berth they had compared to, say, farmers, mechanics, over the road truckers or, indeed, anyone who actually worked for a living.

The owner of *Chez François* believed his restaurant would eventually provide a meeting place, a neutral ground, if you will, where these two disparate peoples could break bread together, meet and mingle. He envisioned a melding of cultures, and something like a new enlightenment emerging. But bad cuisine is bad cuisine, irrespective of whatever higher calling one may have, and the townspeople were not about to pay four times the minimum hourly wage for rubbery baked chicken even if it was called "cocoa van."

Karl paused and looked up. "What's up with you, Sam?"

"Up? Nothing's up with me."

Did she sound short? She didn't mean to. She forked through the greenish tangle on her plate. The menu had called it *épinard en crème* and that sounded good. It wasn't. Spinach, creamed or otherwise, never rated very high on her vegetable hit parade. She felt cheated. She grew up in a part of the country where meals consisted of meat, broiled, boiled, or roasted, and starches, always boiled. Green things were a dietary obligation usually ignored. She put her fork down and planned dessert. *Chez François* might be a bust at anything except roast beef, but M. Francois did do desserts.

"You look, like, faraway or something."

"Oh. I'm sorry. It's just...I really don't like spinach...and, um...when is your hearing?"

The hearing was, in fact, what was *up* with Sam. For the last three and a half months, Karl had been on temporary assignment in Picketsville. She feared he might be just a temporary assignment to her as well. And that could change soon. If the board cleared him, he might be heading back to DC. That would mean, at best, a return to the commuter relationship they'd had before the big blow-up with his boss. That would be a step backward. And he might be transferred to almost anywhere, and that seemed more likely, given the circumstances.

"I should know in a week or so," he said, and sipped his wine. The label featured a frog and the words Jeremiah. "Nice wine."

The room seemed warm, close. She could almost smell fermented grapes. Wine made her sneeze and she was afraid she would do so at any moment.

"Is going back so important?"

He looked at her. A deep V formed between his eyes.

"Sam, all I've ever wanted was the FBI. Other kids in my neighborhood were heading to the carwash or jail, but not me. I worked. I studied. I hoped I would find a way. The lucky ones, like me, who could play a sport, got their ticket out of the neighborhood."

"You played basketball at college, I know, but…"

"It was my ticket out. There were kids in my neighborhood who were better than me, you know? They could sink a three pointer from outside the line with their eyes closed, but they stayed back."

"If they were that good…"

"Good at b-ball. Not good at life. They couldn't get past all the stuff out there, petty crime, and gangs. I could have been part of it, you know. It was there—the drugs, the scams, the players, and the easy money."

"But not you."

"No, not me. If you have a record, most coaches won't recruit you. I say most. There are still some real felons in schools, here and there, but coaches won't take a chance any more. Too many 'spoiled athlete' stories in the news. Too many brushes with the law, rapes, robberies, bribes, DUI, you know. But, like I said, FBI is all I ever wanted." He mopped a crust of bread through the dark sauce on his plate and bit off an end.

"Those guys I played ball with? They went to class only often enough to get by, to stay eligible. They spent their time on the hardboards shooting, passing, dribbling, and more shooting, getting ready to be drafted by the NBA. Some of them were at the university for six or seven years. As long as they had some eligibility left, they stayed and played, hoping some NBA scout would catch their act, so to speak. I was in the books, not shooting threes, shooting for A's. FBI is tough. They don't take dummies in the Bureau."

"No, of course not. Were you drafted?"

"Me? No, no way. I was in class or in the library, not working on my hook shot, not shooting one hundred foul shots a day. No, I played just well enough to stay on the team, ride the bench, to keep the scholarship."

"If you had gone with those other guys and practiced what then?"

"Who knows? I might have made it. Might have been picked in the late rounds and then…there was this guy, Ducky, from my old neighborhood and he—"

"Ducky?"

"Yeah, he walked funny, waddled, so we called Duck, Ducky. Well, he was a couple of years ahead of me and he was drafted in a late round. His agent worked a deal for him and all of a sudden, Ducky is a millionaire. Or so he thinks. He goes out and buys a pimped out Beemer, two carat diamond ear studs, and girls. He played for five years in the NBA for four different teams. He was good, but not quite good enough, see. There are thousands of kids who can shoot and play and who are hungry. One percent will make it to the NBA and stay there. One percent. You have to be better than all of the hungry kids who show up every summer and try to take your job away. Ducky had too much, too soon. You don't come out of the south side with ten cents in your pocket and a pair of one hundred dollar basketball shoes you got 'from a friend' and then land a million or two, guaranteed, and not screw up somewhere along the way. If you can recover and fend off the hungry kids, you'll be okay. But Ducky…"

"He couldn't?"

"Out on his rear end, owed child support to three different women, and had a thousand dollar a day coke habit."

"But the money?"

"Gone. No play, no pay. He's doing time in Joliet."

The conversation had drifted away from where Sam had hoped it would go. Karl pushed his plate away and signaled the waiter.

"I'd like dessert," she said. She couldn't be sure if he would be asking for the check and she wasn't finished.

"Oh? Well, sure." The waiter brought them dessert menus.

"So, if Ike asked you to stay on as a deputy sheriff, to take Whaite Billingsley's place, would you do it?" Whaite Billingsley, Ike's former second in command, had been run off the road by an idiot in a snow storm. A good man, a fair, hard-working cop, gone but not forgotten. His slot had not yet been filled.

"Well, he hasn't asked and he won't."

"Won't? Why?"

"Sam, you are a sweet thing. But you come from another world, I think."

"What do you mean?"

"Look at me, Sam. What do you see?"

"I see a man who is good and loyal..."

"And black."

"You're not...well, I mean..."

Karl smiled. "I know what you mean, Honey. You're wonderfully color blind, though there are days when I wonder if I was really black, instead of what...beige...? Whether you'd ever have looked at me twice."

"I would have."

"Yeah, I think you would. But everybody else in this town don't see it the same way. We are south of the Mason-Dixon Line, Sam. Folks around here are still not quite past Brown vs. the Board of Education."

"I don't believe that."

"You see that old couple get up and leave when we walked in?"

"No. Well, maybe they were finished."

"I don't think they had even ordered, and then there are the notes I get with the mail."

"What notes? I don't remember any notes."

"That's because I intercept them. They're not nice. They want me to know that some of the good people in the town do not approve of you and me, and they intend to save you, a nice white girl, from this black devil."

"That's what they say?"

"That's the nice version. See, even if Ike were foolish enough to offer, what kind of life would I have as a black sheriff? You should have seen that guy, Lydell. He about called me boy. When Ike said I would be leading the investigation, he near fainted on the spot."

Sam's heart fell. She had never even considered the possibility that he wouldn't stay if the circumstances were right. She had planned to urge Ike to keep Karl and thought the only obstacle would be his FBI career. Now, all that seemed far away. She pinched her nose to stop the sneeze and spooned her flan.

Chapter Eleven

Essie Falco blew on her cup of morning coffee. While she faced her computer screen and radio paraphernalia, she kept Karl Hedrick in the corner of her eye. She didn't trust him. She couldn't say why, exactly. It wasn't because he was a black man, she was pretty sure of that. After all, Charlie Picket had been in the sheriff's office since before Ike even, and she didn't have trouble with him. Of course, when Ike took over, he gave Charlie a full duty assignment. Before then, Charlie had been assigned to the south end of town which was where most of the African-American families lived, at least until lately. Some of the older folks didn't cotton to Charlie's being in their part of town now-a-days, especially out in Bolton, where that murder took place. Now that was something interesting, considering…The radio on her desk crackled, which distracted her momentarily, and when she finished talking to the deputy who'd called in, he was gone.

She heard his laughter in the hallway. He must have found an excuse to wander over to Sam's space. Now, that was another thing. She liked Samantha Ryder…Sam, even though she stood, like, over six feet tall and had them green eyes and red hair. She could've played basketball for Ireland or something. And that Karl was even taller. He could probably have played for the Harlem Globe Trotters. Theirs was not a match Essie cared for, or folks in the town approved of, though most of them wouldn't come right out and say so. But there you are. It's a whole new world, and Ike said she'd better get used to it, so she guessed she should. Anybody but Ike saying that, and she'd probably take a walk. But Ike...well, you couldn't say no to him, even if he was, like, Jewish and all. And Ike liked Karl, so that was that. She shook her head. No, she thought, it's not Karl's being colored that mattered—well not much—it's that he's FBI, and the office got nothing but grief from that quarter. She wondered what Karl did that got him a suspension from the Bureau, and then a phony assignment to Picketsville.

"Hey, Mr. FBI guy," she yelled, "you working that shooting up in Bolton?"

"What?"

"Get your rear end out here, and leave Sam alone, or I'll tell Ike you've been smoochin' on company time. What I asked was, are you working on the mess out at the old Lydell place."

Karl reappeared. "I am. You got something for me?"

"Maybe. There's a story that I heard, when I was growing up, about Lydell's place."

"A story?"

"I think there was a murder out there in that house, back in the Civil War day, same as this one."

"What do you mean, *same as this one?*"

"The dead guy was, like, locked up, wasn't he? That's what Billy's brother told Billy."

"Yeah. A locked room murder. So?"

"Well, that's the way it got done before, I think. You could look that up and you'd have a solution right then and there."

"Sam," Karl shouted, "Google locked room mystery, Picketsville, Virginia."

◇◇◇

Betsy Blessing's husband described her shop as her hobby job. She resented the notion that she wasn't serious about her store, but had to admit that business needed to pick up, and soon. She barely made enough to cover her expenses, never took any money home. The IRS would have something to say about another Schedule C, declaring another loss, if she didn't get something going. She needed to show a profit. The bell over the door clanked a welcome and she looked up to see Ike pushing through the door, his new clock under his arm.

"I hope you're here to buy a whole suite of furniture to go with that clock. You are, aren't you?"

"Why would you think that?" He moved a stack of gilt edged books aside and set the clock down on a fragile Hepplewhite chair.

"Well, talk around town is you and the brainy Dr. Harris will be setting up housekeeping soon and knowing, as I do, how you live, I expect you'd need a house full of furniture. I doubt Dr. Harris would put up with the Goodwill rejects you have in your apartment."

"Goodwill rejects? I happen to think retro décor is very with it. I may be a trend setter, even."

"Really? You think? Well then, I have a friend who has an '85 Yugo for sale. I'll have him give you a call."

"Thanks, but no thanks. I have enough trouble being inconspicuous in a police car."

"No furniture?"

"No. I need a different key for the clock. This one doesn't fit."

She opened the case and tried the key, with the same results Ike had the previous night. She retrieved a box from under the counter and rummaged through a pound of clock keys.

Ike's eyebrows raised a bit, "Where'd you get all those?" he asked.

"I've been collecting old hardware for years. Even before I had this shop, I had a little business matching keys, locks, hinges and so forth. I made some money at that."

"I'll tell Jonathan Lydell. He's restoring that old place of his and could use some help in that department, I imagine."

"No need, but thank you, anyway. Jonathan is a regular."

"He buys clock keys?"

"Clock, door, all kinds. You name it. The last time he came in, he wanted a key for an old travel trunk he had in his basement or attic, I don't remember which. And I wouldn't call Bellmore 'that old place,' at least not within his hearing. It's an historic building, and in the register as such, and he insists everyone know that."

"I read the plaque on the wall, sorry, you're right, but relics of the past, animate or inanimate, are not a passion of mine."

"What do you call all those old movies you collect, if not relics of the past?"

"They are classics. Bogart, Cagney, Rita Hayworth, Hedy Lamar are not relics, they are treasures."

"Right-oh, and if you plan to stick with your lady love, you may have to change your tune about houses and history. She is an historian, after all. Here…" Betsy fitted a device into the clock and gave it a series of turns.

"That doesn't look like a key."

"It's a winder." She held up the crank-like device. "See, it has a square hole in the end that fits over the winding stem. It's like a key that way, only with this little crank handle you can wind it more quickly, and with less strain on your fingers when it gets tight."

"I've seen one of those before…speak of the devil…Lydell had one like that mixed up in a box of rusty keys in his basement. Only it was bigger."

"Probably used to wind a cabinet clock, a grandfather clock. He owns at least three. Did I tell you, he wanted me to furnish some of the rooms in Bellmore?"

"That would be a nice sale."

"Oh, no, he wasn't planning on paying for the furniture. He wanted me to place pieces in the rooms, as advertising. He said I could leave my business card on the pieces and if anyone wanted to buy it, they could contact me."

"Very generous of him. I'm guessing here, but I bet he wanted a piece of the sale, too."

"You guess right. Okay, your clock is wound and I've set the striker. If you need to reset it, you see this wire thingy in back of the works? Well, you push it up and count out the strikes to match the hour you have set."

"I got it."

"Good. My best to the lovely Ms. Harris. When are the two of you coming to dinner?"

"You need to talk to her. She's the one with the unmanageable schedule and time problems."

"You know, when most of this furniture was made, people lived at a more leisurely pace, and still had time to hold balls, give parties, and fight a bloody civil war."

"You're planning on throwing a ball, or starting a war?"

"It's an idea. Not the war part. We could do a costume thing. Women in hoop skirts, men in antebellum dress suits. All *Gone With the Wind*, or something."

"And the folks serving the punch?"

"Oh, yeah, can't go there anymore, I guess. Well, it was a thought. Maybe we should do the roaring twenties. Zelda and Scott Fitzgerald, *The Great Gatsby*, all that jazz. Better?"

"Better. Well, *tempus fugit*."

"And also with you."

"What?"

"Sorry, inside church joke. Ask the Reverend Blake Fisher."

She watched, as Ike laid the clock carefully in the trunk of his car next to the riot gear, a collection of crumpled paper coffee cups, and a change of clothes she guessed he must keep handy for those days when things really went south.

Chapter Twelve

Jonathan Lydell riffled through the file case again. There was no doubt about it, pages were missing. A great many pages. Who could have taken them? The only person with access to his study was his daughter. Well, that was not, strictly speaking, true. Henry, that boy with the ridiculous hair and tattoos, came in and out from time to time. His brother worked in the sheriff's office, of all things. One of that tiresome Sutherlin woman's brood. Why that new Vicar let her kind run wild in his church never ceased to amaze him. It seemed impossible to him that so much had changed in the past forty years. The sheriff's tone of voice still rankled. In the past, people like that Schwartz person would show some respect for a Lydell. The fact that Schwartz was Jewish only confirmed his despair over the sad pass the country had come to.

"Martha Marie," he shouted, "have you been rummaging through my papers again?"

No response from the second floor. He tried again, with the same results. "Drunk at…" He checked his watch and returned it to its nesting place in his pocket. "…Three in the afternoon." He sighed, and wondered again about Henry Sutherlin, and whether a boy like that would steal papers. There were more valuable things in the room and in plain sight. Not likely he'd steal documents. He'd have to read them first, and he was barely literate. Still, you never knew with these sharecroppers' descendants. An untrustworthy and sly group, never loyal, the last to enlist, the first to surrender. He wondered if the sheriff would be interested enough in his files to send that red-haired idiot in to steal them. He doubted it, but decided to make some discreet inquires.

"If those papers were to fall into the wrong hands, my books, my life's work, everything, could be destroyed. I could be…"

"Daddy, did you call me just now?" Martha Marie stood in the doorway, swaying a little. She put out her hand on the door jamb to steady herself.

"Yes, I did. I wanted to know if you'd been in my papers again."

"Papers? What papers would that be? You mean your research papers. The stories you tell yourself about how we won the war."

"You are drunk. It's barely three in the afternoon and you are three sheets to the wind."

"Momma used to get there by noon."

"Your mother drank no spirits stronger than a little sherry, on special occasions. How dare you speak of her that way?"

"She was in her cups after breakfast, Daddy. You were always too busy being a Lydell, being the lord of the manor, to even notice. It was how she escaped."

"Escaped? Escaped from what, may I ask? You don't know what you're talking about."

Martha Marie reeled to the sideboard and poured herself another three fingers of amber liquid, which she tossed off in one quick gulp. "From you," she said, and sprawled on the couch. "She couldn't stand listening to you go on and on about good genes and bad. She said if she heard one more lecture on breeding, or about the gentry and the common folk, she'd fetch the bird gun and shoot herself. She never did, just drank. She'd fix breakfast, send us off to school and hit the vodka."

"She did nothing of the sort. You are drunk and mistaken."

"You got the drunk part right. We'll see about who's mistaken." Martha Marie proceeded to pass out. She wouldn't stay that way long. But for now, her drinking had formed a solid wall between them, protecting her from the inevitable tongue lashing her father would have bestowed on her, had she attempted sobriety on a permanent basis.

Lydell glared at her for several minutes. He wished her gone from his presence. Dead would be better. After all he had done for her, and now this…this…He slammed the file box shut and stalked from the room.

After a few minutes had passed, Martha Marie cocked one eye open, stood, and shuffled to the desk.

Too late to replace the papers in the box. He'd already searched there. She paused and then, a sly smile lighted her face. She slid a sheaf of papers under the blotter on his desk. Her father had a habit of doing that when people came into the room, unexpectedly. Satisfied, she refilled her glass and slipped away.

"How's your hand?"

"What?"

"Dr. Harris, you poked your hand with a pencil yesterday, remember? I asked how it was."

"It's fine, Agnes. Thank you. The sheriff says it may turn into a tattoo."

Agnes lifted an eyebrow and turned to leave the office with the mail to be filed.

"Agnes, can I ask you a question?"

"Certainly."

"Sit down. It's a little personal."

Agnes perched on the edge of one or the other of two crewel upholstered chairs opposite. Ike, when he visited, would usually slouch in one or the other. That's how Ruth remembered him. The first time he'd visited, she'd chewed him out royally. She blushed at the memory. How wrong she'd been. The second time he'd come into the office, it was her turn to receive a verbal spanking. She thought that if she ever had to leave Callend, she'd ask for the chairs as part of her severance package.

"Yes?" Agnes still held her dictation pad in her hand.

"What, exactly, do you have against Sheriff Schwartz that makes you dislike him so much?"

"I never said I did."

"Never said, but action, Agnes, action speaks louder than… whatever."

"Well, as long as we are being personal, I believe your behavior, your *actions,* are causing a major scandal on the campus. What sort of example do you suppose you set for the girls when you openly sleep around with that…well, that man?"

Ruth's face reddened. She'd always admired Agnes, appreciated her willingness to shield her from the endless intrusions visited on her office and time. She thought of her as efficient, smart, and loyal. On the last item, she discovered, it appeared she'd been wrong and felt betrayed.

The two women faced each other, each waiting for the other to continue.

"By 'that man' you mean what, precisely?"

"Nothing. Only that he is not the sort of companion I would choose, and I think your faculty and the girls feel the same."

"They are young women, not girls, and fully capable of assessing the circumstances of my relationship, without prejudice as, it appears, you are not."

It was Agnes' turn to turn red. "If my presence is not wanted…"

"Agnes, you and I have been together a long time. You came with me when I accepted this job. You, better than anyone else, know my faults and, God forgive me, my past, including, I should add, past relationships. You were fine with them then, at least you never said anything. Why now, all of a sudden, are you acting like a South American duenna, watching over some sixteen-year-old virgin? You know that I am neither. So what's the problem?"

Agnes lowered her head and said nothing. Ruth, whose patience was already worn thin by work, rumors, and several important postponed decisions, slapped the desk with her hand, and sent another pencil spinning in the air. This time no trauma accompanied the gesture. One serendipitous tattoo was enough.

"Agnes, say something, for God's sake. You act as though I have become the town tramp, or worse, a Hollywood celebrity. Speak to me."

Agnes removed a handkerchief from her sleeve and blew her nose. She sounded like a kitten sneezing. The scent of lilies of the valley wafted toward Ruth from the cloth, which transported her back in time. She hadn't seen a hanky up a woman's sleeve since her maiden aunt from Muncie came to visit, and that was in a previous century.

"President Harris," she began.

"For heaven's sake, Agnes, we've known each other since God made dirt. Call me Ruth."

"Oh well, then that's the thing you see?"

"See? See what. No, sorry, I don't."

"We've been together for all those years and this is the first time you've ever asked me to call you by your Christian name. I'm always Agnes. Agnes, do this, Agnes, do that. And I am happy to do it. I think you may be the most remarkable woman I know but—"

"But I take you for granted, and just once in a while, you'd like to be taken into my confidence. After all these years. Is that it?"

"I think so."

"Is that why you give me a hard time about Ike…Mr. Schwartz?"

"That's part of it. I guess."

"And the other part?"

"Some poet said we should see ourselves as others see us."

"Robert Burns said something like that, yes."

"How does it look? I mean you are the president of the college, and you are acting like the naughty teenager you just said you weren't. What were you thinking? Sneaking around with a policeman. 'Shacking up.' What do you imagine people are saying about you?"

"Agnes, I—"

"Gracious, I don't care about your love life. I never have. Maybe in the past, I even envied you a little, but this is so…blatant. Don't you see? You are not one of the girls…women…you are the president of the college."

Ruth sat, mouth open, in mild shock. Agnes rarely said more than a half dozen words on any subject. And, in this instance, she knew she had it right. One's private life should be that. And when she labored, as a professor or as a department chair, she had one. But now, she was in the public eye twenty-four seven. No wonder…

"Then there is the other thing."

"The other thing?"

"I'm older than you, President Harris…Ruth, and grew up in south Baltimore, Pigtown. We…we had certain feelings about certain people."

"Certain people meaning Jews?"

Agnes hung her head again. "I'm sorry. It's just…well he really is a nice enough man, but with my being angry about everything, well, I'm a little…"

"Pissed?"

"Yes, pissed," Agnes made a wry face that could have passed for a smile and rubbed her hand across the rough fabric on the chair's arm, "and I just let those old feelings come out to hurt you, I guess. I'm sorry."

"Not sorry, Agnes. We should have had this talk a long time ago. And you are correct to tell me. I was so caught up in…well caught up will do…and I lost sight of things. Will you do me a favor now?"

"Yes, of course."

"The situation around here is going to turn into a zoo in the next few weeks. I need protection and I need a means of escape from time to time. Will you help me?"

"Yes."

"Escape with Schwartz, Agnes."

Agnes gulped and smiled. "With the sheriff, for your protection. When things get zooey, you need your own personal cop. Is that it?"

"It'll do. Let's you and me blow this joint and go out to lunch."

Chapter Thirteen

Henry Sutherlin stretched, braced his shoulders, and mopped his newly shaven head. He had only three more sections to split into firewood. A light breeze blew across the yard and carried the sour odor of newly hewn oak along with it. The cord he'd already chopped sat neatly stacked against the fence. By fall, it would be dry and ready for burning. Lydell was particular about his firewood. He liked a twenty-eighty mix of soft and hard. Henry had carefully mixed the pine and apple with the oak lengths so that no matter how Lydell gathered his logs for the day, he'd get the correct combination.

Henry licked his thumb and ran it carefully across the cutting edge of his axe. He was particular about that. Lydell supplied him with axe and wedges, but Henry brought his own to work. People like Lydell rarely kept their tools in good shape and hadn't a clue how to hone a workable edge. He set the next piece on end and split it in half. This one was big enough to take down to eighths.

"Henry? Is that you?"

Lydell had managed to slip up on him without his notice. He did that a lot.

"Sir?"

"When you're done with that, I'd like a moment with you inside, if you please. What happened to your head?"

"Gave it a mowing, goatee too, Mr. Lydell. Plan to change my persona."

"Your what?"

"How I look."

"I know what persona means, Henry. I'm just surprised you do."

"Oh, well, I read a bit…" *you old jerk, do you think us ordinary folk are morons or something?* "…newspapers, comic books, historical documents and such."

Lydell's face fell into worry. "Do you indeed? Inside when you're done, then." He turned and reentered the house.

Now what's up with that, Henry wondered, and split the second length.

◇◇◇

Strange young man, Lydell mused. His *persona* for God's sake. What's he up to? One day he's the local freak show, the next he's normal looking, well except for the tattoos, but they don't show with a long sleeved shirt. Is he working for the sheriff, and if so, why? He sauntered back to his desk and studied his file case. The last book would never be written with those papers out. Someone could always dig up the facts before he could get them down the right way, and then…

"You wanted to see me?"

Henry stood at the door. He did look remarkably different without his coxcomb. Almost presentable.

"Yes, come in. Oh, wipe your feet first. No, maybe you should remove those boots."

Henry did as he was told. Lydell noted the unmatched socks, one with a hole in the toe. He did not ask Henry to sit.

"I am missing some papers, Henry, and I wondered if you had any idea where they might be."

"Well, I can't be sure. What kind of papers would they be?"

"You mentioned a moment ago that you read historical documents. Those kinds of papers."

"Oh, well, I was talking general, sort of. I read the crime reports that come into the house with Billy and sometimes old newspapers. Like, yesterday I dug up the old *Staunton Spectator* story about the murder in your stranger room back in the big war. 'Course, you know all about that, I reckon."

"Are you playing with me, Henry?"

"Sir?"

"I think you are working with someone in the sheriff's office on that murder, and I don't like it."

"Well, actually, I am, but it ain't formal or anything, you know, just me and Billy trying to see who can figure it out first, is all."

"You and Billy. That would be your brother, William?"

"He ain't a William, just Billy. Yep...that is, yes sir."

"Not working with that Schwartz fellow?"

"Ike? No, he ain't dealing with me at the moment."

"I see." Lydell didn't see but he let it pass. Clearly, more discreet inquiries were in order. "About the documents. Again, have you seen anything like them...like these?" He pulled a few sheets from the file case and waved them in Henry's direction.

"I might have, now you mention it."

"Where?" Lydell could not hide the excitement in his voice.

"Maybe...I can't be sure, but I saw Miss Martha Marie reading something that looked like them the other day. Out by the log pile you have out there for making the slave cabins."

"My daughter?"

"Maybe. But it could have been some letters she had. She's back there a lot with her old letters. I think they must be love letters or the like. Sometimes she cries. But that could be because she's...you know."

"Yes, yes. Well, thank you, Henry. That will be all."

Henry gathered his boots and left. Lydell saw the small clumps of mud that fell from their soles and frowned. *Bumpkin. So, Martha Marie was reading letters out by the shed, was she? Or was she reading his papers? If the latter, what had she done with them? And she'd been talking with that man, Grotz. What did they talk about?*

"Martha Marie," he shouted. "Where are you?" No answer, as usual. He stepped outside. No sign of Henry. The axe leaned against the shed wall. The wood pile had been split and stacked.

The thought crossed his mind that he might have underestimated Henry. Henry was a very clever fellow. The question was, how clever?

"Martha Marie," he repeated. He thought he heard a noise in the shed. "Em, is that you?"

"Nobody here but us chickens," she giggled.

He pulled the shed door open. His daughter sat on a box of his books, a bottle of wine in her hand.

"You caught me, Daddy. Now I have to find a new place for my stash."

"You are a disgrace." He turned on his heel and stalked back to the house. "A disgrace," he repeated, although he doubted she heard him or, if she did, cared. He thought he heard her reply but did not respond. A disgrace, a bad apple that fell from the family tree. How did this happen?

The phone was ringing when he reached the cool gloom of the house. He picked up. Betsy Blessing. He listened as she recited the details of Ike Schwartz's last visit. She wanted to know if he was in the market for more keys, winders, or lock parts. What was that woman after? Did she think she knew something? This whole project was becoming much too complicated. He'd had enough. It was time to call the mayor.

Chapter Fourteen

When Ike entered the office, everyone began talking at once. Sam and Karl wanted to tell him about the previous, historical, murder at Bellmore. They'd Googled the information and printed out portions of the local newspaper for the date. Essie needed a moment of his time. She had a problem. The mayor's office had called and would again. The mayor sounded upset, and Ruth left a cryptic message, something about Karl Marx. Ike would understand. Did he? He held up his hands for silence.

"Yes, boys and girls, I do know about that murder. Those of us raised in this part of the world grew up with it. I can give you five minutes, Essie, but it better be important and I think she meant Groucho, not Karl, and he said a lot of things but I think I know what she's referring to, yes, but with Ms. Harris you can never be sure."

The three of them paused and then began again.

"Stop. Enough, already. What I want to know is, has anyone done any constructive work on the case? What came over from the medical examiner's office and the evidence techs?"

Karl cleared his throat and reported that Lydell's daughter had no information. She'd had a drink with Grotz, chatted briefly, and then taken sleeping pills and gone to bed. She didn't hear anything, see anything, or know anything. He was inclined to believe her. "Booze and pills, bad combination."

Billy Sutherlin strolled in, sailed his Stetson across the room where it lit on a peg by the front door. With a superior smile, he announced that he had, in fact, gone over the evidence technician's report.

"At last, a policeman reports for duty." Ike waved Billy into his office and beckoned the others to follow. Essie started to protest. "Later, Essie, I promise."

When they were seated, or arranged against the wall, Ike nodded to Billy to begin. The phone rang. Essie wig-wagged for Ike to pick up. Neither she nor Ike had mastered the intercom. He put the call on speaker. It was time his people heard some of the nonsense he had to deal with every day.

"Hello, Tom. How're things in the mayor's office?"

"Funny you should ask that, Ike. I just had a call from Jonathan Lydell and he wanted to know the same thing. 'Fore I could answer he lit into me about you and yours. What's going on with his investigation?"

"Not *his*, Tom, ours. We are making progress." He looked to Billy, who grinned an assent.

"Lydell wants his keys back."

"He can have them…" Billy put thumb to forefinger in an okay sign, "tomorrow. That is, unless we need to run a trace." Ike wasn't sure what *run a trace* meant, exactly. He'd heard the term used on one of the seemingly infinite permutations of TV's CSI and thought it sounded important. He had an idea, but except on the TV, and perhaps at the Bureau, no lab to his knowledge, could do much more than run fingerprints and, if they had time, DNA samples, but that could take weeks or months.

"Well, that's good," the mayor said. Obviously, he watched the same shows. "Ballistics turn up anything?" Billy shook his head. Ike frowned a *what?* Billy waved a page at Ike. "Have to get back to you on that, Tom. Apparently, there are some questions needing answers." Of course there were. That is the nature of questions, but the mayor seemed not to notice. "The victim's wife will be in on the weekend and we're hoping she can fill us in on what he was doing in the valley."

"She's just getting in? I'd a thought she'd pop right down being it's her husband. Where's she from, anyway?"

"New Jersey. She said she couldn't get off work. I gather she and Mr. Grotz were not getting along lately."

"Well, you put your A-team on this one, Ike. Lydell is a player."

"You got it, Tom."

He hung up. "Our mayor watches too much television. Okay Billy, what's the story on the ballistics?"

"On page five," he said. "The lab says the weapon used was pretty old and probably not fired lately. Whoever did it wasn't a gun expert. They think it probably hadn't been cleaned in a coon's age. The slug, they say, is, like, an old fashioned lead one. The kind they ain't made in years."

"Caliber, make?"

"Now, that's the good part. It's a..." Billy consulted the report, ".455 caliber, from a Webley, MKII, they think."

"What's good about that?" Sam asked.

"How many World War I or II Webley's can there be in the neighborhood?"

"Point made," Ike said. "But there is no guarantee that it's local. Talk to me about the condition of the slug."

"Old, out of date, lead, from a pistol that had not been fired, perhaps even cleaned in a long time," Billy repeated.

Karl scratched his chin. "Which would indicate an amateur who pulled the piece from a drawer or cabinet or—"

"A woman," Sam said.

"Why a woman?" Ike asked.

"I can count on the thumbs of one hand, the number of women of my acquaintance who have even a rudimentary knowledge of guns—cleaning, maintenance, and so on. It sounds like the person who did this found the gun locked away or stored, lugged it to the scene, and blam. That, to me spells angry female, spur of the moment."

"Anybody who watches TV knows how to aim and shoot. At close range, they can probably kill their victim. Cleaning up afterward is another matter," Karl said.

"You know what I like about them TV shows that show people shooting? They have the bad guy hold the gun sideways, you know, with the gun butt parallel to the ground. Man, that has probably saved more lives than the Red Cross," Billy said.

Essie, tired of being left out of the conversation, had joined the group, asked why.

"'Cause the only way the barrel gets pointed in the right direction is if you cock your arm sideways or twist your wrist all funny. Otherwise, you're shooting off to the right every time. That gives the shootee a chance."

"Okay." Ike reassumed control. "Theoretically, we can't rule out the daughter. Although why she'd do it is pretty hard to figure. What else is in the report?"

"Nothing on the clothes or furniture. Fingerprints all belong to Grotz, the lady who cleans, that'd be Charlie Picket's mom, and a few of Mr. Lydell. The only thing I can see that might be worth something is the books."

"Books? What kind of books?"

"Well, he had a library book checked out of the Passaic Public Library, *The Shenandoah Valley Campaign of 1862*, by some guy named Gallagher. There was an overdue notice with it. And then there were four notebooks with hand written stuff in them."

"Fingerprints?"

"His and a bunch of unidentified ones in the library book. On the notebooks, only his, except the techs found smudges on the covers and the upper right hand corner of some of the pages. Don't know what that means."

Karl took the report from Billy and skimmed it. "It probably means someone wearing dirty gloves leafed through them. And here's something else, all the books are numbered and book four has a half dozen pages in the back razored out."

"Who would do that?" Essie asked, enjoying the chance to be part of real police work for a change.

"Either he did, or the killer did. My guess, he did. A killer would just rip them out," Sam said.

"Okay, Karl, you're on the books. Sam, see what you can find out about Grotz and the Passaic library. Billy, I want you to go back out to the Lydell place and search that room from top to bottom. Check out Mrs. Winslow—that's the daughter—with the neighbors, and get me the picture the ET's took at the scene. Lydell says he sealed the room off from the rest of the house when he restored it, but there have been a slew of contractors working out there and anything is possible. Rap on the walls. Make sure they're solid. Sometimes it's easier to build a new wall in front of an old one that's past replastering. If there's enough space between the new one and the original, it's possible to slip in between. Then, who knows? Anyway, look. There has to be a way in and out of that room with the door locked."

"Or to fire a shot into it with the door locked," Karl added, catching Ike's drift.

"Got it." Billy stood and the rest gathered themselves together.

"One last thing. Try not to annoy Lydell any more than necessary. Essie, notify me the minute Mrs. Grotz arrives. That's it."

Chapter Fifteen

Essie lingered as the others filed out. Ike glanced up from the report in front of him.

"Okay, Essie. What can I do for you?"

"Well…Okay, first, I need to ask if it would be okay to take some time off next week. Rita said she'd work an extra shift if she had to and Darcie Billingsly is pretty much up to speed as the on-call, and she's good to work the eleven to seven when her kids are asleep. She has an old aunt that's moved in with her since Whaite died and…"

"Whoa. Stop. It'll be okay. Sure. Where're you going?"

"I was figuring on going with my sister's kids to Disney World. They got passes at work. But…"

"But?"

"I just sat here and listened to you all, and I'm just…wondering. You're going to think this is pretty silly."

"Perhaps, but you won't know until you say it."

"If I was to go to that police academy school, would you be interested in hiring me on as the deputy?"

Ike gazed at Essie. She had been in the department as long as anyone, longer than most. Always cheerful, she'd become a fixture at the dispatch desk. He tried to visualize her as his deputy. He couldn't. People frequently compared her to Dolly Parton with Dolly coming in a distant second. Put all that in a uniform…She was certainly smart enough. Was she tough enough? He sighed.

"Tell you what, Essie, you go on down to Orlando with your nephews and nieces and give it a good think. The next class at the academy won't start until June. There's plenty of time between now and then to get you sponsored and enrolled."

"But if you keep Hedrick...Karl, there won't be a place for me."

"Three things you need to know. First, deputies come and go. It's a perilous, underpaid business. Men like Whaite, for instance, lose their lives in the line of duty and leave widows and kids behind. Some grow tired of the hours and the danger and find something easier to do. Second, you don't know how you'll react to the academy. Not everyone is cut out for this work and the training is designed to find that out. Finally, I haven't asked Karl and I'm not convinced he'd say yes even if I did. He's committed to his career at the Bureau. So, just stay on your course and see what happens."

Ike returned to the report. Essie hesitated.

"Something else?"

"Ike, you know I don't like to gossip..."

"What's on your mind?" he asked, avoiding the opportunity to comment on that bit of off-the-mark self-assessment.

"I came in this office before you did, you know." He did. For the first weeks of his tenure, cronies of his predecessor had tried to make his job impossible. Only a clean sweep of most of the entrenched personnel had kept the sheriff's office from becoming a war zone. Essie had flirted with the dissidents but had been won over. "Ike, they're at it again."

"Who?"

"The deputies you let go and some of the boys down at the feed store. The deputies signed on with a security firm up in Staunton. It's gone out of business and now those guys want to fix it so you can't operate and they get back to the way things were."

"Our late sheriff, Loyal Parker, can't very well hire them back. He's dead."

"Yeah, I know, but they're saying you're responsible for that on account of he'd be alive if you didn't take his place."

"That makes no sense, Essie. What in the world are they thinking?"

"I don't know, but, like, I hear things. They want me to, you know, spy on you and then maybe help them plant some stuff that can be found by the State Police."

"You're kidding. Who're they?"

"God's truth, I wished I was. Like, have you noticed anything where it shouldn't be lately?"

Ike's reputation for being disorganized was legendary. He had a sign over his cluttered desk that read, *I'm not disorganized. I'm creative.* The odds he'd notice anything out of place ran from slim to none.

"Where? Lord, Essie, you know I don't keep track of stuff."

"See, that's what they're counting on, like, what's in your car?"

"Um…" he tried to think about the cruiser. Did anything seem different, out of place? "Nothing…well, there were the coffee cups in the trunk. I don't remember putting them in there. Come to think of it, I never put trash in the trunk of the car."

"Maybe you'd better check it."

"If what you're telling me is straight, I'll need a witness. You said you liked police work…okay, let *us* check it out."

He walked Essie to the car and popped the trunk. The paper cups were scattered in untidy batches. He stared at them for a moment. Essie reached in to gather them up.

"Don't touch," he snapped. "Sorry. Run in and get me a few of the big evidence bags. And a couple of small ones, too."

The two of them, latex gloved, picked up the cups and bagged them. Then Ike removed his spare clothes and emptied the pockets. He bagged three powder filled glycine envelopes and some slips of paper, which had what appeared to be phone numbers scrawled on them with area codes he did not recognize. He made sure Essie signed the tags next to his signature and then had Charlie Picket photograph the trunk and the interior of the car. He directed Charlie to take it, the cups, and papers to the county crime lab.

"Okay, who?" he asked. Essie averted her eyes. "Essie, time to stand up. This town is changing and can't go back to the days when the sheriff's office was the enemy. Who?"

"I don't know for sure, but Daryll, down at the garage where the cars is worked on…he's kin to George LeBrun. You remember him."

Ike did. LeBrun at one time served as second in charge, and acted as the former sheriff's bag man.

"Pull both their prints and send them along with the other stuff. If there's anything going on and I can make a case, those bozos are going to jail."

Essie looked distressed.

"Problem?"

"They'll know I was the one that ratted them out."

Ike hadn't thought of that. "Tell you what. You pack your bags and get on down to Orlando. I'll let the word leak out that I put you on disciplinary paid leave. That is partly true and it ought to make them look elsewhere. Essie, now you see how it is. Police work is messy and sometimes it gets dangerous. But if we don't put the bad guys away, if we turn a blind eye because they might come back to hurt us, they win."

She nodded unhappily and walked back into the office with him. "I reckon you're right. Whew."

Chapter Sixteen

Norbert's Lock and Load sold a combination of security devices, surveillance equipment, and other marginally legal items, as well as guns and ammunition. Rumor had it that some of Norbert's clientele traveled from as far away as Washington D.C. to browse through his inventory. When it came to selling hand guns, Norbert had acquired a reputation, which he vehemently denied, for being somewhat loose in his background checks. In any case, he remained a politically incorrect institution in the very shadows of Callend College, Picketsville's major, and perhaps, only point of interest and bastion of correctness. Ike pulled into the gravel parking lot and waited a moment for Norbert to recognize him and make whatever adjustments he needed before welcoming the town's law enforcement arm.

"Morning, Sheriff." Norbert, as usual, greeted Ike with a display of expensive dental work framed in what Ike assumed passed for a sincere smile.

"Behaving yourself, Norbert?"

"Absolutely, Sheriff. All on the up and up, as you know."

"Right. Just a caution, nothing personal, you understand, but we've been jotting down the license plate numbers of your out of town customers and notifying the states in question. I'm sure there'll be no problem, but on the off chance one of your sales turns up in the commission of a felony, there could be some serious consequences. Just a heads-up. Oh, and the Commonwealth is suing the state of New York to keep them from videotaping gun sales down here. They may or may not have frequented your store. I hope the suit fails."

Norbert blanched and stole a glance at his sales receipt file.

"No worries in that department," he said, but looked worried, nonetheless. "Is there anything else?"

"Webley .455 caliber. You carry loads for that?"

"Webley? I haven't seen one of those for years. Collector's piece. You have one? I'll buy it."

"No, I was wondering if you sold one recently to anyone local and if not the pistol, ammunition for one."

"Not much call for .455. Now, some of the newer Webley's used .380. I stock that."

"Anybody in here asking for .455?"

Norbert frowned and looked thoughtful. Ike recognized the sign of a man wrestling with the truth and trying to find a way to tell it while avoiding it at the same time.

"Nobody from around here, no sir."

That would have to do. Whether a box of shells found their way to Pittsburg or Philadelphia was not Ike's concern at the moment. He'd heard enough to know that the shooter at Lydell's either had shells or acquired them elsewhere. The report suggesting an older composition of the slug probably meant the shells had been around for a while.

"Norbert, I should know this, but if ammunition sits around a while, will it still fire?"

"Theoretically, yes. It depends on the make and conditions—you know, weather, damp, corrosion—but kept dry and clean, it's probably good forever. Might lose some punch, though. I had a fellow in here t'other day had an old Sharp's rifle. It had been hanging on the wall for maybe a hundred years or more. Might not have been used since the Civil War, who knows? Anyway, he said he sighted down the barrel and pulled the trigger and damned near killed his dog. So, yeah, it could work."

"Thanks, Norbert. Do me a favor, let me know if anybody comes in here asking for shells for a Webley, or wants to sell you one, will you?"

"You bet I will. Say, if you-all want to upgrade weapons, I can get you a deal on a Glock 31. You've been lugging that Smith and Wesson around for years, Sheriff. Nice lightweight Glock'd be better. The thirty-one fires a .357 round, same as your S and W but it's lighter and a whole lot easier to handle. Make you a good deal."

"I'll think about it. Thanks." Ike paused and turned back to Norbert. "Has Jonathan Lydell stopped by here lately?"

"The stuffed shirt that's restoring his house over in Bolton?"

"Yes."

"No. Wait a minute. Yes, he was…about a week ago, maybe two. He wanted to know about security systems. He wants to burglar proof that dump of his. Like, what's the chance of that?"

"That all? He didn't want to buy shells for a pistol, did he?" It didn't seem likely.

"No, but he did rummage through that box of old keys, and bought one."

"Okay, well, thanks, try to behave, Norbert. I'd hate to run you in."

"Never happen, Sheriff."

Three miles away, and in what could pass for another century, the object of their conversation sat at his desk fretting. Lydell had not written a word for days and he wanted to finish his last book in time to teach at Callend. That ridiculous Ms. Harris may have put him off, but if the rumors were true, she wouldn't be in a position to say much one way or the other, soon enough. The contractor who promised to have the log structures up by Friday, this Friday, had dropped off the face of the earth. And his papers were still missing. That fact bothered him the most. The papers were important to the future, and Bellmore. He searched the surface of the desk, as if it might provide a clue as to their whereabouts. His hand brushed the blotter and the edge of one of the documents peeked out from beneath it. He lifted the blotter and found the rest. His relief was short lived. Some were still missing, the important ones, and he knew for a certainty that he had not put these there. No one else...he paused. The only persons who would know he sometimes slid papers under the blotter were Mrs. Picket, the cleaning woman, and Martha Marie.

The Picket woman had a son in the sheriff's office. But she didn't figure to have done it. Simple woman. He felt as if he were suddenly surrounded by police relatives. Martha Marie...what had she said? *We'll see...* something. But she was drunk, as usual. He drummed his fingers on the mahogany, subconsciously beating out the rhythm to *Dixie...* land o' cotton. Mostly soy beans nowadays.

"Martha Marie, where are you?" he shouted. Probably still in the shed. He stood and walked to the side board. Lydell did not drink much. The drinks table served more as a prop than a functioning service. At least it had until Martha Marie came to live with him. He poured several inches from the decanter, with the sterling silver *Bourbon* hanger on it, and drank. He coughed and raced to the porch and spat over the rail. Mrs. Antonelli who had just stepped out for air, gaped. He heard a chuckle behind him.

"It's apple juice," Martha Marie said.

"What...what's that you say?"

"You heard me. It's apple juice. Now you know my secret."

"Secret? What secret? I don't understand."

"Well then, I'll explain. I don't have my mother's cast iron stomach and frankly, whiskey can give me the hangover, before it gives me the drunk, lately...bad liver from too much partying in my misspent youth. I can manage one, maybe two or three drinks at a time and that's it. I have to space them out, you see?" She strolled to the divan and sat down, squared her shoulders and looked him in the eye. "But to keep you off my back I, like Mother before me, find it easier to be drunk. You are nasty when I'm that way, but you don't work at it. When I'm sober, you're always in my face, and if you're not lecturing me on something…my past mistakes, the tragedy I represent to the family, or some other damned fool topic, you are boring me to death with your version of history, which, as we both know, is ninety percent bullshit, one hundred percent self aggrandizement. So, I play drunk. Now you know. Sorry I'm such a disappointment to you. I can't even be an authentic drunk."

Lydell listened to his daughter with growing alarm. "History, fiction? That's a terrible thing to say, Em. Why we Lydells were—"

"Don't," she screamed. "Don't even start. Please do not give me 'How the Shenandoah Lydells Saved the Country' lecture. It's all crap. You know it and I know it."

He sat heavily at his desk and stared at his daughter. What had happened? He shuffled through the papers on the desk and looked up at her.

"What on earth are you going on about?"

She lifted one eyebrow and smiled.

Chapter Seventeen

George LeBrun caught up with Essie outside Shop N Save. He grabbed her arm and pulled her aside.

"Ow, George, that hurts. What are you doing? Let go of me."

"Not until I find out what's going on with you, Judas woman."

"What are you talking about? Let go." Essie wrenched her arm free and headed toward the shop's door. He reached out and spun her around by the shoulders.

"You know. Or you'd better know. That Jew boy's car was sent to the crime lab before I could call it in, and now they're all over it. Who sold me out?"

LeBrun had a reputation for cruelty and violence that, when he acted as the deputy to Ike's predecessor, guaranteed that money flowed, favors were done, evidence stayed suppressed, and witnesses remained reluctant to testify. As she looked into his heavy lidded eyes, Essie felt fear freeze her heart.

"You ain't been talking, have you?" he snarled. "'Cause if you has, certain things might could happen to you. You remember how it was, back before Schwartz came?" She remembered and took a step backward.

"I didn't say anything," she stammered. LeBrun stepped forward and put his face close to hers. His halitosis nearly knocked her off her feet. His teeth were rotten and she wondered what had happened to him. Bad as he acted in the past, he always dressed smart and took pride in his appearance and good looks. Those days were over and done with.

"You're sure about that, Sweetie? 'Cause if we find out you're in with him, somebody could get hurt real bad. You recall what happened to Doris Lampley?"

She did. Doris was found on the wrong side of town, beaten, raped, and unwilling to talk about what happened to her. She left town shortly thereafter, and the case in which she was scheduled to testify had to be dismissed.

"Look," Essie said, trying not to let him hear the fear in her voice, "I'm being put on paid leave, for crying out loud. They suspect me of having something to do with all that stuff you put in Ike's…in the sheriff's car. I'm in trouble because of you and your idiot nephew. Maybe you should be talking to him." Lying was not one of Essie's strong suits and she kept her eyes averted, hoping LeBrun wouldn't see through her.

LeBrun stepped back, apparently considering her remarks. "It's true? You ain't in the office no more?"

"Temporarily relieved, you might say."

"So, who's taking your place?"

"Temps, Rita, I don't know. I don't care. Jeezus, George, just knowing you can cost me my job. Where am I going to get another job in this town?"

"We'll take care of you just as soon as we're finished with Ikey." He started to walk away. Essie felt the relief flow over her but before she could breathe it in, he spun back toward her.

"We'll be watching you, girlie, so you be careful."

While Ike waited for the arrival of Anton Grotz's wife, he pulled bags from the shelf in the evidence locker. He replaced the notebooks, relocked the cabinet, and took the ancient keys back to his office. Karl sat in the chair reserved for visitors.

"Lydell wants his keys back. Are we finished with them?"

Karl had nearly slipped into a post-lunch coma. Ike's voice startled him back to consciousness. "Yes, I guess so. You see anything interesting?"

"There's something about those keys. I can't quite put my finger on it. Take some pictures of them for me first, will you, Karl? Then ask Essie to call Lydell and tell him he can pick them up."

"Essie's not in."

"Oh, right, I put her on paid leave, but that wasn't supposed to start until tomorrow. Where is she?"

"Beats me. Darcie Billingsly said Rita called to ask if she could finish Essie's shift."

"No explanation?"

Karl shrugged. Ike dialed Essie at home. After the tenth ring, he hung up and tried her cell phone.

"This is Ike. Where are you? Why aren't you here? Your leave doesn't start until tomorrow." He thought he might have sounded abrupt and added, "Are you okay? What happened?"

"What'd she say?"

"Voice mail...Karl, unlike your girlfriend, Sam, you trust your instincts. Should I be worried?"

"Has she ever ditched like this before?"

"No, well, not lately. And she always calls when she has to change her shift."

"Always?"

"Yes."

"Then you should be worried."

Ike heaved himself out of his chair and walked to the outer office. "Hey there, Darcie, how are you? Where's Essie's Rolodex?"

"I'm pretty fine, thank you, Sheriff. I think it's over there." Darcie pointed toward the chipboard credenza behind the desk.

"Everybody calls me Ike in here, Darcie. Did Rita say why Essie wasn't coming back from lunch?"

"No, she just said it was an emergency or something."

"Essie had an emergency?"

"No, I think the emergency belonged to Rita, which is why she called me. She couldn't cover for Essie. Is there a problem?"

"I don't know. I hope not, but since...ah...Lebrun. Do you happen to know if LeBrun is in town by any chance?"

Darcie shifted backward in her chair and inspected the ceiling. "George or Randy?"

"Either or both."

"Well, now that you mention it, I think I saw George over to the Shop N Save earlier. Randy left town a while back and is driving one of them big, over the road, trucks for an outfit up in Winchester. Drives down to Florida, up to New Jersey, and back again, they say. He's not a nice man, Ike."

"Randy?"

"George, well, both actually."

"Why would you say that?"

"On account of what he did. You know it wasn't more'n a week after Whaite's funeral than George is on the phone to me. Says I'll be needing a man to look after me now since Whaite's passed and then he said…well, you know. I said, 'George, you stop that talk and, anyway, you ain't a deputy no more,' and he said, 'Not right now, woman, but maybe that'll pretty soon change.' He scares me, Ike. Him and his brother, both. To tell the truth, those LeBrun boys are nothing but trouble. They're like the mafia or something."

"They aren't quick enough or smart enough to be mafia, Darcie. They are just a couple of schoolyard bullies that never grew up. One day they'll overstep and we will put them away."

"Sooner the better."

Karl picked up the envelope containing Lydell's keys. He dumped them on the counter top and pushed them around with his finger.

"You notice anything odd about those keys?" Ike asked.

Karl picked up the two keys and studied them for a moment, turning them over in his hand and weighing them.

"Is this a test, Ike? Keys are keys. This one is shorter. They're both pretty old. The rust on them is, like, permanent. And here's something, only the one shows any evidence of use, you know, scratches and so on." He held the key up to the light. "This one has a longer shaft but the tumbler face, or whatever the tab-like thing at the end is called, that throws the lock, is flush at the end on the long one but the shaft extends past it on the short one."

"You think any of that might be important?"

"Right now, we're stumbling around in the dark. For me, that means we have to treat everything as important."

Ike took the keys from him and repeated Karl's weighing and study. He closed his eyes, grunted, and dropped the keys back in their envelope.

Chapter Eighteen

Esther Grotz arrived in the middle of the afternoon. She looked like she'd spent the previous fifteen hours on a Greyhound bus which, in fact, she had. Her sleep encrusted eyes peered myopically through Elton John inspired, metallic flecked glasses. Dressed in pink polyester capri's, matching flip-flops, and a Kelly green blazer over a burnt orange blouse, she could have passed as the poster child for Goodwill dressing gone wild. She introduced herself to Darcie and asked to see the sheriff.

"What is this? Dodge City? What kind of town has a sheriff nowadays?"

Darcie escorted her to Ike who ushered her into his office. He asked for coffee and an extra chair.

"Darcie, see if Sam is available to join us."

"Okay," the wife of the recently deceased Anton Grotz declared, "I'm here. What do I have to do so I can go home, and who's paying for my bus ticket? I had to use my mother's credit card."

Ike had not expected the reaction. He assumed that a wife of a homicide victim would be eager to claim the body and cooperate with the investigation. The last thing he expected was a bill for a bus ticket. Mrs. Grotz took a breath and began again.

"Anton spent every dime I made on his stupid investigations. He thought he was on the way to winning a Pulitzer prize. 'Esther,' he'd say, 'this is the big one.' Like he's that Robert Redford character, whoever that guy was, that caught Nixon. 'The big one, my foot,' I'd say. 'A big piece of—'"

"I'm sorry, Mrs. Grotz, for the inconvenience. It's just that your husband was murdered and there are some questions we must ask and you may be the only person with the answers. And we thought you'd want to make arrangements for burial."

"What I gotta do is find me a cheap hotel, grab some Z's, and catch the next bus outta here. I'm due at work on Monday in the AM. I ain't burying anybody, either. They have a program at the VA, don't they? He was in the Army. Desert Storm, he was. Only time he had a regular paycheck. Let the VA plant him."

Darcie brought in the coffee.

"You got any food? I ain't had a bite since last night."

"Darcie, run over to the Crossroads and see if they can put a plate together for Mrs. Grotz."

"Will chicken be all right?" Darcie asked and gave Ike a look.

"Anything as long as it don't have peppers or okra. You people eat a lot of that crap, don't you? Okra, terrible stuff. My uncle Frank used to grow it and he'd fry it and put it in soup and, God, it was awful."

Ike felt his neck turning red. He could be a patient man. Indeed, some of his friends accused him of being too patient. But, in less than ten minutes, Esther Grotz had managed to elevate his blood pressure to a medically significant level. He stepped to his door, leaned out, and yelled.

"Sam, where are you?"

Sam loped around the corner, her face slightly flushed.

"Sorry, I thought I ought to bring the notebooks and Mr. Grotz's personal things."

"Thanks, yes, good thinking. Sam, this is Mrs. Grotz. Mrs. Grotz, this is Deputy Ryder. She will conduct the interview. If you don't have anything else for me, I will excuse myself. Duty...and...all that." Ike ducked out of the office and the building. He met Darcie with a covered plate on the way in.

"Meatloaf is all Flora had ready for quick delivery. It might have a few peppers in it, I can't be sure."

"She'll eat it. She'll complain, but she'll eat it."

Darcie continued on her way to the office. Ike traced her steps back toward the diner. Coffee, he thought. Coffee and a slice of diabetes inducing cherry pie. That will do the trick.

Sam watched Ike's retreating back and wondered what had gotten into him. Darcie handed her the plate.

"It could have peppers, so be careful." Darcie whispered in her ear, watching Esther Grotz out of the corner of her eye.

"What…Peppers? Will somebody explain to me what is going on?" Sam closed her eyes, took a deep breath and, a smile carefully arranged on her face, carried the plate into the office.

"No okra, right."

"Okra? I don't think so…no, there won't be any available until late spring and anyway, Flora, the woman who runs the diner, can't stand it so, no, no okra."

Mrs. Grotz nodded and dug into her meal. Sam sat opposite her and marveled at how quickly the food disappeared.

"Got any more of this?" the lady said, and extended her coffee cup. Sam poured her another cup. Mrs. Grotz mopped her face with a tissue, drained her cup, and looked up at Sam. "You're a telephone pole, girl. Good lord, your legs must reach up to your arm pits."

She proceeded to rant for nearly twenty minutes, detailing her problems, her husband's failures, the inconvenience she had to bear, all mixed in with *ad hominem* attacks on Sam, Darcie, and the police in general. The only good news, she hadn't noticed the green peppers.

Finally, Sam had enough. She silently cursed Ike for a coward and turned to the woman who was still belling like a hound after a rabbit.

"Mrs. Grotz, cut the crap."

"What? What do you mean? I don't have to listen to this."

"Yes, you do. Here's why. We have a murder. Your husband took four bullets and ended up locked up in a room at the home of Jonathan Lydell. The only person we've come across with a motive is you. So put a sock in it, and tell me what your husband was doing in the valley."

"Motive? You think I killed the stupid son of a—"

"Why was he here?"

Esther Grotz took a deep breath and let it out in a low whistle. She shook a cigarette from a crumpled pack of generic smokes.

"Not in here," Sam said and took the offending item from her.

"Jeez, you people are something."

"Why was he here, Mrs. Grotz?"

"Like, I don't know for sure. He said the usual, 'This is the big one, Esther.' I asked what and where. See, I needed to do that because the last 'big one' turned out to be a story about some of the family members in the area. You know what I mean about the family?"

"He planned to expose the mob?"

"The New Jersey family, right. Like, people ain't seen enough on *The Sopranos,* so before he gets that one done...remember, he hasn't earned a dime in six months at that point...two goons show up at the door and take him for a walk around the block. He came back a little rumpled and white as a sheet. He told me I should burn his notebooks."

"And did you?"

"He thought I did. He told the goons I did. When they come around, I showed them some ashes. I don't think they bought it. But you never know."

"What happened to the books?"

"Well, when that all went away and he got started on this new project, I told him I still had the books. He said, 'Jesus, Esther, you want to get us killed?' I said, 'These books are worth money to somebody, and since you aren't earning out, I'm testing the market.' He went really white then. You should've seen it."

"What happened to the books, Mrs. Grotz?"

"That's the thing. I don't know. He was working on this new project. He says he found some old papers down in the library. There was this guy, Brian...I don't think I ever heard of anybody in the family named Brian. Most of them are goombas, you know? Vito, Tony, Vince…like that, so this guy had come from outside the neighborhood. There's a kid in the neighborhood, Brian O'Neil is his name, but I don't think that's who he meant. Anyway, the next thing I know, he's gone and so are the books. You have a mafia down here? Maybe he came to sell them here."

"We'd like to keep the books for a little while longer. Would that be all right with you?"

"They're worth money."

"They're worth your life. But if you insist, we will send them back to you."

"You keep them for now. I'll let you know."

Sam spent another half hour trying to extract some useful information from her. Beyond the unlikely idea that her husband came to rural Virginia to peddle insider information to a local Mafia Don, she learned nothing new. Ike returned at the end of the session.

"Anything?" he asked, after Mrs. Grotz had been directed to the local Holiday Inn Express.

"Unless we have an organized crime family in the area, nothing. She is ignorant of what her husband was up to and didn't seem to care. Do we?"

"Do we what?"

"Have a mafia chapter in town?"

"That would be too simple. No. All we have here is the usual collection of misfits, bullies, and an occasional homicidal maniac. Just your typical southern town."

Sam missed the irony and nodded.

Chapter Nineteen

God watches over children and drunks, the saying goes. Jonathan Lydell snapped his cell phone shut and contemplated his daughter sprawled at the foot of the stairs, her limbs splayed in an awkward array, head twisted at an unnatural angle from her torso, and dead eyes staring at the ceiling. Apparently that protection did not extend to fake drunks. The expression on her face looked as if she'd just opened the door to a dark room to find all of her friends waiting to celebrate her birthday. Surprise! Unconsciously, his gaze followed her line of sight to the junction of wall and ceiling where a spider's web held a newly captured house fly. The more the victim struggled, the worse its predicament became. Trapped in a tangled web. He shook his head in appreciation of this intersection of metaphor and reality. *Oh what a tangled web we weave…*

"Poor girl, so many mistakes, so many wrong turns, and now this," he murmured. He slipped the pillow in his hand under her head, as if it might make her more comfortable. He sat back and waited for the Picketsville volunteer fire department to arrive. He wiped his eyes. He thought he ought to shift her body, rearrange it in a more decorous way. Why bother? Certainly she was past caring and so, he supposed, was he, yet…as much as they had differed and fought over the years, she was his only daughter, the mother of his grandson, and the last *doyenne* of Bellmore. What would he do now? Living with her had been difficult, without her…?

◇◇◇

Sam explained to Karl what she'd learned from Mrs. Grotz.

"Where is she now?" he asked.

"Darcie sent her to the Holiday Inn Express." She turned to Ike. "I asked you before about organized crime here in the valley. You said it didn't seem likely, but it's still a possibility. Karl, can your friends at the Bureau help us?"

"Assuming I still have friends there, yeah, maybe. At least I can call."

Ike swiveled around in his chair. The air in the room had become stale. From too much Grotz or just too many people for too long, he couldn't be sure.

"Before you do," he said, "let's think this thing through. The likelihood that there is a local mafia connection is slim at best. But allowing there might be one, why would Grotz want to approach them? What does he gain? Families look after each other when an outsider interferes. Doesn't it seem more likely the New Jersey crowd would be the shooters or at least put out a contract? If they discovered the Grotz woman did not destroy the books, and her husband might still have them, then wouldn't they be anxious to punish Grotz, follow him down here, or tap a local connection, and dispatch him? And then take out the missus. If I were that lady, I would disappear for a while. At least until we clear up this mess."

"Do you think we will?" Sam asked.

"Part of it, maybe. I hope we will figure out the why, and maybe even the who. It's the how that has me stumped. And until we get that worked out, knowing the who and the why isn't worth squat."

Karl wiped his forehead. "But at least then the bad guys would know we knew and they'd be looking over their shoulders from then on."

"Small comfort in that. This whole set-up just doesn't make sense. We need to know what he was tracking when he came here. What was he up to?"

"You're not buying a mob hit?"

"No. He's too easy a target at home. Kill him right there in Passaic. Why come here?"

They sat in silence for a moment. "Sam, any other thoughts?"

"Yes, two things. First, I saved the cutlery and cup from Mrs. Grotz's dinner so we'll have her prints and, if we need it, a DNA sample." Ike tilted his head, peered over the top of his reading glasses.

"Okay, Ike, I know that the DNA thing takes fifteen forevers, but you never know. Second, he had an overdue library book with his stuff. I can search that library's files and find out what else he was reading. That may give us a clue about what his 'big one' consisted of."

"Good. Karl, your turn."

"I'm still stuck on the why he ended up in a locked room. It is so idiotic. Nobody, except mystery story junkies, thinks about locked rooms. I mean, it must take hours to set one up, and did you know there's a whole book about them? Locked room mystery stories, that is. Somebody catalogued them, I looked. Every conceivable way is discussed. Amazing and entertaining, but murderers aren't in the entertainment business."

"Maybe," Sam said, "maybe the two are not related at all."

"What do you mean, not related?"

"A hypothetical to consider. The murder is separated from the lock up. One person did the shooting, another locked the room. Possible?"

"Possible," Ike said, "but the question remains, why bother?"

The three fell silent again. Ike cracked the window and let in some cool spring air. The phone rang in the outer office. Darcie frowned and then called Ike, a tinny voice on the intercom. "Ike, the dispatcher over at the volunteer fire company just called. She thought you'd like to know there's been an accident out at Mr. Lydell's house."

"What kind of acci…can you hear me?"

"You have to push that little button that says MIC," Sam said, and pointed at the phone.

"Oh, okay…Darcie?"

"Yes?"

"What kind of accident?"

"Seems like his daughter fell down the stairs and broke her neck, bless her heart."

Ike pulled up behind the fire company's bright red pumper. The Picketsville Volunteer Fire Company, like its big city counterparts, responded to 9-1-1 calls with a full complement of equipment. The captain would then release the units not needed after he assessed the situation. Picketsville firefighters were cross-trained. The pumper crew could double as an EMT team. Lights from roof mounts flashed asynchronously and the neighborhood residents lined both sides of the road, gawking. He slid out of the cruiser and walked toward the house.

"Sheriff," Lydell said, barely loud enough to be heard over the noise of idling diesel engines and shouting fire fighters. "These men insist that my daughter's body must be taken to the coroner's office. I won't have it."

For once Ike sympathized with Lydell. It did seem harsh and unnecessary to quarantine a body in that way, particularly in the case of an accident, but the town statute was firm. Any death that might be construed as suspicious, no matter how slight, had to pass muster with the coroner. The statute had been placed on the books as a result of some egregious, and highly suspicious, accidents involving court witnesses and municipal reformers in years past.

"Sorry, Mr. Lydell, but it's the law. I'll speak to the doc and ask him to give a quick release."

Lydell did not look particularly mollified. "It's outrageous. My daughter fell and I cannot even make decent arrangements. I must contact my grandson…he's an attorney, you know, he may have something to say about all of this."

Ike disengaged from the angry old man. He climbed the stairs to the porch and stepped into the hallway. The stranger room door had been closed but the lock did not seem to have been repaired yet. The fire company captain met him in the hallway.

"Best guess, Buck?"

"Drunk as a lord, Ike. She reeked of whiskey. The decanter on the sideboard is empty. It looks like she tried to go upstairs, maybe to sleep it off, missed a step and tumbled down."

"Who called it in?"

"The old man."

Ike circled the body, peered up the steps and frowned. He climbed halfway up and bent over to inspect the carpet runner on one step. He pulled an envelope from his pocket, lifted the flap and scooped something that looked like a press-on fingernail into it. It wasn't much, but you never know. He nodded to the ambulance crew who slid Martha Marie Winslow, nee Lydell, into a body bag, zipped it shut, and carried her away. Lydell stood outside the door, his face shattered with grief. It looked like grief, but you never know.

Chapter Twenty

Henry Sutherlin mingled with the crowd watching the fire trucks and, later, Ike's arrival. He asked what happened. One of the EMTs stopped loading his equipment long enough to tell him. Poor Miss Martha Marie. He ran his hand over his newly shorn head and chin, and had a brief moment of panic, until he remembered he'd been to Lee Henry's salon and had his Mohawk removed. The goatee fell to a set of sheep shears he found in Wainwright's barn.

"Don't fret none, Honey," Lee had said. "Hair grows. If you get to missing your little old up-do, you can always grow it back."

As he watched Ike emerge from the house, he wondered if he would be interested in hearing his take on the murders, not that he had anything new, but with this latest death, maybe...

"Yo, Tattoo Boy. You still playing at being a deputy?"

Henry turned to face George LeBrun. Some believe that a lifetime of saintliness will shape a concomitant expression on a person's visage. Similarly a lifetime spent in degradation and ugliness will also find its way to your face. George now qualified as an extremely ugly man.

"What?"

"Well, since Ike the Kike turned you down, I figured you were out here playing at being a policeman and trying to impress him."

Henry frowned. He had no interest in pursuing a conversation with George LeBrun. He remembered him from the old days when the sheriff's office had become the town's black eye. And though he'd been a teenager at the time, he recalled the rumors circulating about LeBrun and his cronies. "Hooligans," his mother described them. His brothers, Billy and Frank, used a few stronger words. George stepped closer. He grinned and Henry recoiled at the smell and sight of LeBrun's rotting teeth.

"I bet you have one of them police band radios so you can show up at all the crime scenes and look smart. You're wasting your time, you know. Schwartz ain't interested in hiring any decent white guys. He's taking on freaks and niggers." He drained a soda can, tossed it aside, and lit a cigar. A cheap cigar, as nearly as Henry could tell, and tried to position himself upwind.

"Careful there, George. My brother works for Ike and, in case you didn't know it, the black guy is FBI on assignment."

"What about the Amazon woman, the seven foot dyke, with the man's name that he hired from the college?"

"George, stuff it. You're off the reservation there. Ryder is okay."

"Yeah? And you got your priorities all screwed up. Time is coming when the Jew and his friends are gonna be history and the sheriff's office will be looking for deputies. You play your cards right and you could be one of them."

"What are you talking about, George? If you're figuring on running against Ike next year, you ain't got a prayer, and even if he don't run, one of Wainwright's cows has a better chance of getting elected than you. And why do you spend so much time hanging around here, George? You got business or are you just nosey?"

LeBrun's face turned scarlet. Billy knew LeBrun could be trouble when he was angry and he regretted the remark almost instantly.

"There's some of us that are looking for friends in this town, weirdo, and we will keep track of who is for us and who ain't. Oh yeah, and if you see Falco, you tell her she'd better stay straight or else."

"Essie? You're kidding. Essie never—"

"Your brother Billy is sweet on her, I know, so you can tell him to keep her in line."

"You know something, George, you ought never to pick on a family that's got seven brothers 'cause as much as we may fuss at each other, if you go at one of us, you get us all. And that goes for people that's close to us as well. See, Essie and Billy, well, they're, like, good friends."

"Friends ain't the way I heard it. I heard he was doing the nasty with her regular like."

Henry did not usually consider consequences when he acted and hitting LeBrun could only end in trouble, but family is family and before he saw it coming, Henry clipped LeBrun on the ear with a roundhouse punch. George could have easily blocked it but he'd just reached for his cigar and, temporarily distracted, missed seeing it coming. It didn't have much power and only stunned. The cigar sailed away into the street. LeBrun whirled and kicked Henry, who promptly crumpled to the macadam. LeBrun whipped a buck knife from his jeans pocket and had the blade open so fast Henry thought for a moment it was a switchblade. LeBrun looked angry enough to carve him up on the spot.

"Hold it right there, George, unless you want a weekend in jail." Ike had slipped up behind them.

LeBrun whirled to face him. "What charges will you be bringing?"

Henry had by this time limped out of knife range. Should he run? Ike would be mad either way. He decided to stay, but keep his distance.

Ike snapped open his holster tab and rested his hand on the butt of his .357 magnum.

"George, do yourself a big favor and let go of that pig-sticker. In the eyes of the law, it qualifies as a deadly weapon and, as you for sure know, that'd justify my jerking out this cannon and dropping you on the spot. I'm not even going to count. Just you drop it now."

Henry shifted his gaze from one to the other, as if he were watching a tennis match. LeBrun glared at Ike. Ike had the pistol cleared just as LeBrun dropped the knife.

"Kick it over here and get out of my sight."

LeBrun scuttled away, cursing.

"Ike, you just bought yourself a wagonload of mess. That guy is mean as a snake and he'll be back."

"He's only mean when he thinks he's got a big edge. I almost wish he had come at me. We'd be done with him by now."

Ike stooped and retrieved the knife, folded the blade, and dropped it in his pocket.

It had taken four of five appointments, but Ike had finally gotten used to the blended aroma of wet hair and shampoo in Lee Henry's salon. She had a cup of coffee and a half-eaten cheese Danish in each hand when he arrived.

"You're late, handsome. You been busy keeping law and order in Dodge?"

Ike dropped into her chair and sighed.

"Why do I do it, Lee? It isn't the money and it sure isn't the prestige, so why do I keep going out every day and put up with all this…stuff?"

She flipped the plastic sheet over him and tied the neck strings. "Beats me, Ike. I reckon you must like it, somehow. I'll tell you this much, though, since you took over as sheriff, the rest of us can sleep at night for a change. Now you take that last crew…"

"I had a run in with one of them half an hour ago. Do you remember George LeBrun?"

"Do I remember having my wisdom teeth out? That man is a piece of work. He should have 666 tattooed on his forehead. He was one of them that hurt my baby sister. Sorry, you know all about that. But I'll tell you this, Ike, if I ever got the chance…I'd kill him as soon as look at him and then you'd be hauling me in for murder."

"Gotcha."

Lee switched on her electric shears. "Okay, now on a lighter note, Mr. Sheriff. You been out to the mall lately?"

"Some, not much, been busy."

"You seen how them young girls is dressing?"

"You mean the belly shirts?"

"No, I mean their pants is falling down. Jeeze Louise, it's like double cleavage. One up top facing front, one down low facing back. Lordy, they bend over and you can see near everything either way."

"Old guys out at the mall tell me they consider it a divine gift. Something sent to brighten their day."

"DOM is what they are. You know what they're calling that, um...rear slot?"

"It was always a 'plumber's crack' before."

"Not no more. Now it's a 'card swipe.' Swear to God, Ike, that's what it's called. Ain't that something? Speaking of which, did I tell you about my cousin Derrick?"

"He's the one with the lazy eye?"

"No, you're thinking of Erick. Derrick is the one who had a piece of his ear bit off in a fight with his ex."

"So what happened to Derrick?" Ike braced himself for *the story*. Lee always had one for him. It had become as much a part of his haircut as the clippers and the mousse. Lee Henry's mission in life, he told his friends, was to provide laughter therapy to folks when they needed it, and the haircut was only a necessary, but coincidental part of the session.

"He showed up here the other day and he's got himself two black eyes. Two! I said, 'Derrick, where'd you get them black eyes?' He says, 'Well, I was up to the church Wednesday night, just minding my business and the preacher asks us to stand and sing a verse or two of *Come to the River*. Now, there's a large lady in front of me whose got her dress stuck in her...card swipe' he said the other word but you know what he meant. 'So,' he said, 'I figured I'd be a good servant of the Lord and help the sister out. I reached over and pulled it loose. That's when she hit me with her purse right here on my right side.'" Lee applied the clippers to Ike's neck.

"So then I said, 'But what about the other black eye?' and Derrick, he said, 'Well, since she seemed so upset about what I done with her dress, I figured I'd better put it back. That's when she got me on the left.' It's the truth, Ike, swear to God."

Ike's cell phone chirped. He flipped it open and held it to his ear.

"Not that side, Ike, I'm working over there." Lee tilted his head and applied her clippers to his side burns. He shifted the phone to the other ear.

"Ike, you got two calls. I wouldn't disturb you but they sounded important."

"It's okay, Darcie. Who called?"

"Essie called and said could you come over to her sister's house on account of something happened that she's scared of, and Norbert over at the gun store called and said he had your...Webley...I made him spell it...what's a Webley?"

"It's a make of pistol. Send Karl over to Norbert's and you can tell Essie, if she calls again, I'll be there in maybe thirty minutes." So Norbert came by a Webley. What were the odds it would be *the* Webley?

"You know what they call the little love handles that pop over the top of them low ridin' jeans?"

Ike resisted shaking his head. Lee had switched to applying her straight razor to his neck.

"Muffin tops. Ain't that a hoot?"

Chapter Twenty-one

Karl waited across the street from The Lock and Load for five minutes. He didn't have any compelling reason to do so, it had just become a cautionary habit he'd developed over the years, and one that had once saved him from a major gaffe and career ending mistake. So, he sat in the police cruiser and watched. Only one man entered and left. He exited the car and walked the few yards to the shop. He wanted to brace Norbert Sills about the Webley with as few witnesses as possible. Norbert had a reputation within the Bureau that even Ike didn't know.

The doorway had been fitted with a warning device and it buzzed as he entered. The shop was not large, a few glass fronted display cases filled with handguns of various calibers and prices, and a one-way mirror behind the cash register. The customer space carried the faint odor of stale tobacco smoke and gun oil. He'd seen the Bureau's file. Sills' picture did not do him justice. The Norbert in the file photo looked meaner and tougher. This Norbert, his sickly smile notwithstanding, looked like a wharf rat.

"Sills, you called and said you had a Webley for us. Is that correct?"

"Who the hell are you?"

"The uniform doesn't suggest anything to you?"

"I want to speak to the sheriff, not one of his boys."

Karl locked on Sills, his gaze like five miles of polar ice. He slipped out his Bureau credentials and slid them across the counter.

"FBI? Cripes. I didn't know. I thought you were—"

"One of the sheriff's *boys*, so you said. I'm both, Sills. I'm on loan to the sheriff. And, in case you didn't know, the Bureau has a file on you and your store that's two inches thick. You are just one questionable sale away from an indictment. So, tell me about the Webley?"

Norbert swallowed. "Hey, listen man, I run a legit operation here. You can ask anybody."

"We have. One more shooting in the District, Pittsburgh, or anywhere else with a pistol traceable to you and you're serving time. Now, are you going to tell me about the Webley or not?"

Norbert's eyes did an Irish jig in their sockets and finally stared at the counter surface.

"Okay. See, this kid comes in here this morning with a Webley. 'I want to sell it,' he says. I say, 'Where'd you get it?' and he looks at me funny, and so I know I ain't going to get the truth. He tells me it's his granddad's old service revolver. I say, 'What war?' He hems and haws and says, 'Korea?' like it's a question. What a dope. He wants to know how much it's worth and I give him a price which he is not happy about. 'That's all?' he wants to know. Well, I know it ain't his dear old granddad's piece on account it's an English service revolver and our guys packed a .45 in those days. But he's nervous and tries to talk me up, but I don't go there. I give an extra ten bucks, that's it."

"Could we cut to the chase here, Sills? Who was he, and what happened to the pistol?"

"Yeah, yeah, I'm getting to that. This is good. See, I know your boss, the sheriff, wants that piece, maybe, so I say, 'I'll need to see some ID.' And this moron hands me his driver's license and the picture is right there and I know it's him. I copy it on the machine and I take the gun and put it away. He wants his dough. I give him a ten spot, but I say, 'the gun has to clear the police screening process.' He doesn't know that that is a bunch of…you know, and when he hears *police*, he grabs the Hamilton and takes off."

Karl shook his head. He had to hand it to Norbert. He'd learned over the years that people, who traded in the shadowy edges of society, were good at what they did because they learned early on how to lie convincingly.

"Where's the Webley now?"

Norbert reached into a cabinet behind him and produced the pistol.

"Ta-dah!"

"Break it open and dump the shells in here. Be careful."

Karl opened an evidence bag. Norbert opened the breach and allowed the shells to fall in, four empty casings and two loads. He dropped the gun in a second bag.

"We have your prints on file. I expect the kid's will be on the pistol, too. Let's hope someone else got careless loading it, assuming, of course, this is the piece we're looking for. I'll take that Xerox of the driver's license now."

Norbert handed him the paper.

"Thanks."

Norbert stared at Karl's holster and said, "Say, is that nine millimeter Bureau issue? If not, I'll take it in trade for a Glock 31. Great little piece. The sheriff is thinking of replacing his old .357 with one."

"It's a personal weapon and it suits me just fine. Thanks anyway."

"Well if you ever change your mind…"

"Ike, I'm scared." Essie Falco huddled on an overstuffed sofa hugging her knees. Ike dropped into a worn recliner with a duct tape patch on one arm. Essie's sister owned a double-wide on an acre that used to be part of old man Craddock's farm. A lone cow grazed a few yards from the front door.

"Because?"

"George LeBrun. You know what he did at the Shop N Save?"

"I heard. I had a run in with him myself out at Lydell's about an hour ago."

"He's not fooling, Ike. He means to get you and anyone he thinks will get in his way. He's...well, it's like he's crazy or something. I mean in the old days he was just a dirty cop with a mean streak. Now he's—"

"A meth-head, I know. He's brought the worst of the drug culture into town."

"But—"

"You'll be safe enough, Essie. When do you go to Disney World?"

"Well, that's the thing. My sister works for the county and they just changed her work schedule. I might have to stick around for a while." The cow outside lowed a mournful counterpoint to Essie's complaint.

"Can you stay here?"

"Yeah, I guess. But he'll find me if he wants to."

"Essie, LeBrun is a bully. He picks on people smaller or weaker than he is. Out in the open, with witnesses, he won't do anything more than threaten, hopped up on crystal meth or not." Ike hoped he told the truth but meth-heads were hard to predict, sometimes violent, sometimes merely irrational.

Essie rolled up her sleeve and showed Ike the bruise LeBrun had made when he grabbed her arm. Ike closed his eyes and fought the anger that might lead him into doing something rash. For the first time since he became sheriff, he pined for his CIA days. Back then, he could quietly dispense some personal and anonymous justice.

"We'll take care of it, Essie. I'll have someone keep an eye out."

"Ike, that'd be a tip off, wouldn't it? I mean..."

"You won't even know they're there. Try to relax. We're on it."

Essie looked doubtful. "Someone will be close by?"

"Absolutely." Ike made the promise but at the same time realized that keeping it would not be easy. Mostly, he wanted Essie to believe it. Then she would feel better, safer, and believe that LeBrun wouldn't dare approach her again. Then he touched the Buck Knife in his pocket and knew he couldn't be sure of anything. LeBrun was like a rabies carrier at the Westminster dog show. The sooner he was put down, the better. He would have offered Essie a gun but that would only lead to difficulties of monumental proportions if she were to use it. Besides, on this side of town, most folks owned a firearm of some sort, and if Essie felt really threatened, she could have one in hand in a heartbeat. He didn't like that idea any better, but at least the department would not be at risk if anything went wrong.

He heard the roar of an engine and had started to turn toward the door when a rock smashed through the front window. Essie screamed, and balled up on the couch. Ike instinctively ducked and rolled. Splintered glass cascaded across the floor. By the time he managed to stand and run to the door, whatever vehicle had borne the rock thrower had careened around the bend and disappeared. The cow bawled and loped off across the pasture. Ike felt his blood pressure spike. Now he was really angry.

"Essie, do you have a firearm?"

"What?"

"A gun, any kind. Do you have one?"

"Yeah." She reached into her purse and removed a Dixie Derringer. "I got this from Billy. He showed me how to shoot it."

Ike whistled. Only in America. So much for caution.

"Okay, Essie, but do me a favor, will you? Keep an empty chamber under the hammer. I'd hate to see you wham someone with that purse and end up shooting a bystander."

"I don't swing a purse, Ike."

"Good. Empty the chamber anyway."

Chapter Twenty-two

"Stuff on your desk for you, Boss." Billy Sutherlin waved in the general direction of Ike's office and headed for the door.

"Hold on a minute, Billy. Did you give Essie a pistol?"

"More like I loaned it to her, Ike. That piece set me back a couple of hundred."

"You know what's going on with George LeBrun?"

"Oh yeah."

"If she gets spooked, she might put a bullet in him."

"Public service, way I see it, Ike."

"Billy, think a minute. If that little .22 caliber popgun misses anything vital, LeBrun will be on her, and kill her in a heartbeat. You know what he nearly did to your brother."

"Ike, I thought about that, for sure, and I figured if she got the drop on him, he'd back away. Nobody wants to take a chance against a pistol. Besides which, it has a magnum load. Do more'n knick him."

"I hope you're right. Still, I don't like it. What's on the desk?"

"Crime lab report, on your car. Karl got the Webley and he's picking up the kid that brought it to Norbert, and they're running prints on the ammo. Sam says she has a lead on someplace in New Jersey." Billy continued his way to the door. "Oh, yeah, thanks for taking care of George out at Lydell's. If you hadn't, I would 'a, and Henry said to ask if now is a good time to talk."

"Sure, where is he?"

"Outside in his truck. I'll send him in."

"On your way to wherever it is you're going, how about dropping this off at the Lab." Ike handed him an evidence bag with a rock in it. To Billy's raised eyebrows he added, "It was thrown through the window at Essie's sister's place. No note. Maybe we can lift a print, though I doubt it. But you never know what will turn up and we need all the help we can get." Billy scooped up the bag, jammed his Stetson down low on his forehead, and left.

Ike settled in his beat-up oak desk chair and swiveled right and left. No squeal or squeak. That was good. As a rule, his desk looked like a burial mound. He told anyone who had the temerity to ask, he had a system to find what he needed in the heap, but lately either he, or the system, had developed a serious glitch and had crashed, which meant he needed to do his semi-annual desk top cleaning. He glanced at the calendar from Unger's Funeral Home on the wall and realized April had arrived the week before. That confirmed it.

Henry rapped on the door and he waved him in. "Hey, Ike, I just wanted to say, I appreciate what you done for me out at Lydell's this morning. That sombitch could 'a cut me up if you hadn't come along."

"You need to pick your fights a little more carefully, Henry. As you said, he could have cut you up proper."

"Yeah, well, he was off on Essie and Billy and I just couldn't stand there, could I?"

Ike pulled LeBrun's Buck Knife from his pocket, jacked open the blade and speared a piece of paper. He pulled the paper free and held it by one corner, drew the knife down its length from the top. It sliced through its length with barely a whisper. Half fluttered to the floor.

"Whoa," Henry said, "now that there is one sharp knife."

With great care, Ike folded it and shoved it into a drawer. "You wanted to see me about something else?"

"Huh? Oh yeah. I was going to tell you about what I heard out at Lydell's this morning. Well, actually there's two things.

First George, that's LeBrun, I seen him hanging around, you know? Like more than once out at Lydell's."

"That's interesting. Any idea why?"

"No sir, sorry. Just thought it might be something, and then there's the other thing. It might or might not have anything to do with anything either, you know, but…well anyway, I was out there in the back stacking the wood I split the day before and I hear him and Miss Martha Marie upstairs going at it."

"That's Lydell and his daughter…going at it?"

"Yeah. And she's yelling, which is no surprise on account of her drinking and all, and he's hollering back."

"And the problem is?"

"He don't ordinarily yell back at her when she's you know, sauced. He just shakes his head, sad like, but not then. They was going at it big time."

"You hear anything helpful?"

"I don't know if I did or not. He's going on about some old documents and how she had no right to do this or that, and she's yelling something like he's a hypnotist—it sounded like that—but that don't make no sense, either."

"Hypocrite."

"What?"

"She probably called him a hypocrite, not a hypnotist."

"Yeah? Well you might be right there. Anyhow, that got me to thinking about documents. See, the day before he called me in on the carpet, so to say, and asked had I seen some old papers of his. I didn't know what he was talking about but he sure acted spooked."

"Documents?"

"Yep. He's on about them papers. I don't know what they were about, but it sure had him riled and then this morning he's hollering at Miss Martha Marie, so I figured you might want to know about that."

"Thank you, Henry. I don't know what to do with it, but something tells me to remember it. Maybe it'll come to me later. That all?" Ike stared at Henry's hair, or more accurately, the lack thereof, and realized in the scuffle at Lydell's, he'd completely missed Henry's newly bald pate. "What happened to your hair, Henry?"

"I had Miss Lee lop it off, the hair, I mean. I can hide the tats, of course, and yes sir, that's pretty much it, unless you got a minute to talk about the academy. See, I know I messed up the first time and maybe I ain't supposed to be in law enforcement, but I'd like to give it another go."

"Henry, you go for it, if that's what you want. You see how your brothers handle it. Billy at work here and Frank over with the State Police, so you know what you're getting into, I guess."

"I was thinking more along the line of being an evidence technician. You know CSI and all that. You'd be okay sponsoring me?"

"Sure, why not? Good luck with that."

Henry grinned a thank you, and Ike noted the small hole in his lip that must have supported a stud not too long ago. Henry seemed to be cleaning up his act. What he'd do about the holes in his ears was something else. Ike waved him out and started to sift through the pile of paper on his desk. He found the Crime Lab's preliminary report under a discount coupon for pizza.

The Passaic Public Library faxed a list of books Grotz had borrowed in the past year and referred Sam to the Passaic Historical Society. The curator—Sam guessed that's who it was—seemed reluctant at first to share any information with her. Sam reminded her she was following a lead in a murder investigation. That did the trick.

"Oh yes, it's not easy to forget a name like Grotz," she said. Sam waited. "Okay, I have it here. He read several old letters in the Walzak file. The family left them with us a few years ago. They had an ancestor who was killed in the Civil War and they thought we might be interested in some old letters and notes he wrote at that time."

"Can you tell me if there is anything in them that might help us?"

"I really don't know. What would you be looking for?"

That was the question, certainly. What indeed. "I'm not sure. We only have some overdue library books and an interest in the Shenandoah Valley campaign to go on. Would it be possible for you to copy the documents he spent his time on and send them to us?"

"Oh dear, I don't know. Well, you see, the problem is, we are missing some of the documents in that file. We assumed Mr. Grotz must have taken them, but…well, we can't be sure and don't like to…"

"We will be more than happy to search for them at this end. Perhaps they are with his personal items." Sam knew better, but she hoped the possibility that the documents might be retrievable would help with the decision. "We would cover any charges, of course," Sam said, although she couldn't be sure if she had it right. She listened as the person on the other end of the line conferred with someone else.

"Yes, we can fax you the documents. No charge for that, of course."

Sam gave them a fax number.

Chapter Twenty-three

Traces of pseudaphedrine, cocaine, methamphetamine, cannabis, ethanol, and caffeine residue...cough syrup, coke, meth, pot, booze, and coffee! The report continued with a laundry list of chemicals that Ike recognized as fillers, solvents, sugars, and other inconsequential materials. He read the report with growing concern. *A few smudged prints on the cup lids, AFIS search tentatively identifies: LeBrun, George, on four points only. The glassine bags yielded small amounts of crystal meth mixed with inositol.* The car had Daryll Jenkins' prints, but then it would. He worked on the car.

Methamphetamine worried Ike. Except for some recreational use of pot and, lately, ecstasy, at the high school and up at the college, the town had managed, so far, to avoid the worst of the nation's pervasive drug culture. Now, it seemed, he faced the double nightmare of cocaine, crystal meth, and God only knew what else. Karl entered the outer office with a young man in tow. Ike moved to meet them.

"Sheriff," Karl said, "this is Tommy."

"Tommy? Last name?"

"He says he isn't saying anything, including his name. He wants to 'lawyer up.'"

"Where do you suppose he learned that? Tommy, what do you mean you want to lawyer up?" The boy looked confused, dropped his gaze and studied his shoes. "What have you done, son, which would require calling a lawyer?"

"Nothing. I didn't do nothing, Sheriff. I was walking through the pasture out by Mr. Wainwright's and I found it."

"Found it? Could you be more specific?"

"What about my lawyer?"

"What's his name?"

"Huh?"

"You wanted to call your lawyer. I'll do that, but I need a name."

"I don't know any lawyers."

"You want us to provide one, is that it?"

"I don't know. Like, on the TV, they get lawyers and stuff."

Ike sighed, and silently cursed the television industry for making his job impossibly complex as thousands of otherwise sensible people assumed without DNA and exotic forensic evidence, even a full confession wouldn't convict.

"Tommy, let's get something straight. You have not been charged with a crime, so you don't need a lawyer unless there is something about finding an old revolver that can incriminate you. Second, we have a copy of your driver's license and we already know your name. And finally, this is a murder investigation, and unless you want to be an accessory after the fact, and do some serious jail time, you need to tell us about the gun." The latter was a stretch but Ike figured if the kid didn't know anything more than televisionland law, it would work. It did.

"I ain't going to no jail. I didn't do nothing."

"You found the gun. You want to give us the details now?"

Tommy squinched up his face and reached into his windbreaker pocket for a pack of cigarettes.

"Not in here, son."

He dropped the pack back in his pocket. "So, now do we go into a room with the one-way glass mirror window?"

Karl started to laugh and then caught himself. With as much patience as he could muster, Ike led him into his office.

"Okay, Tommy, talk to me."

"See, I found it out in the woods. You know, like, where Wainwright's back pasture touches Mr. Lydell's? Well, there's this old hollow stump back on the fence line. I used to hide stuff there when I was a kid." Ike smiled at Tommy's *kid*. "Anyway, Mister Lydell chased me off a couple of times so I ain't been back for a while. Well, old Wainwright just plowed that back lot and I was out there looking for arrowheads. They're worth some money at the souvenir shop. So I think, I'll just stroll over and have a look-see in my old stump. And there it was."

"Why did you try to sell it? When I was your age, I'd have cleaned it up and kept it."

"I figured it was worth some money and I wanted to get me some."

"For?"

"I ain't saying."

Ike let that pass. "Was there anything else in the stump?"

"Just some old junk, like it's been there forever."

Ike swiveled around to catch Karl's eye. He, in turn, produced a notebook and pen. "What kind of junk?"

"There's a match box, all rotted up that had some old pennies. I think they must have been Billy Shorter's, but he's moved away somewhere. Me and him used to hide stuff in that stump back awhile. And an old key."

"Key?"

"Yeah, like an old time door key. It was in there, too. Oh, and a box of bullets."

Ike gazed at the boy who shifted from side-to-side and looked at him and then Karl. "Am I in trouble, Sheriff?"

"There are traces of marijuana on the pistol grip. That wouldn't have anything to do with your needing money would it?" Karl glanced sharply at Ike. No test had been run on the piece and he had no idea what Ike was up to. The kid's lower lip began to quiver.

"It wasn't my idea," he said. "It were Daryll's."

"Daryll. That would be George LeBrun's cousin, Daryll Jenkins?"

"Yes sir."

"He wanted you to sell or buy?"

"Sell, out at school. I owed him for some…you won't tell my folks?"

"Thank you, Tommy. I'm going to call your mom and dad now, and release you in their custody. I want you to tell them to bring in all the stuff you found with the gun when they come to pick you up. And Tommy…"

"Yes sir?"

"You don't want to get mixed up with drugs, you hear?"

"Yes sir."

"Karl, go pick up Daryll Jenkins."

Karl walked into the garage where the man he assumed to be Jenkins stood under a rusted out Ford Explorer up on the grease rack, and struggled to free its oil filter. Karl let him unwind a string of obscenities before he spoke.

"Jenkins?"

"Yeah, that's me," Daryll said, without ducking his head to see who addressed him.

"You want to pop out here for a minute?"

"Who's asking."

Karl considered for a moment and said, "FBI."

"O…kay. Now we're talking. You're here about the stuff in the sheriff's car, right?" Daryll ducked out from under, and took in Karl. Jenkins had the same beetling brows as his cousin. That constituted the only similarity between the two. "Hey, wait a minute," he muttered, "you ain't FBI, you're the sheriff's boy, ain't that right?"

Karl slipped his nightstick free and tapped Daryll on the right knee. The knee buckled and Daryll Jenkins dropped to the floor.

"Hey. Ow. You can't do that. I'm reporting you to the cops."

"I am the cops, Stupid. Now stand up and put your hands behind your back."

"You got nothing on me, boy."

There was that word again. Karl tapped the other knee, this time harder. Daryll went down again. "There's nobody here but you and me, you little dirt bag, so it's your word against mine. Judges never listen to drug dealers anyway, so, you're done. Now, get up and put your hands—"

"Behind my back. Okay, okay. Just keep that stick away from me. What's the charge?"

"Solicitation to sell illegal drugs, for one, planting false evidence in a police car, and, I expect, we'll find some more things to throw at you before Friday."

George LeBrun needed to talk to his cousin. Either the Falco bitch sold him out or his cousin, Daryll, did. He rounded the corner of the garage in time to see Karl Hedrick lead Daryll away. He ducked back behind a stack of used tires. Neither man saw him. When the two had driven away, he slipped into the office. He riffled through the top drawer of a three drawer filing cabinet and emptied it of its contents, which he shoved into a dirty gunny sack. He spun and walked back into the garage area. It wouldn't do to have the sheriff's office return with a warrant, and they surely would. He had no illusions about his cousin. The jerk would blab his head off inside a half hour. He removed a key from his jacket pocket and unlocked a door to what appeared to be a small storage room. Nothing in it would survive a fire. There would be no usable evidence other than some scorched cans and jars. He'd already disposed of the cough medicine bottles in the dumpster down the alley behind Schwartz's place. He carried in a gallon can of gasoline, poured it on the counter and floor, stepped outside, and tossed in a lighted match. He slammed the door and walked away. Now that's some real meth cooking. Too bad about Daryll's garage. He hoped the moron had insurance.

Chapter Twenty-four

The fax machine hummed to life and began spitting out sheets of paper. The cover sheet indicated thirty pages would be forthcoming. Sam glanced at the first, a letter written in elegant copperplate, to a Mr. F. Brian, from an acquaintance in Frederick, Maryland. The Walzak file, apparently. Sam skimmed the pages as they collected in the tray. Ancient folds and creases, and the fading occasioned by the passage of over a century and a half, made them difficult to read. She wished she could have seen the originals. It appeared the late Mr. Franklin Brian of Trenton, New Jersey had some very interesting things to say about some of Virginia's more illustrious citizens, now long departed. Bolton, Virginia appeared in several later documents.

She collected the stack and retreated to her office where she spread them out on a countertop with the list of books Grotz had borrowed from the Passaic Public Library. She sorted them by date, and then cross referenced them to the books on the list. An hour passed. As she read, a frown creased her forehead. Later, it was replaced by a puzzled look, and that, finally, by one of comprehension. She scooped up documents, the book list, and headed for the college library.

◇◇◇

Jonathan Lydell refused to speak to anyone other than the sheriff himself. Rita, who'd come on duty at four, wigwagged for Ike to pick up.

"Sheriff, I want to report a theft." Lydell sounded distracted, worried.

"Mr. Lydell, you do not have to call me personally. The dispatcher will send a deputy to speak to you and take your statement."

"Thank you, I'm sure that is the routine, however, you must understand this is a matter of some urgency and I do not wish to place myself in the hands of anyone less than the top man, so to speak."

Ike guessed, Lydell had probably already called the State Police, and had been rebuffed by them. Now he had to deal with the locals, a breed with which he had little or no patience.

"Okay, tell me what was stolen and I will put someone on it immediately."

"A weapon, a family heirloom, you might say, a very old firearm, to be exact. It has some sentimental value. It was given to my late brother by his opposite number in the British Army—Cairo, Field Marshall Montgomery, Rommel, El Alamein, military intelligence, and all that."

"I see. By any chance, would the weapon in question be a Webley, .455 caliber?"

"Excuse me, but how did you know?"

"It, or one very much like it, turned up as part of our investigation. What can you tell me about the weapon?"

"Well, I just spoke of its origin. What else would you like to know?"

"When did you miss it?"

"Why, today, of course."

"Today?"

"Yes, most certainly, today. I was searching for some documents that I had…misplaced and, well, in the excitement of Martha Marie's accident and…" his voice broke.

"Yes, I see. You were searching for some papers. Could the pistol have been stolen earlier?"

Lydell sighed and collected himself. "I suppose it could have. Are you suggesting it might be the weapon that killed that man?"

"It is possible, certainly. How are you holding up?"

"Holding up? What on earth…oh, you mean because of poor Martha Marie. Very well, under the circumstances, I think. She drank, you know. Spirits were her undoing, I'm afraid."

"We will need to hold the pistol for a while, Mr. Lydell, at least until the ballistics tests are run and we can establish or eliminate it as a murder weapon."

"Yes, of course."

"I'll have to ask you to come in and identify it."

"Yes."

"Did you find your papers?"

"Papers? You mean the missing documents? Ah…Yes, I did, thank you." The line stayed silent. Ike started to hang up when Lydell spoke again. His voice seemed far away. "About Martha Marie, my daughter…"

"I had a word with the coroner. The post is complete and you can make whatever arrangements necessary."

"Was there anything…did he mention…?"

"I'll have the report tomorrow. If there is anything you need to know, I will call you."

"Yes, thank you." Lydell hung up. Ike drummed his fingertips beating out the rhythm to *The Teddy Bear's Picnic*.

Karl studied Daryll Jenkins. The clock on the wall, a survivor of another, simpler era, ticked away, marking time. Jenkins fidgeted, squirmed, and wiped his hands on his greasy jeans. Karl waited. He knew that only hardened criminals, the really tough guys, could sit and endure long periods of silence. Amateurs, like this one, would soon cave in and start talking. Jenkins first tried a stare down and lost. His gaze darted away from Karl's unremitting one and settled on the window. Outside, a lone, unkempt lilac seemed ready to burst into bloom a week before all the others in town, the beneficiary of high doses of carbon monoxide and heat from the parking lot next to it. The temperature in the room climbed.

"Hey, how about we open a window. It's hot in here," Jenkins said.

"I think it's just fine, Daryll. Beautiful spring day. Time to sit and chat about this and that. You want to tell me about your cousin and what the two of you have been up to? Or, should I call my friends in the Drug Enforcement Agency and see if they can't find a whole lot of things to drop in your lap?"

"Hey, you can't do that. You got nothing on me."

Rita walked over to Karl and whispered something in his ear and left.

"You know, Daryll, you might just be right about that. What were you up to in that back room of yours?"

"What back room?"

"At your garage, Daryll. That back room."

"I don't know what you're talking about."

"Well, whatever it was, it's gone now. Someone torched your garage just after we left. Who do you suppose would do a thing like that?"

"What? What do you mean, torched?"

"Up in smoke—took most of the rest of the building, too. Witnesses said it looked like a bomb went off back there. We'll know more when the arson investigators are done, but first they have to finish putting out the fire. Too bad you can't be there to help."

"I gotta get out of here. You have to let me go."

"Not today, man. We have enough charges on you to put you away for a while. If you have a lawyer, you might want to call him, or her. In the meantime you will be in the local lock-up."

"Yeah? I'll be out by dinner time."

"How will that work? Cousin George going to put up your bail? Unless the moon is made of green cheese, he's the dude who did your garage. All those chemicals and solvents. Did you know that just starting a car around all that stuff could set the whole building into orbit?"

"What chemicals? I don't know what you're talking about."

"Right. And then there's old George, who, when he hears you've been talking to us, might just want to have a private little chat with you, too. You think?"

"I ain't said nothing to you."

"You will eventually, and anyway, George won't know that, will he?"

"I'll tell him otherwise."

"Let's hope he believes you. He's got a mean temper, they say, and isn't one to delve very deep into things, so you'd better talk fast."

Daryll's face paled and he began to bite what was left of his fingernails. "Look, I can't say nothing, you got that? You need to protect me. I have rights, you know. I got the whatchamacallit, fifth amendment thing, right?"

"Oh yeah."

"You have to do something."

"Hey, if you call your lawyer, he will move for an arraignment. The judge will set bail and out you go. I can't help you there."

"If I don't, you know, like, call right away?"

"Well, we can hold you for a while on suspicion, stuff like that. Of course the longer you stay with us, the more likely it'll seem we flipped you. So either way, you're on your way to becoming toast. Your call."

"I want to think about this."

"I'll find you a cell with a window."

Chapter Twenty-five

The scent of burning hardwoods and pine slowly filled the room, as the heat from the marble faced fireplace took the edge off an early evening chill.

"A fire is a cheerful addition on a day like today," Ike said. What a lame thing to say, he thought, and smiled at Ruth who stood near the hearth frowning as if unsure whether she should pace, stand still, or sit. He could not read the expression on her face. That made him uneasy. Always in the past, whether she was angry, worried, happy, or sad, he could measure her mood, see through her. Tonight Ruth was opaque.

"Are you feeling all right?"

"What? I'm sorry, Ike, my mind must have drifted away for a moment."

"A bit more than a moment."

"Yes? Well…what would you do if you were me?"

Ike had been promised a light dinner in exchange for some conversation and advice. Apparently the advice part came first and what form that would take had been left vague. His stomach reminded him he had skipped lunch.

"If I were you," he began, smiling…

"Before you start, Schwartz. I'm not in the mood for word games, salacious suggestions, or redneck humor. This is serious."

"I surrender. I don't know from what, but I recognize a woman on the war path when I see one. However, I still need to know the context at least. What would I do if I were you—about what, exactly?"

"The merger business. Isn't that what we were talking about?"

"Actually, you were muttering to yourself while I was consuming some of your excellent single malt. How much do they pay you so that you can afford expensive scotch like this?"

"Not enough. It was a gift from Armand Dillon, if you must know. So help me out here, Sheriff. What do I do?"

M. Armand Dillon had, at one time, served on the board of trustees of Callend College, and remained its largest donor. He, though retired from a life spent accumulating additional assets to his enormous net worth, still retained his skills as a ruthless capitalist and entrepreneur. His, that is, the Dillon Art collection had been stolen from the Art Storage facility located on the campus the previous summer and subsequently recovered by Ike. Not without some confusion, a few shots fired, and a grateful Dillon who generously blessed the school with cash. The robbery, and its sequelae, also served as the fulcrum that leveraged Ike and Ruth together in the first place.

"Dillon always had good taste, I'll say that for him."

"Bushels of money will do that for you. I need to figure out where we go with this merger business. CU…"

"Who?"

"I told you, Carter Union, the college that's breathing down our backs."

"So it's official now. They are seeking a merger."

"Where have you been? Of course."

"Been? Ruth, I think the term is 'out of the loop.' Just because you have had extensive conversations with me in your head, doesn't mean I've heard any of them, you know? That is what you've been doing, isn't it?"

"What? No. Have I? When did we talk last?"

"At the A-frame, you were in a funk and otherwise, we were studying tattoos mostly, or, in your case, the lack of them. Remember?"

"Really? That long ago? I guess I have become so used to talking things over with you that, yeah, the conversations in my head are…Oh, well. Here's the thing, CU—you're with me now? Okay, they've put up some numbers that have me scared. The board is listening to them like they're first year students at orientation."

"And the scary part is what?"

"My board is not blessed with business types. Oh, some of them are okay, I guess, but for the most part, they are members because they fit the Board Rule Profile."

"Sorry, you've lost me again. What is the board rule profile?"

"Board members should be givers, getters, or get out of the way."

"Ah. So, your board is in over its collective head when dealing with the shrewd city slickers from Carter Union."

"Precisely. The negotiators from CU come from their business school and they're throwing their weight around. We could be completely absorbed by them and that worries me."

"And maybe lose your job?"

"That too, but believe me that possibility, as hard as it would be to accept, is not what has me upset. Callend is a fine liberal arts college that has served its constituency well. I'd hate to see it flushed away by a bunch of MBAs."

"It's all about the Benjamins, isn't it?"

"The whats?"

"Money. Benjamin Franklin's picture is on the one hundred dollar bill."

"Oh, cute. This is more like one hundred thousand dollar bills."

"That would be Woodrow Wilson."

"How do you know all this stuff?"

"The magic of the internet. I am starving. How about we eat whatever it is you promised me and I will cogitate on your problem at the same time."

"Cogitate? Don't you start in on me."

"Perfectly good word. It was today's entry on my word builder calendar. 'Cogitate, to ponder or meditate on, usually intently…' etcetera, etcetera."

"Since when did you need a word builder calendar?"

"Ever since you introduced me to your loquacious faculty friends."

"Loquacious? Then you need to get me a Jeff Foxworthy dictionary so I can communicate in redneck with yours."

"Very wise. Now what about that food?"

"You promise to help me after?"

"Help you with that and more."

"Don't get ahead of yourself there, lover."

Sam leafed through the last of the books she'd pulled from the shelf. A stack of Jonathan Lydell's books were on one side and several local history books on the other. Somewhere between them lay the answer to what Anton Grotz was doing in the Shenandoah Valley. The librarian tiptoed over and slipped another document reproduction in front of her. Sam read again the report of the locked room mystery in the pages of the *Staunton Spectator*. She riffled through her notes and frowned. She didn't notice Karl slip up behind her.

"Okay, Library Lady, time to pack it in for the day. The folks here want to close up."

"Help me out, Karl," she said, ignoring his suggestion. "All of the documents Grotz studied, and all the books he'd checked out of the library were about a particular time during the Civil War, and seem to have something to do with the Lydell family."

"Maybe he came down to interview Lydell for a book he planned to write or something."

"Maybe. But his wife indicated he thought he had found something she called big. That sounds more like a scandal or something controversial. Maybe something to do with the war?"

"Lord, Sam, that war was over a long time ago. Who cares about what happened then?"

"You need to live in these parts a little longer, Karl. The people down here are not done with it. They celebrated Robert E. Lee's two hundredth birthday a while back. You do know who he is."

"Southern general or something."

"Oh my, you do have a lot to learn."

"Not much call for that knowledge where I come from, and I mean both geographically and culturally."

"Not a big deal in northern Minnesota, either. But down here? It's like talking about God."

"And you think I should bone up on southern culture and history, famous people?"

"And local heroes, if you plan to spend any time here, yes."

"That's the thing, though. I don't plan to do that. Not on my radar screen." Karl saw the cloud cross Sam's face. "Hey, we'll be okay, you'll see."

"Yeah, sure. Anyway, Grotz has this thing about the war, and the Lydells, and the murder in the room back then. There has to be a connection."

"The only connection we can work on is, he was writing about the time and place and wanted to talk to a descendant of the original. That would explain why he was happy to change places with the other guy and move over to Lydell's room."

"I think it's more than that."

"Look, Sam, they want to close. Grab your stuff and we'll talk over dinner."

"Whose turn to cook?"

"Mine, we're eating out."

Chapter Twenty-six

Ruth stacked the dinner plates in the sink, poured two glasses of wine, and absently pounded her fist against the counter top. Ike sipped his wine.

"This is nice. What is it?"

"What? Oh, it's an ice wine. Local. From the Rockbridge Winery up the road in Raphine, I think. Anyway, Agnes found it." Ruth downed her glass and poured another.

Ike glanced at the label on the bottle, *V d'Or,* and fled into the living room, glass in one hand, bottle in the other. He found a place on the sofa and watched as Ruth stalked in, kicked off her shoes and prowled.

"Ike, you know about things and you can't be bamboozled. You need to help us with the negotiations." She put her glass down on a piecrust table, and padded to the window. The temperature outside had dropped when the sun set, and even though the room still held the fire's warmth, she hugged herself against the chill air sliding off the panes.

"Need to? Not me, Ruth. When it comes to hard-nosed financial maneuvering, I am a babe in the woods. Now if you wanted me to put out a contract on one or more of them…"

"No, be serious, and anyway, it's not just about the Franklins—"

"Benjamins."

"You know what I mean, the money. It's the snotty attitude they bring to the table. Like, 'We're here to help you. Trust us.

We know what is best for you.' It's as if they think of us as slow-to-learn children or something."

Ruth made a slow circuit of the room and paused by the entryway. She ran her hand along its brocade hanging, fiddled with the tieback, and turned back toward Ike. He rose and stirred the coals in the dying fire. Small sparks leapt out only to be captured and extinguished by the fire screen. He shook his head and studied her as she continued her path back to the piecrust table and her glass.

"Back to the issue—I hate to say it, Madam President, but when it comes to this sort of thing, your faculty often behave as though they were children."

"I know, I know. Something like half my tenured professors bought into a Ponzi scheme last winter. See, that's what I mean. You don't fall for all that stuff. You are a quintessential skeptic..."

"Oh, oh, we're back to the word builder."

"Stop it. I need your help. What I mean is, you could sit at that table and they couldn't fool you."

Ike resumed his place on the couch and sipped his wine. After a moment he looked up and said, "It's a thought, Ruth, but not a good one, I'm afraid."

"Why?"

"I am the sheriff of Picketsville, not a business guru. Your board, your faculty, the committee, whoever, would not take it kindly if you were to wedge me into the discussion, believe me."

"Again, why?"

"How will it look? President Harris asks good ole Sheriff Ike to come to the table and save the college from a fate worse than death. To them I am Buford T. Justice complete with mirrored sunglasses and...you get the picture. And then, 'what are his qualifications for the job?' they ask...hmm...let's see...well, he's her boyfriend, no, make that her lover. He has no background in business, mergers, academics, education, or anything whatsoever that's relevant or needed."

"You're smarter than any of them, and you know it."

"I don't know it. What's worse, you're not paying attention. Ruth, merger or no merger, you and I are 'an item.' Your faculty is unhappy about me sneaking into their president's house and, may I say, bed. They have a low opinion of me and what I do. I have absolutely no credibility whatsoever. They will be so distracted by me and by our relationship, CU will eat them alive."

Ruth plopped down on the chenille sofa next to him and slouched back, legs outstretched, revealing a very unladylike expanse of thigh. She studied the dregs of the wine in her glass and extended it toward him. He poured another dollop for her.

"Thanks." She sipped at her wine and puffed out her cheeks. "Then what will I do? As it now stands, I think we will be eaten alive anyway. Your being there can't make it worse."

"Perhaps not, but if that were to happen, and if I were in the mix, guess who'd get the blame, and then who'd pay for it?"

"You and then me. Damn!"

"My advice to you is to load your side of the table with some heavy hitters from the business community. You must have alumni, parents of students, friends, people, who can help you out. I've seen you work a room full of potential donors and I know you can get them to do almost anything you ask. Go spin your rolodex and bring some professionals in."

"You think?"

"No question."

Ruth tugged halfheartedly at her skirt, which had retreated alarmingly close to her waist. She toyed with the top button on her blouse and sighed. A log collapsed into the coals. A shower of sparks crackled and snapped—miniature fireworks.

"Ike, I know this is mean of me. I guess you had plans for later…tattoos and all that…but I am bushed. Will you be very angry if we call it a night?"

"Angry? No. Disappointed? Well, maybe a little. You need your beauty rest, so I'm out of here."

"It's not *beauty rest.*"

Ike grinned and stood. "Glad to see you are still in possession of your sensibilities. I'll call."

"What'll you do? I feel awful."

"I'll commandeer the rest of this nifty wine and tune in the classic movie channel—my major off-duty pastime. *Casablanca* is on in a half hour. And don't worry, schweet heart, we'll always have Paris."

She gave him a rueful smile and waved him out the door.

Sam sat upright, blankets pulled up to her chest, scowling in concentration. "There has to be more to this than just an interview. Look, the man was murdered. That alone tells you something else had to be…"

Karl sighed. The clock read one AM. He had the seven to three shift and was not a morning person. "Sam, give it a rest. We have two, no, three, cases running now and not only can the murder wait, it will have to. No matter what Grotz had turned his hand to, who struck John with this or that, as long as we can't unlock that stranger room door and show how it happened, it won't matter a lick."

"Okay. I know, I know. But suppose I'm right. Suppose Grotz knew something about Lydell, like, maybe he's a blackmailer or something."

"Who's a blackmailer, Lydell or Grotz?"

"Well, I guess it could be either one, let's say it's Lydell. Those old history nuts are always digging up stuff about people. And, so then Grotz is sent down to put him away only something goes wrong and—"

"Grotz is the bad guy and Lydell shot him in self defense? Come on Sam, the guy is so old he probably couldn't pull the trigger of that antique pistol, assuming the Webley we have in custody is the weapon. And, if it was self defense, why lock the stiff in a room, assuming he could. Why not just call the cops? Besides, who'd send Grotz?"

"His wife said he had something on the New Jersey Family. Maybe it wasn't what she thought. Suppose he actually worked for them and his being a writer was a cover. Like maybe they would overlook the stuff he dug up on them if he did them a favor or something."

"So he spends months in the library studying Lydell's books and more time at the historical society, and then comes down here to shoot him. Why waste the time? If someone wanted Lydell or Grotz, for that matter, why not just kill them and hot foot it out of town. Same nagging question, why the big mystery?"

"I don't know. Shoot, I just think there is something really fishy about this whole business and weak old man or not...he could have had someone else pull the trigger, you know."

"Oh, so now there're three people involved. So it's not a spontaneous shooting any more?"

"Maybe Grotz tipped his hand and so he put in a call."

"To whom?"

"How about George LeBrun."

"Love it, if it were true. The guy's a real bottom feeder, but, same problems, Sam, too many dots to connect, not enough numbers."

"Dots?"

"Yeah. Real connect the dot puzzles have lots of dots. The only way to get the picture is to connect the right ones, in the right order, and to do that you have to follow the numbers. We are long on dots and short on numbers."

"But what about—"

"Goodnight, Sugar. I'm bushed. Big day tomorrow. Why don't you come in with me early and sort through all the material that we do have, go over the coroner's reports, the junk from Ike's car, all of it, and then see if you can come up with some new dots or, better yet, some numbers."

"Numbers. Right. Okay, that's a good idea. Make sure I'm up."

Sam switched off the bedside light. A new three quarter moon lighted the room. In a week it would be full. She smiled at the thought and dropped off to sleep.

Karl, now fully awake, spent the next twenty-five minutes mulling over what she had said. He got up and pulled the blinds tight. The moonlight, he decided, was keeping him awake. Sam had a point. *Fishy* barely touched what they had their hands on. And what about the other guy—the one who got away—the man who switched places with Grotz. What did they know about him? Where to start?

The stone smashed through the window and scattered most of the double hung glazing on the floor. Sam catapulted from the bed, rolled and came up in a shooter's crouch, Glock held two-handed, safety off, and cocked. Karl hit the floor.

"Jesus, Sam, hold your fire."

Chapter Twenty-seven

When Ike walked into his office he found Karl sitting on the desk's edge with one leg swinging, the other on the floor, foot tapping.

"I thought you were out on patrol?" he said and dropped into his chair. His hands wandered over the desk, shuffled some papers, and raised one eyebrow at the stone that anchored one small raggedy stack.

"Bad night, Ike."

"You too?"

"I don't know…what?"

"Sorry, a little before morning coffee humor. What's up?"

"That's up." Karl pointed to the stone.

"I thought I told Billy to take that over to the lab."

"He did. That's my stone."

"Looks like the one that landed in Essie's sister's living room. Where'd you find yours?"

"Came through our window last night. Knocked out the entire pane. Landlady is really ticked, like it's my fault." Ike started to say something and thought better of it. Now was not the time. "What? You think it's my fault?"

"No, no. Go on."

"Well, it busted through the window and, no kidding, I swear before it hit the carpet, Sam, who is in REM sleep, rolls out of that sack and has her Glock out and cocked and trained on me. I thought I was a goner."

"She's quick."

"Well, yeah. There she is, moonlight streaming in through the busted window, in a full crouch, pistol in both hands. And I swear to goodness, unless she's part kangaroo, I don't know where that pistol came from. You should have seen it."

The image formed in Ike's mind and he quickly pushed it aside. A picture of a Sam, all six feet two inches of her, naked, crouched in the moonlight, gun at the ready, did not need to get past short term memory, if that. If his brain were a hard drive, that image alone would get him busted for downloading porn.

"Why would somebody toss a rock through my window?"

"I can think of several reasons. But first, check the stone out with somebody at the lab. See if it's possible it came from the same place as the one tossed at Essie."

"What reasons?"

"Later."

"Why not now?"

"I said, later." Karl must have heard the uncharacteristic edge in Ike's voice and stepped away from the desk. The scowl on his face did not look good.

"You da boss."

Ike let that pass. But he and Karl would need to have some words, and soon.

"The lab sent back these pictures," Karl tossed a stack of photographs on the desk. "They're of the stranger room. Lab guy says they can't get anything from the rocks except they think they're from the same place, but quarried limestone is pretty much the same all over this area." Karl lowered himself into a chair. "What reasons?"

Ike inspected the photographs briefly and set them to one side. "Okay. I said several. How about two?"

"Two will do."

"First. There is always, in a small town like this, a group of people who, for reasons that defy logic, can't stand change. In your case, they can't accept an African-American as a deputy sheriff."

"You have Charlie Picket. He's been here, like, forever."

"Yes, but he is our African-American."

"Excuse me? *Our?*"

"He's been around, as you say, forever. Everybody knows him. His family has lived in the area for centuries. This town is named Picketsville, for crying out loud. Does that tell you anything?"

"I thought the town was named after one of those confederate general guys."

"No, that *guy* spelled his name with two T's. Charlie's mother cleans houses for the gentry out on Main Street. Before I took over this office, he was the designated black deputy. His job was to patrol the predominately black neighborhood. People got used to that. In their eyes it made some kind of sense. When I put him on general patrol, the white folks did not like it much, wrote me a few letters, said they'd never vote for me again, but they got over it. As I said, he's ours."

"And me?"

"You are...pardon the language...but, you are that uppity you-know-what from up north somewhere, not ours. You might as well be from the IRS. Do you follow?"

"I guess. And since I am that person, some of the ingrained...I almost said inbred...would I be far off on that, I wonder...they want me to go away, and a rock through the window is their way of inviting me to leave town?"

"That's reason number one."

"Okay. You're saying I don't have a career developing here in 'one T' Picketsville. So, that's no big tragedy. I wasn't planning on one anyway. You just confirmed what I already suspected. You need to explain that to Sam, by the way."

"I expect she already knows and also knows that it's not necessarily true."

"Not?"

"You could become a citizen, so to speak. Listen, everybody from outside has to work their way into a town like this."

"Yeah, yeah. Not me. What's reason number two?"

"Sit." Karl sat on the only other chair in the office. Ike rolled his chair to the door and pushed it shut with his foot. "I wouldn't toss Picketsville away so quickly, Karl. Okay, reason number two—Sam."

Karl got to his feet, planted his palms on Ike's desk and glared at him. "Oh, I get it, de bad back debbil is asleepin' wid de nice white gal and we gotta do sumpin' 'bout it. Time to get out the white sheets and the kerosene soaked cross? Miscegenation, Oh Lordy. "

"Stop right there, sit down, and listen. This is a nice town. We do not now have, never have had, and never will have Klansmen. The bad guys are pretty much limited to the bozos you've already met—the LeBruns and their cousins, maybe a half dozen others. If you just paid attention to the folks on the street, you'd know that."

"Huh? I know a bigot when I see one, Ike, and here I am in de Ole South where they grow like weeds…"

"Folks lean too much on stereotypes and never check to see if they are accurate. Up north they assume down south is home base for racists and worse. Karl, I'd bet you a breakfast there's probably as much racial intolerance and violence in your hometown of Chicago, as you'll find around here. At least we have never had a skinhead march."

"So, you're saying…what? It exists everywhere, so it's okay?"

Ike drew in a breath, counted to ten, and exhaled. Conversations like this one never went well, which was why, he supposed, most people avoided them. There is something in the human psyche that is either reluctant to engage, afraid of giving offense, or riled by the topic, that will lead to ugly confrontations. Either way, he realized this was not going to go down correctly and he would soon be in hot water. He plunged ahead anyway.

"No, what I'm saying is, like it or not, you are going to find it everywhere, not just here, or there. It is pervasive, mean, and unacceptable in a civil society. But at the same time, I am sick and tired of people who can't seem to live in the here and now without playing their victim card."

"Their what?" Karl's eyes flashed dangerously.

"Victims. Everybody, it seems, wants to be a victim of some sort. Victims because of their race, their gender, education or lack thereof, because of abuse suffered as children, low self esteem, restless leg syndrome, or any of the hundreds of sociological catchphrases, buzz words, real or imagined, and psychobabble that hobble progress. It doesn't matter a rip to people where you come from. It's where you're headed they're interested in." Ike ran his fingers through his hair. "People draw lines in the sand. They separate themselves from one another for all kinds of reasons. Mostly because they are different in some way—color, language, origin, breeding—all that crap. Greeks and Persians, Muslims and Christians, Algonquians and Sioux, white and black, urban black and…who?"

"Koreans."

"You see? If you are born in a particular place or time, you acquire all the prejudices of that place and time. It's a damned shame, but it's true. Most of us have learned not to respond to those old biases. We sit on them. Some pretend they're not there, but to do so denies them, and is disingenuous at best. I know it is not politically correct to say so, but most of us *are* socialized early on with all sorts of negatives about all kinds of other people. We are bigots in one way or another. If you come from a place like this you are probably a racist at some level. A few never rise above it. Those are the ones who toss rocks, join the neo-Nazis, shave their heads, burn crosses, burn schools, or become suicide bombers. The rest of us just muddle through as best we can, trying to do and say the right thing, no matter what bigoted thoughts are dancing around behind our eyes."

"You're beginning to sound like Bill Cosby, man."

"I could do worse." Ike paused and caught his breath. Karl did not look convinced. He had a right not to. "Anyway, return-ing to your midnight missile. The second reason the rock came through your window, believe it or not, is not so much about miscegenation, but cohabitation."

"What?"

"Sorry, but folks around here still cling to an old fashioned set of values and one of the things they object to is, what they consider the decline of our social institutions, in your case, marriage."

"You're kidding, right? This is the twenty-first century, Ike. It's what people do. It's on prime-time, it's a cultural norm, for God's sake, it's—"

"Not acceptable to the folks up on Main Street."

"Main Street? This is who? Sinclair Lewis?"

"Look, I'm in no position to preach here. My relationship with Dr. Harris is causing both of us a peck of trouble with her people and mine, but the difference is, we don't actually live together. People can always pretend we're not...well. It's not what you are as a man, Karl, it's how you function as a man in a small town like this one which is, after all, suspicious of all strangers."

Karl knuckled his forehead and stared at Ike for a full minute. "So, you haven't offered the deputy position to me because...what? I don't fit in? Because I'm shacked up with the pretty deputy, or because you don't like my attitude 'cause I tend to play my 'victim's card?' You're spinning a whole mess of shit here, Ike. So which?"

Ike shook his head. As he had presumed from the outset, he wasn't handling this very well. "If you must know, offering you a job is a wholly separate issue. But since you asked—I haven't offered you the job because I think it's important for you to go through with your hearing. I expect you will prevail, but even if you don't, you still must do it. See, if I offered the job now and you accepted rather than face a possible negative result at your hearing, you might regret the decision forever. You'd always wonder 'what if.' Could I have made it in the Bureau? If you walk away from a career in the FBI, I want you to do so as a positive choice, not as an escape."

"You offering me a job?"

"Not yet. Now, go talk to your lady and see what you can do about reason number two. But, just so you know, reason number one is what bought you the rock."

Karl left, closing the door a little harder than usual.

Chapter Twenty-eight

Henry Sutherlin didn't spy. When he worked for Lydell, he made a point of keeping his eyes away from the house. The year previously, Miss Martha Marie had slipped past an upstairs window just as God created her. Henry figured if she'd seen him looking, she could make trouble, so now he kept his gaze focused on the task at hand. The disassembled cabins had been delivered two weeks before. The logs were coded and numbered to aid in reassembly. Lydell wanted them sorted so that the crew he'd hired somewhere in town could begin reconstructing his slave quarters. Something, a noise, a premonition, he would never be sure, made him turn and look at the house. Shadowy figures moved behind darkened windows. Just silhouettes, but he'd know George LeBrun and, of course, Lydell anywhere. He ducked behind a pile of the logs. He reckoned he couldn't be seen. He remembered what the knife had done to Ike's piece of paper and George was not someone to go through life with only one blade. He didn't want to be noticed.

Sounds of an argument filtered through the closed doors. He couldn't make out the words. He peered out between two of the heavy chestnut beams. In a few minutes, he heard a door slam and then, silence. He stayed crouched behind the logs. Not yet, wait. Lydell walked out through the back door, took two or three steps in his direction, and looked right and left. He carried something heavy in his hand. Henry squinted through the gap in the logs. As Lydell turned to reenter the house, Henry saw the glint of sunlight on metal. Lydell carried a double barreled shotgun. Henry scuttled backward, slipped behind the shed, and then into the woods. He reckoned he was done working for Mr. Jonathan Lydell forever.

Sam, true to her word, went to work early. Somewhere in all those papers, books, reports, and guesses, she believed she would find the answer to the murder of Anton Grotz. She held that view as an act of faith; the practical side of her nature was near despair. TMI. Too much information, too few connections. What did Karl say? They needed some numbers to show them how to connect the dots. She spread the papers, the faxes from New Jersey, and the library books on one desk. The photographs, evidence technician's reports, ballistics, and coroner's reports went on another.

Earlier, she thought she had a lead from the papers accumulated by Grotz. She needed to go back to it and think it through once more. The facsimile of the *Staunton Spectator* caught her eye and she read it, frowned, and reread it. She picked up the stack of pictures taken of the stranger room. She held one up and studied it myopically, dropped it, and rummaged through the materials for the CD with the pictures stored on it.

"Be right back," she said to no one in particular, and headed to her office. Her computer was already booted up and she slid the disc into its D drive. She had a moderately sophisticated photo processing program, so it was an easy matter to find the picture that had caught her attention and bring it up on her screen. She selected a portion and enlarged it. There was no doubt. The traveler's trunk had a brass plate fastened to it, and the plate had elaborately engraved initials etched into its surface—F.B.

She reread the *Staunton Spectator* once more; *The traveler is reported to have been a Mister Franklin Brian of undetermined address. He had no baggage and...*

No baggage…F.B., Franklin Brian. It had to be. Of course the lines of communication would have been unreliable during that time, what with Union raids. Of course, they might have misunderstood. But suppose they weren't. Suppose that trunk had belonged to Franklin Brian. What did it contain that the original Jonathan Lydell felt compelled to keep it? And who was Franklin Brian? Why was he murdered? Sam sat down and whistled.

"I'll bet a week's pay that if we could figure that out we'd have the rest."

"What?" Rita said. "Figure what out?"

"Who would I talk to about the Civil War around here?"

"The War of Northern Aggression, you mean."

"Whatever. Gracious, you'd think in over a century and a half you could settle on a name. Anyway, this is a today murder, but its roots go back to that time, and I don't have time to be choosey with my words. Sorry."

Ike walked in the door and looked at the display of material scattered across the table. "Who wants to know about the war?"

"I do. I think the two murders are linked somehow." Sam was almost dancing in excitement.

"Well, the best source, locally, excluding Jonathan Lydell, would be Dr. Leon Weitz at the college. You remember him?"

"Yes, I do. Look, I'm not on duty yet so I'm going to drive up to the college and see him. You have anything you want to know while I'm there?"

"Like what?"

"I don't know. But if I'm right, you'll need to do some heavy duty research on the Lydells."

"I will? Okay, get me his books from the library."

"Already got'em. I'm off."

Ike watched her leave. "What's she up to, Rita?"

"Beats me. She spread all that stuff all over the place, ran back to her office and then…well you heard the rest. She thinks the old Lydell murder back in the day is, like, connected to the new one."

"Hmmm…Any news from Essie?"

"Not today. Is this forced leave you have her on got an end point? My husband is getting antsy with my new hours."

"Sorry, Rita. Tell him it won't be much longer."

Ike picked up the two coroner's reports and the results of the ballistics test from the spread Sam had created. He settled in his office with a cup of lukewarm coffee and opened them one at a time. The ballistics confirmed that the weapon used in the shooting was the Webley they had—presumably Lydell's. The coroner's report on Grotz was straight forward. He'd been shot three times in the back and once in the forehead. Three bullets had been retrieved and matched those from the Webley. The coroner's report on Martha Marie Lydell Winslow told a different story. There were only slight traces of alcohol in her system. Her blood alcohol was well below the DUI limit. But there were indications of cocaine use, the presence of a few petechial hemorrhages in the eyes, face, and neck area, and four small and one larger bruise on her back. He hadn't expected any surprises. It appeared he was wrong.

Ike sat back and studied the reports. Lydell testified his daughter was drunk. The body reeked of whiskey. But no trace? And cocaine? If she wasn't drunk…how much cocaine? He read again. Not enough of either to affect her motor abilities. She could navigate. So why did she fall down the stairs? What about the bruises? She did tumble. Still…Henry Sutherlin said he heard Lydell and his daughter arguing.

Why? The case is full of whys. Never mind how the murder was done…it's the whys. Someone shot Grotz who then went to the trouble to make it look like a locked room mystery. Martha Marie, for no reason at all, launches herself down the stairs. If we figure this one out, Ike muttered, I'll have earned my pension.

He would have to look up petechial hemorrhages.

Chapter Twenty-nine

Karl completed a circuit of the town's west sector. The least interesting part of being a deputy, he believed, was patrol. Picketsville lacked the problems that characterized big cities. Patrolling the streets involved scraping up a drunk or two on the weekends, breaking up a kegger in Craddock's woods, and handing out a few speeding tickets. Not much in the way of excitement. On the upside, it gave him time to think. He had Sam on his mind lately. Sam and what Ike had said about "One T Picketsville." The whole concept of the town's antediluvian, middle-class morals boggled his mind. But Ike wasn't one to dance around facts. If he said the townsfolk thought his relationship was suspect, he was probably right. Karl's problem revolved around whether he cared enough to change his living arrangements, and if so, how and when.

One complete circuit done. He nosed into a parking spot at the Seven-Eleven and exited. Time for coffee and, stereotype or not, a donut. Yuri, the manager, greeted him as usual, that is to say, effusively, and also, as usual, insisting there'd be no charge. They had a running disagreement about paying for donuts and coffee. Yuri maintained it was a custom in his country—Karl wasn't sure where that was, he guessed one of the former soviets—that people showed their appreciation to the *polizei* for their services. Karl, in turn, accused Yuri of offering him a bribe and declared he might have to arrest him if he didn't accept the money. The argument would go on until Karl filled his cup, selected the donut with the heaviest coating of glaze, and paid. Yuri would roll his eyes, shake his head, and that would be it until the next time Karl came in.

His transaction complete, he exited the store, Yuri's disappointment trailing after him. He put the cup and donut on the roof of the car while he opened the driver's side door. He had it halfway open when a blue Chevy Malibu roared past, doing at least twenty miles over the limit. He only caught a glimpse of the driver but could not mistake either the car or the driver's profile. A determined Essie Falco, eyes fixed on the road, had the car floored and headed out the Covington Road. Karl slid behind the wheel, backed up, and sped after her. He glanced in the rear view mirror just in time to see his coffee and donut sail off the roof and into the road behind him.

Rita fumbled with the send button and repeated her call. She frowned and called Ike on the intercom.

"Ike, I can't reach Billy Sutherlin. He's supposed to be out patrolling the east sector and I've had a call from someone reporting a possible prowler."

Ike fiddled with the intercom and took a stab at the buttons. He hit the right one.

"A prowler at nine in the morning?"

"That's what she said."

"Who said?"

"A woman named Mavis Bowers. Do you know her?"

"Sort of. She was one of the ladies at the church when we had that murder last fall. She's been a little spooked ever since. I wouldn't worry too much about it. But what's up with Billy?"

"I'm calling, but he's not answering. If I didn't know him better, I'd say he has his radio turned off."

"You can tell?"

"Well, I don't know, maybe. Back before you were sheriff, the guys would do that…turn off their radios so they wouldn't have to answer a call. It was usually when they were up to no good. Anyway, I had a feeling that I could tell. It was the way the call would sound from this end. See, when the radio's on, there is this, like, echo sort of sound. But when they're off, you don't hear it."

"How?"

"Okay. You set all the radios on a common frequency and then we have a different, alternate one for each set that allows us to talk to a single person without cluttering up the common one, right? Billy didn't answer on the general so I tried his alternate. That's when I figured he's off the air."

"Show me."

"Okay, so your radio is on, right?"

"Yes."

"Put it on the alternate frequency, leave it on your desk, and come out here."

Ike unclipped his radio, switched to the alternate channel, placed the set on the only clear spot on his desk, and walked over to the dispatch desk. Rita called him on his frequency. Sure enough, there was a hint of an over-voice. At Rita's direction, he returned to his office and turned the set off and returned. She called him again. The difference was very slight. The echo had disappeared. Rita had been at this for years and to her ear, it was obvious.

"Billy knows better than to turn off his radio. What's he thinking? Keep trying, and see if you can raise Karl."

"Roger that."

"And keep trying to find Essie, too. Something is not right here. Did Billy know about the radio off thing?"

"We talked about it once but I don't know if he knows or not."

"Okay. I'll drive out and see Mavis Bowers. Keep trying."

Karl watched as a silver Chrysler flattened his mid-morning snack and sent the coffee cup skittering across the road. He tried to catch Essie but she had the Chevy flat out. For a split second he thought to use the siren but something, instinct maybe, kept his finger off the toggle switch. After all, it was Essie and whatever she had in mind, he felt pretty sure she did not want company. The way she was pushing her car convinced him she would be better served if she did. He managed to keep her in sight out the Covington Road, past Craddock's Woods. He braked abruptly when he saw her tail lights brighten. She turned right and bounced into the state park. Karl slowed to a crawl and then pulled into a copse of maples and got out. He'd follow on foot. Something was not right. His radio crackled and he quickly shut it off.

◇◇◇

"Ike. Are you there?"

"I hear you, Rita. Did you find Billy?"

"No, still no answer. So, I called Karl like you said, and he didn't answer either, so I tried his alternate and I swear, his set is off, too."

"What was his last location?"

"His latest twenty was the Seven-Eleven out near the Covington Road. But that was fifteen minutes ago."

"What's going on here? Did you raise Essie?"

"I got through to her sister's place. She wasn't there. Her niece answered the phone. She said Essie had a call from her boyfriend and took off in a hurry."

"Her boyfriend?"

"She meant Billy."

"What in the world is going on? Listen, you get hold of Mavis Bowers and tell her we have an emergency and we'll check out her prowler later. Tell her we're sorry."

"No need, Ike. She called back a few minutes ago and said not to bother, it was just the gas man."

"Sheesh. Okay, Rita, I'm heading out to the Seven-Eleven to track Karl. You keep after Billy."

"Ten-four, Ike."

This is not good.

Chapter Thirty

Jonathan Lydell had a problem. Martha Marie indicated she'd seen the documents but hadn't mentioned where she'd put them. She had slipped three of them under the blotter but the others...the important ones...were nowhere to be found. Henry said she often read out in the yard. She hid things in the shed. He'd turned it upside down. Aside from boxes of his books and a half empty wine bottle, he'd found nothing. He didn't think Schwartz, or any of his Keystone Cops, would be back, but he hated loose ends. And then there was the business with that odious LeBrun person. He wanted money. Everybody wanted money. Who did they think they were dealing with?

Cocaine? LeBrun expected him to pay for Martha Marie's drugs. He had no idea she used cocaine. Young people did nowadays, but where did she get the money to pay for them in the first place? He was sure the alimony she received went into her bank account but, you never knew. And who connected her to that foul-mouthed person? He drummed his fingers on the desk top and absently turned the blotter aside as if he might find his missing documents under it after all. Did he dare call the sheriff about LeBrun? Where might that lead? He needed to close some things down. First he'd bring Martha Marie home and make arrangements with Unger's Funeral parlor. Then there was the problem with the pistol. That might be difficult to explain. Police were so suspicious. They never seemed willing to accept a simple explanation for a thing, were always looking for something darker. None of this would be happening if society had maintained a sense of respect for families and history. A Lydell should not be subject to the sort of treatment by the local constabulary he received.

Where could those papers be? His thoughts had become increasingly angry and now his fingers beat a noisy tattoo on the desk. His face reddened. Finally, he slapped the desk and cursed. Flossie Picket, dust cloth in hand, stopped and turned.

"You say something, Mister Lydell?"

"What? Were you snooping? I won't have servants snooping and eavesdropping, you hear?"

"You keep shouting at me for no reason and you won't have no servants, period."

"What's that you say?"

"You heard me. I took this job on because I thought you needed some help bad after your other cleaner got sick and had to quit. Now I see she maybe wasn't sick at all."

"That will be all. You are dismissed as of this moment."

"That's good with me, Mist' Lydell, but you owe me for two weeks now. You didn't leave no money last Friday like usual. And I expect cash money this time."

"Of all the effrontery. You will be paid in good time and now you will vacate the premises."

"Not without my one-hundred-fifty dollars, I won't."

"You will or I shall call the police."

"Now that would be good. I'm sure they'd be more than happy to have a reason to get another look-see around here. You know my son? He works for the sheriff."

"Are you threatening me, woman?"

"I'm asking you to pay me my wages. That's all. You the one brought up police."

Lydell had risen from his chair and now, as if deflated, sat down again. Lights flashed behind his eyes. He was only minutes away from a migraine. He fumbled in his wallet and took out one hundred and fifteen dollars in crumpled tens, fives, and ones.

"That's all you get. You didn't give me a full day today."

Flossie Picket had come into the room in the first place to tell him what she'd found tucked under the bolster in the third floor bedroom. Now she stared at the angry old man and, with a pitying look that accelerated the onset of his migraine, scooped up the money and stalked out the door.

Somewhere on his journey from corrupt sheriff's deputy to crystal meth addict, George LeBrun had changed from a man considered to be clever but mean, to just plain mean. What the chemicals had done to his central nervous system would be the subject for a toxicologist at some future time, but now sheer meanness drove him.

Bushwhacking Billy Sutherlin had been easy...too easy. In his day, George thought, you had to get up pretty early in the morning to trap a deputy with a phony call. Billy fell right into it. Now that deputy sat in the driver's seat of his own cruiser, with a sawed off twelve-gauge shotgun duct-tapped to his neck.

"Don't even think about doing anything stupid, Sutherlin. My finger is on this here trigger and it's real touchy. Hell, I might blow your head off and not even mean too. That's how quick this trigger is." George began to giggle. "Don't you think that's funny Billy? Laugh, Billy."

Billy remained stone faced.

"You want me to do it now, boy?"

"You won't, LeBrun."

"I won't? Why, won't?"

"You have something else up your sleeve. You want Essie for some reason, and you won't do anything 'til she gets here."

"Well, you ain't as dumb as I figured. Yep, we'll wait."

"Why'd you have me call her?"

"She ratted me out. My cousin, Daryll, is in your jail because of her. My business is up in flames, you might say, and she's gonna pay."

"You won't get away with it. Sooner or later, you're going down."

"Who's gonna do that? Not you, Billy. You're toast. Sheriff Ikey? Not likely. He'll want to, but prove it was me way out here in the park that done it? No way. And not that big, black...here she comes."

Essie Falco braked and jumped out. George LeBrun punched Billy in the ribs.

"Okay, Sutherlin, slide out slow and easy. Make sure she sees the mess you got yourself in."

Essie watched Billy open the door and took another step forward.

"Billy, why'd you call? You sounded like you were in trouble and—" She caught sight of LeBrun and the shotgun at the same time. "Oh."

"You shouldn't have come, Essie. I tried to warn you, sort of, but..."

"You shouldn't have come, Essie." LeBrun mimicked Billy. "Ooo, now I've got you both."

Essie paled. "I didn't understand. You said it's about the...I didn't understand."

"Poor Baby. She didn't understand you, Billy, you dumb suck."

"What do you want, George?" Essie moved slightly to her left.

"Want? Well, first off, I'm going to have to blow your lover boy away so's I can free this gun. Then I'm aiming to send you to wherever traitor women go when they're found out."

"What do you mean, traitor? I never—"

"Don't get smart with me. You sold me out to that sheriff buddy of yours and Daryll's in jail. You done it." Billy had moved to his left at the same time. "You hold still." Billy stopped. LeBrun's eyes swept over Essie. He smiled.

"Seems a shame to waste all that," Lebrun said. He licked his lips and stared at Essie's chest. "Ought to have me a taste first."

Essie stared back. She seemed to consider her options, measured LeBrun's mental state, glanced past him into the woods behind him, and then said, "What's stopping you?"

LeBrun had not figured on that response. She began to unbutton her blouse.

"Don't do it," Billy said and stepped to his left again.

"Shut up, Sutherlin. You've been there a hundred times. I been thinking about this woman for years. Come on, Sweetheart, skin out for Georgie."

"Not here, George. In the trees. Someone might see us from the road."

"Nobody drives out here this time of day." As he said the words, a pickup whooshed by. "Okay. Back up slow, Billy. Essie, you just keep doing what you're doing. We're moving into the woods."

Essie pulled her blouse away from her slacks. And stepped forward. They had ten yards to cover to the seclusion of the woods. The woods and LeBrun's lust were the only thing between her and a shotgun blast in the face.

Chapter Thirty-one

Karl peered through tree branches at the open field into which Essie had driven. Billy Sutherlin's cruiser idled next to a picnic table and, for a moment, he thought he'd chased Essie for no reason—Essie and Billy were just meeting, for lunch? He could only guess why, and then what Ike would say if he found out that his deputy and dispatcher were getting it on during duty hours. He nearly returned to his car and cursed himself for wasting his time and losing his coffee and donut. But something akin to premonition made him pause. He watched Essie walk toward Billy's cruiser. She didn't seem to be moving like a person eager to be meeting her boyfriend for a tryst. Billy slid awkwardly from his car. Odd. That's when Karl saw LeBrun, and the gun attached to Billy's neck. It took a moment for the scene to register. He'd been in a hostage situation like this once before in DC and it hadn't turned out well. He had to do something, and soon. A bridle path intersected the road to his right. It appeared to circle through the woods and around the picnic area. If he were to follow it, it might lead him around the field and behind LeBrun. He moved away from the road and onto the path. It had recently received a new layer of tanbark. He could move along noiselessly, working his way deeper into the woods, and closer to the figures in the field.

The trees effectively hid him from view and he reckoned if he moved slowly enough and stayed low, there was a good chance he could get behind LeBrun, without being spotted. What he'd do when he got there was less clear. He doubted he could dash from the woods, cover the distance to LeBrun, and disarm him without being heard or seen. He could try a head shot, but the odds were not good. And if either failed, Billy would have his head blown off. Still, he'd have to try. At least he could stop the same thing happening to Essie. If he could get a shot off...he'd pray for some luck. He got it. The path did, in fact, circle around behind them and a breeze picked up, moving branches and bushes, and making it easier to move quickly. Essie seemed to be saying something to LeBrun. He jerked at the gun, which Karl now saw clearly had been taped to the nape of Billy's neck. The trip around the bridle path seemed to take forever.

Ike pulled into the Seven-Eleven and jumped out of his car. He didn't even switch off the ignition; a move that would have produced a tongue-lashing by him had one of his deputies done the same thing. *Surest way to give a stranger a police car,* he'd have said. Yuri greeted him as he pushed through the double doors.

"Ah, Sheriff Ike, so nice to see you. I was just talking to the nice tall deputy of yours. That would not be the beautiful deputy Sam, who is also very tall, but—"

"Which way did he go?"

"Go? Oh I am not sure. You see, we were discussing how in my country, it is the duty of humble shop keepers to show their support for—"

"Yuri, shut up and tell me which way he went."

Yuri looked hurt. "Sheriff, I was about to. You see, he insisted on paying for his coffee and donut. It was not necessary. Can I get you a coffee and something...no charge, of course?"

"Yuri, in two seconds flat, I'm going to lock you up for obstruction of justice. Now think, which way did Karl, the tall, black deputy, go?"

"Oh, yes, of course. I cannot be sure, I was with another customer, but I think he went out the Covington Road."

Ike bolted out of the door, slid behind the wheel of his car, and cut off a FedEx truck as he pulled out of the store's parking lot. He ran over a sack and cup which were lying in the street. He assumed some litterbug had dropped them and snarled at the whole world of wasteful, careless people.

◇◇◇

Karl scuttled along the path but kept his eyes focused on the three people in the field. He muttered a call for backup into the radio on his shoulder and then remembered he'd shut it off. The squawk and chatter it would make when he turned it on could alert LeBrun and that could only end badly for Billy. He watched as the two of them shuffled toward Essie. He could not make out what LeBrun was saying, but Essie looked distressed and Billy ready to take his chances with the gun. Essie moved to her left. It looked like she wanted to move LeBrun to one side and away from Billy's back. Billy tried moving as well. Instead of a straight line, now the three of them were separated. Karl finally reached a point to their rear. Essie looked into the woods and saw him. Her face betrayed nothing, no wide-eyed look of recognition, nothing. He put his finger to his lips. He heard her say, "What's stopping you?" A very cool woman. Not the ditz he'd seen in the office.

Then he watched as Essie began to unbutton her blouse. What now? She kept moving to her left. He found a tree trunk to LeBrun's left rear and slipped behind it. He thanked his lucky stars he was black and wearing a brown uniform. In the woods he was practically invisible. If he kept very still, LeBrun would not see him. If Essie could get LeBrun to back up to him, there was a chance he could take him out. Since LeBrun held the shotgun in his right hand, it would be his right index finger on the trigger. Finally Karl understood what Essie had in mind. She kept moving to LeBrun's right forcing him to turn sideways.

Essie pulled her blouse free from her slacks. A truck sped past on the Covington Road. Essie said something and LeBrun hesitated and then started to back up. LeBrun seemed wholly focused on Essie's bright red bra. It's like a bullfight, Karl mused, and shook his head to dismiss the thought. He needed to stay focused on the gun. Essie had LeBrun backed up almost even with Karl, but as he had moved to face Essie, his back was now to him. Essie unsnapped the front catch of her bra and held it together momentarily. Karl could almost hear LeBrun's blood pressure rise.

She did not smile or show any emotion. She opened her hands and let the brassiere slide off her shoulders. She threw her shoulders back, and faced LeBrun. If he wanted to grab her, he'd have to do it with his right hand. If he did, his finger would come off the trigger and there would be a split second before he shifted to his left and in that moment, Karl would have to act. He slipped his baton loose from his belt.

"Well, well, woman, you surely do present a pretty picture. Don't she, Billy?"

LeBrun reached for her with his right hand. The gun wavered as he moved his left hand from the stock toward the trigger. Karl stepped forward and brought his baton down with a loud crack on LeBrun's left wrist. He howled and released the shotgun. Karl reckoned he'd broken at least one bone. He shot one foot behind LeBrun and sent an elbow to his face. LeBrun fell backward and let go of the gun stock. Karl dropped to the ground with him, put a knee firmly in his back, and cuffed him. LeBrun yelped when the cuffs snapped shut on his left wrist. Karl gave it an extra squeeze.

Essie ran to Billy and started to reach for the gun.

"Don't, Essie, stop." Essie froze, wide-eyed.

Karl lurched to his feet. Lebrun tried to twist around. Karl tapped him behind the ear with the baton and LeBrun slumped forward on his face, and lay still.

"Essie, take the knife out of my belt and when I tell you to, saw away at the tape close to the barrel's end. Not now! Wait. This thing may have hair trigger and we don't want to blow Billy's head off. We'll let Ike do that when he hears what happened."

Karl gingerly took the gun by the stock, raised it slowly and set the safety. "Now," he said, and Essie attacked the tape first freeing the gun, and then she reached to remove the rest from Billy's neck.

"I can get this, Babe," Billy said. "I think maybe you need to, like, cover up."

Essie looked down at her bare chest, turned a bright crimson, and retrieved her clothes. She turned her back to the men and hastily dressed. Karl pumped out the shells from the gun and leaned it against a tree. Essie was tucking in her shirttail when Ike bounced across the picnic area in his car. He scrambled out and, arms akimbo, stared at the four figures in front of him.

"I'm sure there is a very rational explanation for all of this."

Essie turned pale and sat down heavily at the picnic table.

"Essie, are you okay?"

Billy walked over to LeBrun who had started to moan and kicked him in the ribs.

"You dirt ball, you dirty—"

"Enough, Billy. He's done," Karl said.

Billy started to launch another kick but stopped. "I should have put you down a long time ago, when I had the chance, LeBrun." He went to Essie, sat down beside her, and wrapped her in his arms. She started to shake uncontrollably.

Chapter Thirty-two

"I've never been so scared in my life," Essie sobbed.

"You should have seen her, Ike," Karl said. "I mean…not seen her, like…you know what I mean. I've never seen a braver, cooler act in my life."

"He was going to kill us. Rape me and kill Billy and me and—"

"You hush, now, it's over, Babe. It's okay." Billy stroked her hair.

"I had your little pistol in my purse, Billy, but I left it in the car. I didn't know…and then I couldn't go back to get it…"

"Shhh, it's okay…"

"You take her home, Billy," Ike said. "Call the doctor for a sedative or something and let her rest. She's had a bad time. Go. Now." He pointed toward Billy's cruiser. The two stood and Billy led Essie to the car but she stopped, reversed her field and walked over to LeBrun who struggled on the ground.

"You pond scum," she screamed and kicked him in the side. "You sleazy, rotten, son of a—"

"Whoa, Babe. It's over."

She kicked him again. "It's never over. These people never go away. They're like the flu. They just keep coming around, year after year."

"Not this time Essie," Ike said. "We'll have enough to put this one away for a long time. Take her home Billy, and you take a couple of days off, too. Go to Orlando with her."

Billy nodded and led Essie back to the car. She began to cry again. Deep wrenching sobs. They drove away. Ike turned to Karl.

"What happened here?"

"I'd be guessing, you'll have to check with Billy, but apparently LeBrun managed to catch Billy off guard and made him call Essie. Anyway, he had Billy taped to this twelve gauge and—"

"Backup. What were you doing here?"

Karl filled Ike in as best he could. He described what he saw from the store and why he followed Essie, what Essie had done to get LeBrun to back into the woods and in range of Karl's baton.

"Essie did that? It didn't just happen?"

"No, I'd stake my life on it. She did what she had to do to keep that gun from blowing Billy's head off."

"And if you had not come along? If you hadn't seen her fly by the Seven-Eleven?"

"I think she would have done whatever she could to save Billy. Even…"

"Okay. So what do we do with this miserable excuse for a man?"

"Do you mind if I sit down? This is just catching up with me. You ever had something like this happen to you?"

"Long time ago. Not fun."

Karl took Essie's place on the bench and exhaled. His hands were shaking.

"That was a near thing."

"You all did good."

Lebrun moaned and tried to roll over.

"Oh, shit, in all the excitement, I didn't pat him down, Ike."

Ike stepped over to LeBrun and went through his pockets and clothes. He removed a knife, some glassine packets, and a revolver from an ankle holster.

Ike broke the revolver and dumped the shells. "Good thing you all kept him on his face and 'sedated.' LeBrun, I think you're finally cooked." LeBrun grunted and spat. "Karl, what charges can we make stick here?"

"Start with kidnapping. That's federal. Then there are two counts of attempted murder. Assault, assault with a deadly weapon, attempted rape, resisting arrest—"

"He resisted arrest?"

"If I say so, he did. I say so. How else would he get a broken wrist?"

"Point taken, okay, what else?"

"Unless I'm mistaken, those envelopes you just relieved him of justify a count or two of possession. And his breath is criminally rotten. That ought to be worth at least a no parole sentence. How're you doing down there, Lebrun?"

LeBrun mumbled something about a lawyer.

"Eventually, George, eventually," Ike said.

The sun started its descent in the west. The parks tress cast long shadows across the open picnic area and the temperature began to drop. Early spring meant cool nights. Ike pivoted in a circle, took in the scene once more, and smiled. "I think it's time to toss him in the car and take him in. I think we'll threaten to put him in with his cousin. That should get Daryll talking."

Flossie Picket had her dander up. Instead of going home to her soap opera and a cup of tea, she drove to the sheriff's office. No old white man would talk to her that way, and that was a fact. She parked her Pontiac in a visitor's space and marched into the office.

"How do, Miz Picket. You looking for Charlie?"

"Afternoon, Rita. How come you're here and not Essie?"

"To tell the truth, it's a little confusing. Seems like there was either some threats made against her…that's the rumor, or she's fixing to visit Disney World with her sister."

"Mercy. All that? What do you reckon is the reason?"

"I'll tell you the truth, I really don't know. Onlyist thing I know is if I don't get back on nights real soon, my husband is going to divorce me…or worse."

"What could be worse than that?"

"He could have his mother come live with us."

"You mean Sadie Mae? Oooh, that's not good. By the way, where is Charles?"

"He's around here somewhere. All kinds of things been happening and he might be out in the lot."

"Momma, what're you doing here?" Charlie Picket walked in the door with an armful of papers in his hand.

"I come to tell you that I don't clean for Mister Lydell no more."

"You drove over here to tell me that?"

"There's more. That man was in a funk this morning. I come to tell him something and he's sitting at that big desk of his muttering and banging away on it with his fingers something fierce. Then he cussed at me."

"Cussed at you? What for?"

"Well, maybe not me in particular but sort of in general."

"How does somebody cuss at you in general, Momma?"

"Never you mind. That's not the important thing I got to tell you."

Charlie ushered his mother to a vacant desk and had her sit down. She didn't want any coffee but she took the cup of tea Rita offered.

"Now, what did you want to tell me?"

"I was going to tell Mister Lydell what I saw tucked up under the bolster in the third floor bedroom 'fore he got snotty with me. I figured he didn't deserve that information but then on my way over here I thought it was maybe something Ike ought to know."

"And that is? Momma there's been a major event went down today and I ain't got a whole lot of time, so tell me."

"If your Momma can't take but a minute of your time, Mr. Important Deputy, then I'll just take myself on home and you can talk to me later."

"Momma, it ain't that. If I heard right, we had a near double shooting involving Miss Falco and Deputy Sutherlin. Things are a little scattered."

"Fine, you just tell Mister Ike when you see him, Flossie Picket has some news might interest him. Goodbye."

Charlie sighed. He recognized the symptoms. When his mother got her dander up there was no use arguing with her. He watched her stomp out the door.

"What do you suppose she saw in that bedroom, Charlie?"

He shrugged. "Could be anything. Dust bunnies from outer space, Jimmy Hoffa, a clue to the murder, who knows?"

The door flew open again and Ike, Karl dragging a cursing George LeBrun, and a gaggle of townsfolk poured in.

Dorothy Sutherlin met Essie and Billy at her door.

"You come on in here, dear. You've had a bad day."

"Mom," Billy began.

"Hush, Billy. I heard all about it."

"Heard? Heard how? We just come from there."

"Your brother Frank got it on the highway patrol radio and checked. You go to the cupboard and get some of your Daddy's liquor. Fix up a dollop for Essie here and you can have one yourself." Billy's father passed on nearly twenty years before but his jug of corn liquor still stood in the pantry for 'medicinal purposes.' Billy poured himself a generous shot and a smaller one, which he watered down, for Essie.

Dorothy Sutherlin held the glass out to her. "Here now, you just swallow this. It'll calm you down."

"No thank you. I'll be fine."

"You will be, that's for sure. But you ain't now. Drink up." Essie obediently swallowed, coughed, and handed the glass back. Her eyes watered but not from tears. "Now, I'm going to draw you a hot bath and then you're going to lie down for a spell. Billy here is going to the market and buy us some steaks for dinner and then he's going to sit down and tell me everything."

Essie allowed herself to be mothered. She took the bath, accepted an over large flannel nightgown, and was asleep in ten minutes.

Downstairs, Dorothy fixed her second youngest with a look that brooked no evasion. "Why'd you bring that sweet thing here?"

"She don't have a real home and anyone to look after her. I just thought—"

"You thought right. Now, you go settle down somewhere and listen to yourself, what you just said to me."

Chapter Thirty-three

The threat of sharing a cell with his homicidal cousin convinced Daryll Jenkins his interests would be served best by cooperating with the police. Like the operatic dickey bird, he sang. He was still at it at seven o'clock in the evening when Ike left the office. He had tried to call Ruth three times but the newly amiable Agnes told him she was in a meeting and it looked like it would be a marathon. Ike didn't bother to point out that marathons were races and her metaphor off the mark. He would have in the past but tonight fatigue overwhelmed him. Enough, he thought, I've had enough. I need a meal, a shower, and eight hours of uninterrupted sleep.

"Would you like me to have Dr. Harris call you when she's free?"

"Thank you, no, Agnes. I'm done for the night. You might tell her I'll try to call tomorrow. It's been a long day."

"Sheriff, is it true about the arrest of a drug dealer in the State Park? Someone tried to kill a deputy?"

"I don't know what you heard, but some of it is probably true. The bottom line is, a bad guy is in jail and, except for the bad guy, no one was hurt. Goodnight, Agnes." He walked across the street to The Crossroads Diner.

The diner occupied the corner of Main Street and the Covington Road for years. Before that, it sat on a lot across the street. It had been relocated in the late sixties when the town council took the property to make room for the municipal building which housed the courthouse, sheriff's department, jail, and the mayor's office. The diner's owner had it hauled across the street to a vacant lot and resumed business within a month.

Unlike its newer, urban imitators with their waitresses in poodle skirts and ersatz fifties décor, the Crossroads was the real thing. The aroma of coffee, bacon, and frying food wafted down the street for blocks. Flora Blevins, who'd inherited the business from her father, kept the chrome and Formica interior spotless. Yet, years of griddle cooking had embedded its essence deeply into the very substance of the building. The result could not be duplicated in an imitation.

Other than breakfast, Ike avoided the diner. Lunches and dinners usually consisted of portion controlled, gray—irrespective of its origin—meat, instant carbohydrates of some sort, it didn't matter what, and all drowning in a sea of canned, suspiciously brown, gravy. The good news, if any…the diner served breakfast twenty-four seven. Since breakfast appealed to Ike at the moment, he sauntered in and took his usual place at the counter. The regulars at night were a different group than the ones he joked with in the morning. He recognized most of them, however. The only constant in the diner was Flora Blevins. She held forth from six in the morning until nearly ten at night when she would surrender the reins to her cousin, Arlene. Ike didn't know how these two old women did it. The hours must be killing.

Flora slid a cup of coffee in front of him and waited. Flora did not see any reason to observe the niceties of wait service with Ike, whom she adored, but ragged on mercilessly.

"I'll have breakfast," he said. Nothing more was necessary. Flora had decided early on what Ike would have for breakfast, no matter what he ordered, or when. She always served him the same thing. She held it as a sacred duty to assure the meals he took under her roof met her nutritional standard. That standard presumed that most doctors were quacks, and heavy was healthy. So she served him what most people would describe as a heart-attack breakfast—eggs, bacon, toast swimming in butter, grits, and if in a good mood, she added hash browns and two very fat-filled sausages. Ike had begged for pancakes, oatmeal, fruit, anything, but Flora vetoed them all and gave him his 'usual.'

"How's our boy Karl holding up?" she said, and shoved the bowl of sweeteners to him.

"By Karl, I assume you mean Deputy Hedrick."

"Of course. Don't you go getting smart with me, Ike Schwartz."

"I ask, Flora, because until this very moment, you referred to him as 'that black guy.'"

"I never."

"You did. And you weren't too nice about it, either. When did he become 'our boy Karl?' And, a word to the wise, I wouldn't be calling him boy if he's in earshot."

"I don't know what you mean, and besides, why's everybody so touchy now days."

"Trust me, he has a right to be. Some oaf threw a rock through his window."

"I heard about that. Some of the regulars here had a talk with them boys about that. It won't happen again."

"Why'd they do that?"

Flora strode over to the order window. "Make the sheriff a breakfast. And he looks a little peaked so put in something extra."

Ike was, at best, a casual exponent of his religion. Bacon and an occasional sausage, although proscribed by Judaism, did not worry him. He ate crab cakes and steamed crabs, if and when he could get them, and without compunction. But the last time Flora added an 'extra' to his breakfast it turned out to be a very large, very greasy, gray pork chop. It brought him back to the faith of his fathers.

"No extra, Flora, thanks. It's late."

"You sure?"

"Very. So you still haven't told me, when did Karl become our boy?"

"You don't do what he done out there at the park, and not have somebody take notice. He saved Dorothy Sutherlin's boy and that nice Essie Falco. They're folks, Ike, you know that."

The small town tom-toms had been busy. By five that evening the core of the town, the natives, knew everything that had transpired out at the state park earlier. They always did. Karl had saved two of their own. Karl was no longer an outsider. It was that simple.

"So he's okay now?"

"I don't know what you're going on about. Here's your breakfast."

"You going to tell him?"

"What's to tell?"

At that moment, Karl, finished with his grilling of Daryll Jenkins, pushed through the glass door and scanned the room. He spotted Ike and was about to say something when one of the men stood and slapped him on the back.

"Sit a spell, Karl, and tell us all what you done," the guy said. The three others at the table shifted their chairs around to make room for him.

"Ah, thanks, later maybe. I need to have a word with my boss."

Karl zigzagged his way around tables and booths to Ike.

"What was that all about?"

"Order breakfast, it's on me."

"Thanks, but I'm not that hungry. I just came to fill you in on what Jenkins told us and—"

"It can wait. Flora, this man needs a breakfast."

"Coming up."

"Wait, I haven't ordered anything yet."

"You don't have to. Flora will decide what kind of breakfast you need, and from now on, that's what you'll get no matter what you order."

Flora slid a plate of pancakes in front of Karl.

"My God, these flapjacks look like manhole covers. I can never eat all of this."

"You just have to try. If you fail, you will hear about it for weeks."

"You let her get away with this?"

"Yep."

"Wow. Just look at the size of those things. And there are four of them. And what are these gray, square things on the side dish?"

"Scrapple."

"What's scrapple?"

"You don't want to know. Pour a little syrup on it, and try. If that doesn't suit, try catsup. There are two kinds of people in the world…people who love scrapple and people who hate it. Of those who love it, there are two kinds of people…those who eat it with catsup, and those who pour on syrup. Both groups think the others are insane."

"You're saying if I eat in this place and order breakfast, no matter what I say, I get fried manhole covers and little gray things on the side?"

"That's the drill."

"Wait, that sounds like what my momma would do."

"Exactly." Ike held out his hand. "Karl, welcome to 'one T Picketsville.'"

Chapter Thirty-four

Ike and Karl paused outside the diner, burdened with too much food, and staring at the moon, partially hidden behind some high clouds.

"You wanted to tell me something in there, Karl?"

"I wanted to fill you in on Jenkins, but I guess that can wait. I left a report on your desk. It's preliminary, but you'll get the drift. There is one other thing, though. I found a letter in my box at the office. It's been there for three or four days. I just now discovered it. See, I never got in the habit of looking for mail there, being temporary and all. But, I forgot that I gave that address to the Bureau."

"You received a letter from the FBI?"

"About my hearing."

"When is it?"

"That's the thing. It's tomorrow at three o'clock. I have to drive to DC first thing in the morning. Sorry, I won't be able to take my shift, but I could be back by seven or eight tomorrow night if that helps."

"No, you just get up there and do what you need to do. We'll manage here."

Karl clenched his jaw. His hands balled up into fists. "It won't amount to jack. The fix is in."

"You don't know that."

"Ike, I know the Bureau. There's, like, an old boys network up there. It won't matter how badly my superior might have acted, he filed insubordination charges against me, and even though what I did turned out to be correct, they will close ranks and cover his ass."

"He's under review, too, isn't he?"

"Yeah, and he's near retirement age. He'll get a slap on the wrist and be asked to retire early—pension and all."

"You're selling yourself short, Karl. You're going to be reinstated." Karl shook his head. There wasn't anything more Ike could add. "Goodnight, Karl. Go home and get a decent night's sleep. Maybe you'll feel better in the morning. In any case, when it's over, get on back here and let us know. A lot of people are pretty fond of you, you know."

"Who, those diner people? Come on, Ike, what's up with that?"

"Those diner people, as you call them, are the tip of the iceberg. Listen, when I want to know what the folks in this town are thinking, I go talk to the people in Flora's diner. Trust me. You're solid here." Karl didn't look convinced. "Sleep on it, go to your hearing, and come back. Goodnight."

Sam uncurled from her place on the sofa when Karl walked in the door. "Hi, are you okay?"

"Okay? Yeah, as a matter of fact. But, I tell you after we unloaded that shotgun I had a moment."

"What was that like? I mean, were you scared?"

"Petrified. If I had missed LeBrun's wrist with my baton…if he'd seen me out of the corner of his eye…if Essie hadn't done what she did…she, Billy, and probably me, would be on a slab down at the morgue. Yeah, I was plenty scared."

"You told me once you were involved in a situation like that before."

"Yeah, I tried not to think about that. That was in DC and it ended up real bad. Hostage dead and two agents down." Karl slumped down beside her. "There's something else." He handed her the letter. She frowned as she read.

"Tomorrow? That's not much notice."

"Look at the postmark. It was in my box at the office. I never check that box."

"What will you do?"

"Drive up tomorrow and face the music. When I get back I may be out of a job. How's the idea of me being your kept man grab you."

"You won't be out of a job, Karl. They'll give you back your job and if they don't Ike will ask you to stay."

"That's only a maybe, Sam, not a for sure. And even if he did…"

"Even if he did…what?"

"Nothing. I had a bite to eat at the Crossroads Diner. The people there…they were different."

"Different good or different bad?"

"I don't know…different good, I guess." They sat in silence for a moment.

"I've been going over the Grotz thing," she said. "I think I have some of it figured out. Just a couple of loose ends you can help me with. When you get back from DC, I'll tell you what I think happened."

"Why not now?"

"You've had a long day, you have another one tomorrow, and I think you need something beside cop talk tonight."

"What did you have in mind?"

"Go take a shower and come to bed."

Jonathan Lydell could hardly keep his eyes open. He seriously contemplated locking up and going to bed. If his grandson couldn't show him more respect than to be two hours late coming down from Richmond, then he could spend the night in a motel. He started to act on that thought, when the sweep of headlights and a short horn tap announced the arrival of Benjamin Harrison Winslow, Esq. Lydell heaved himself off the settee. The door had been left unlocked. He listened to his grandson's footsteps resound on the porch.

"Hiya, Gramps," he said.

Lydell had a thing about colloquialisms and diminutives of people's names. The use of nicknames, first names with strangers, and sloppy speech set his geriatric teeth on edge. "Gramps" could cause him to crack a crown.

"You're late, it's late, and I'm going to bed. There is food in the ice box, and we'll talk in the morning about this police business and your mother's arrangements."

"You never told me what happened."

"If you hadn't seen fit to lollygag around Richmond for days instead of coming home, you would have had ample time to hear the details. Let's just say, your mother, in her cups as usual, slipped and fell down the stairs."

Winslow forced himself to overlook his grandfather's rudeness. "Where were you when this happened?"

"What are you playing at...prosecutor?"

"Is that what it sounds like? No, maybe, I mean, should I? I want to know what happened. Your call said accident. Five minutes on the phone, Gramps, that's all I got from you."

"Stop calling me that. I'm your grandfather. Call me Grandfather, dammit."

"Sorry, Grandfather then. So tell me what happened."

"Tomorrow. We'll talk tomorrow. Goodnight."

Winslow watched the old man labor up the stairs and disappear into the shadows at the top.

"You're in the old guest room next to the bath," he shouted and then slammed his bedroom door.

"Nice," Winslow muttered. He went to the kitchen, dug a ham shank from the refrigerator—his grandfather's ice box—and assembled a sandwich. There was no beer to be found so he settled for a diet soda, the only soft drink in sight. He guessed it had been his mother's.

What did the old man mean about *police business?* Was there some question about the accident? Winslow knew his limits. He

made a living suing and defending corporate entities in a variety
of complex and occasionally remunerative civil cases. He had
no illusions about his abilities in criminal cases. He wouldn't
touch one with a ten foot pole. He'd represent the old man up
to, but not through something like that. Why did he think his
grandfather would need counsel? Something didn't ring true,
but he couldn't put his finger on it.

He gazed at his surroundings. The old man said he intended
to restore Bellmore to its antebellum status. If the kitchen served
as an example of what he'd accomplished so far, he'd have to say
the war still raged. He finished his snack, turned out the lights,
and found his way to the guest room. Big day tomorrow.

Dorothy Sutherlin peeked around the bedroom door to check
on Essie. She slept soundly, folded in the fetal position, her hair
in a golden tumble around her face. Dorothy listened and, reas-
sured by her regular breathing, closed the door, and retreated
to the first floor. She settled into her rocking chair to wait, an
afghan across her knees. Ordinarily she would not sit up for
her children. When they were teenagers she'd worry and wait,
but not any more. Tonight, though, she needed to speak to her
youngest. She didn't have long to wait. Henry pulled into the
driveway and let himself in the house. The figure of his mother
in her chair startled him.

"You're still up?"

"Been waiting for you."

"Now, you didn't have to go and do that. I only went to bowl
a few games with the guys."

"I wasn't worried about that. Did you hear what almost happened to Billy and Essie Falco?"

He hadn't. His mother had been fully briefed earlier by Billy,
except the part about Essie taking off her clothes. Billy didn't
think his mother needed to hear that part and certainly not from
him. She recited the story to Henry.

"They okay?" Henry wished he'd been there. Wished he'd had a shot at LeBrun.

"They're fine. When you go upstairs, you be quiet. Essie is in the twins' old room and fast asleep."

Henry turned toward the stairway. "Will do. Goodnight, Ma."

"Whoa. I'm not done here. Billy said you were putting in an application to the police academy again."

"Yes'm, I am."

"I don't want you to." She started to rock in the chair, its motion measuring her mood.

"Why?"

"Why do you think? Every one of my boys is in some kind of dangerous service. Billy near got his brains blowed out today. Jack's dead. Danny got himself shot or something, he won't say how or where. Frank like to died in that high speed chase last year. I can't give another son to that kind of life no more. I don't need anymore of my children in danger. You get a job at the hardware store like your Daddy. I want one son safe. You hear?"

"Ma, I ain't going to be a cop. I want to be an evidence technician. It's a whole lot different."

"I seen them on TV. You ain't going to do that." Dorothy's rocking now had the same cadence as the grandfather clock ticking in the hall.

"Ma, that's just TV. Those CSI people aren't real. ETs don't do any of that stuff. They just process the crime scene and the evidence, take pictures, put suspicious things in bags, like that. Once they're done, they give it to the police. I'm not even sure if I get a badge and the only gun I'd have is my hunting rifle on the weekend."

"On the TV they drive around, shoot, and—"

"Ma, I promise you, there're no hot babes in, like, fashion magazine clothes, and guys driving around in Hummers. It'd be more like, say, Mr. Harquvist down at the drug store, filling prescriptions or like working in the biology lab at the high school. You remember how I used to like doing that. There's no danger, honest."

Dorothy slowed her rocking. She sighed but still looked worried. "You're sure? I still don't like it. You think hard about the hardware store, Henry. And don't make any noise going upstairs."

Chapter Thirty-five

The scent of freshly brewed coffee greeted Ike as he pushed through the door. He paused, and gazed around the outer office.

"Whoa, I must be in the wrong building. Where's the always day old, thick as tar coffee I've come to love?" He spun and caught sight of Essie. "I thought I told you to take off, go to Disney World…rest, what are you doing here?"

"I'm going there, but not right now. And I'm here because here is where I belong. And I need to talk to you sometime, Ike, when you have a minute."

"I have several, as a matter of fact, right now. Let me get a cup and make sure I'm not dreaming." Ike filled his mug, added creamer and sweetener, and retreated to his office. Essie followed him in and sat. "How are you holding up, Essie? I got the whole story from Karl. He said he'd never seen anyone as brave as you were."

"I've never been so scared in my life, Ike. It was Karl that did the deed, though."

"Not without what you did."

"I didn't do anything much."

"You were off the charts, Essie."

She stared out the window and swallowed. Her hands plucked at the fabric of her slacks. Ike waited.

"Is that what it's like?" she said.

"Is what, what it's like…?"

"Being a police person. Is that what they do…put their life on the line like that?"

"It can be, is sometimes, but not often, at least not in a small town like Picketsville. You've sat at that dispatch desk. How many times have any of us had to face something like what you went through?"

"Come on, Ike, there was Whaite just last winter. I mean poor Darcie's left with them kids…and I don't know what happened in that motel last summer. You never said anything about it to anybody. It happens more than enough. I can't do it."

"But you did it. You were thinking about attending the Police Academy. I told you before, you get a test somewhere along the line. None quite like yours, I guess, but sooner or later you see first hand what's involved. Now you've seen it. If that was your test, you passed. You are ready to go up to Weyer's Cave to the academy."

"That's the thing, Ike, I didn't and so I'm not. I wasn't thinking about anything except Billy. If it had been anyone else…well, I wouldn't have been there in the first place, I guess, but no way would I take that chance."

"But—"

"No, you don't understand. I couldn't do that for anyone else. Like, if I had been in Karl's shoes, I'd have run away. I wouldn't have done anything. Maybe I might've run to the car and called for help, blow the horn, or something like that. But, no way could I do what he did. I only wanted to help Billy, save his life. Police work is not for me. I know that now." She started to shake. Not much, but enough to worry Ike.

"Everyone has doubts, Essie. What you don't have to wonder about is, will I be brave? That's what gets to everyone."

"Brave? No, scared and…just scared. I just saw that dirt bag with the gun on Billy and I just…"

"You did good, Essie. You're a natural."

"I'm not. You didn't hear me. Anybody else, anywhere else, and I'm gone, outta there. Not brave, not close to brave. I can't do police work."

"You're ditching the academy?"

"Yes. Like I said, Ike, it was for Billy. See, all these years, me and Billy was just, like, friends. That's what we told each other. Friends with…" She blushed, looked at the floor, and took a deep breath, "…like they say, 'friends with privileges.' But out there in the park, all of a sudden I realized that it wasn't true. He wasn't just a friend. He had become something more. You know what I mean?"

"I think so. How's Billy feel?"

Her face brightened, "I guess that's the upside. We spent early this morning on the porch swing, talking. We never did much serious talking before. It was mostly fun. So, I told him what I came to realize out there in the park, and he sat there looking out across the field, quiet like. I swear there was this tear in his eye, maybe. And then he said, 'What were you thinking about out there, woman?' and I told him what I just told you, and he said, 'I didn't know Karl was back there. I aimed to turn and even if he pulled that trigger, I'd get him in a grip and pull him down so's you could run.' He just sat there shaking his head and looking at me like I was some…I don't know…really important person, or something. Then he said…this is the good part…'You know, Essie, you and me have been playing around long enough. I reckon it's about time we grew up a little.'" Essie's eyes filled with tears. Ike put his hand on hers.

"Then he said, 'Last night I told Ma that you didn't have anyone to look after you proper and she made me think about that.' I was about to say, 'I'm okay,' when he says, 'Marry me, Essie Falco.' He did, Ike, just like that."

"And you said?"

"Well, what do you think? I said yes, of course."

"When will you get married?"

"Miz Sutherlin is arranging it all. She's pretty big in that old church of hers. She says June, so that's that."

"Disney World off the books?"

"Nope. Honeymoon."

"I'm happy for you, Essie. I still think you'd make a fine deputy."

"Miz Sutherlin says no way she's going to have another police in the family. Besides, the way I'm put together, I'd spend more time on maternity leave than on duty."

It was Ike's turn to blush. Essie stood and strode out the door just as Henry Sutherlin walked in.

"Just one thing, though, I'm still the head dispatcher around here." She flashed him a smile. It fell short of her usual dazzler. That would come back, he guessed in time. "Hey-o Henry. What're you here for?"

"Hey there, Sis to be, I come to see Ike. You got a minute, Ike?"

Ike waved him in.

"Essie tell you the news? Great, huh?"

"She did, it is. What's on your mind, Henry?"

"It's like this. My Ma is dead set against me going to the police academy on account of what she sees on the TV. She thinks I'm going to drive around in a cop car, arrest folks, and get shot at, you know like on them shows. What nearly happened to Billy like to scared her to death. I told her that TV stuff was all made up. The evidence technicians just, like, work out puzzles."

"What do you want from me?"

"Could you, like, talk to her? You know, tell her it ain't dangerous and all?"

"I can do that. Anything else?"

"Nope, thanks. Say, is that coffee fresh?"

"Help yourself. Your 'Sis to be' made it. One question for you, Henry."

"Shoot."

"You said you heard Lydell arguing with his daughter the day she fell down the stairs."

"Yes, and that struck me funny because—"

"I remember that part. Tell me again where the voices came from, do you remember?"

"Came from?"

"Upstairs, downstairs, one up, one down?"

Henry scuffed his boot on the floor. His face lit up. "Both were upstairs."

"That's what I thought you said."

"Is it important?"

"You're the evidence tech, you tell me?"

"I'll think on it. Here's a free one for you. George Lebrun and Lydell were getting into it hot and heavy the other day. Sounded serious."

"Lebrun and Lydell?" Henry nodded.

The phone on his desk blinked and Essie wigwagged for Ike to pick up. He waved Henry out. Frank Sutherlin was on the line and asked for a few minutes. This must be Sutherlin day, he thought. He listened to Frank talk and then to his proposal. His eyebrows slowly climbed his forehead. When Frank finished, Ike paused, squinted through the glass windows that formed one wall of his office.

"It sounds okay at this end, better than okay, actually. You clear it with your Major and we'll work out the details." He hung up and scratched his chin.

"One door closes, another opens," he muttered. He stepped back into the main office to refill his cup. Henry waved goodbye and banged out the door. Essie looked expectantly at Ike.

"What'd Frank want?"

"How well do you know Billy's brothers?"

"Not all that good. Michael and Johnny are away somewhere in the Army. Jack passed, and, of course, you know Henry. I was out to their place on Christmas. Frank was there and Danny. He's one of them SEALs, they keep him on a short string, I think, and Henry, Billy, and that's all."

"What's Frank like?"

"Frank is…how do I say it? He's, like, the opposite of Billy. I mean, time was when Billy was sort of wild. No more, though, and Frank is solid. He gave Billy a talking to at the party. He was looking at me when he did it, so I guess I was supposed to be included." She pursed her lips and frowned. "I'll tell you what he's like. He reminds me of Whaite." Her radio crackled. She turned away.

"Essie, when you're done with that call, get me Jonathan Lydell on the phone, and tell him he needs to come in and identify his pistol. And tell him I have some questions for him about his daughter's accident."

Frank reminded Essie of Whaite.

Chapter Thirty-six

Ike had the items that were found in the tree stump spread out on his desk. The matchbox, containing a handful of Indianhead pennies, had nearly disintegrated. The pennies were corroded. Obviously, they had been in the stump for years. The box of bullets, aside from being damp, was in reasonably good shape. There was one rusty key similar in shape to the dozens he'd seen in Lydell's basement. There appeared to be a partial print in the red rust, but insufficient to identify. The pistol still showed some powder from the evidence techs attempt to lift prints, but was otherwise in good shape. The report detailing the items lay next to them.

He studied it, looking for something, anything that might move the investigation forward. As it now stood, there didn't seem to be any light at the end of his tunnel. He slipped on a pair of latex gloves, even though the report had been written and they were not necessary, and picked up each of the items in turn, pennies, rusty key, bullets with their box, and the pistol. The prints on the gun belonged to Tommy, the kid who found it, Norbert from the gun store, and Lydell. The shells in the box had prints as well, Lydell's. They were old and the techs deemed any match they might make as unreliable. Old prints would be consistent with Lydell's story of the gun having languished in a drawer for years. The casings in the pistol's cylinder and the two unfired bullets had cleaner, relatively recent prints, all Lydell's.

He turned his attention to the two coroner's reports. Grotz's posed more questions than it answered. Three shots to the back, one in the forehead. That would mean Grotz was probably shot first while his back was turned to the shooter, and the one in the forehead was to make sure he wouldn't get up. Ike mulled over the wounds. He could see how someone might shoot Grotz in the back in a locked room. How big an aperture would you need to do that? A not noticeable hole in the wall, door probably. Ike made a mental note to check the door again. But the difficulty with that scenario was how do you get the forehead shot? Maybe it was first. Knock on the door…who's there?…mumble, mumble…walk to the door and bend forward—bang, stagger back and turn—bang, bang, and to make sure, bang. It could work except, Ike didn't remember any holes in the door. He'd have to check under the doorknocker. That might be a possibility.

He reread the other report. Martha Marie Lydell Winslow fell down a flight of stairs. She reeked of whiskey but her blood alcohol was below the legal limit for impaired. She showed traces of cocaine but none recently. LeBrun sold cocaine. Was that what Lydell and he were arguing about? Lydell said she was drunk, but she wasn't. Except for a possible misstep, why did she fall? And what were the two arguing about before she fell? He still had to look up petechiae. Ike pulled a scrap of paper from the pile on his desk and jotted down the things that puzzled him. He wanted to be ready for Lydell.

Jonathan Lydell arrived at the office a little after noon. He had his grandson in tow. Ike ushered them into his office and had them sit. He shuffled some papers, offered them coffee, which they refused, sat and stared off into space for a moment.

"Sheriff? Excuse me, but I am a busy man. You wanted to see me. I'm here." Lydell seemed irked which was exactly what Ike wanted. He wasn't sure about the grandson.

"I take it this is your grandson. Is that correct?"

Lydell struggled to remember his manners. Normally any semblance of civility he reserved for people he assigned to his "class." Ike Schwartz, the upstart Jewish sheriff, did not so qualify. But he knew enough not to aggravate him. "Yes, this is my grandson, Ben, Benjamin Harrison Winslow. You are aware of the Winslows, I believe." Ike was. He'd made a phone call to his father, Abe. Abe knew everybody. He, in turn, had shaken the cherry tree and filled Ike in on Winslow, his law practice, partners and success, such as it was.

"Nice to meet you." Ike extended his hand which Winslow took. A fish hand, Ike thought.

"The same," Winslow replied.

Niceties over, Ike spread the items from the tree stump before them. "Can you identify any or all of these?"

Lydell sifted through them. He looked greedily at the pennies. With the right dates they could be worth a fortune. Ike knew they were worth anywhere from two dollars apiece to fifteen hundred dollars for an 1877 coin, depending on condition. Ike had not looked at the dates on the pennies in the box. Lydell fidgeted and looked like he was tempted. He'd called himself a packrat, and Ike wondered what held him back. Lydell avoided the key entirely and settled for the pistol, which he'd already acknowledged as his, and the box of ammunition.

"The key? It's not one of yours?"

Lydell hesitated, a split second of indecision, should he or shouldn't he? "No, not mine. Only these two things," he said, and gestured toward the gun and shells. Then, as if the temptation became too great, he said, "Those pennies. What will you do with them?"

"We'll try to find the rightful owner, of course. Someone named Shorter, possibly. Failing at that, we'll put them away until they can be appraised, and then we will sell them."

"But the boy who found them, wouldn't they be his? I'd be more than happy to give him some money for them."

I bet you would, you old crook, Ike thought. "The problem with that is, he has been booked on a felony and released to his parents. There is a legal issue here as to whether he can profit from it, you see." That was more than a stretch. Winslow's eyes flickered. Ike could almost hear the wheels turning. In a minute, he guessed, Winslow would try for a value guess on the pennies.

Thirty seconds later, Winslow cleared his throat. "Would you have any idea of the value of those pennies? They are rare, aren't they?"

"No idea," Ike lied. "There are about forty of them. Last I heard they were going for two dollars apiece, but you never know." Winslow deflated. "Okay, then as I told you, Mr. Lydell, I will have to keep this pistol as evidence for the time being. The box of ammunition I will keep as well. You can retrieve them when our investigation is complete."

"Do you honestly believe you will find that man's murderer? It certainly doesn't seem very promising to me."

"Oh yes, we'll get him. Just a matter of time and good police work." Ike lied for the second time. He guessed he might be headed for a liar's record because he had a few more for Lydell before he'd turn him loose. "Are you sure I can't get you something, coffee, water…?"

"I'll take a bottle of water," Winslow said, and loosed his collar. Ike had deliberately closed the window before they came. Sweat'em, he'd thought. He retrieved three bottles of water from the little refrigerator in the break room. The bottles were recycled, probably illegally. They were all refilled at the water fountain after being emptied by one or the other of the staff. Ike hoped they had remembered to wash them first.

Lydell snapped open his pocket watch and made a show of checking the time. "Is there more?"

"I need to take a statement from you about your daughter's accident."

"I told you everything you wanted to know at the time. I can't add to that."

"No? You see, there are a few things that seem out of place. Perhaps in the stress of the moment, you misspoke."

"What do you mean, misspoke? I told you exactly what happened."

"Yes, I see. You said your daughter had been drinking and that caused her fall."

"Yes, certainly. You were there. She positively reeked with bourbon."

"The coroner reports that all of the alcohol was on her clothes and in her mouth, not her stomach. Her blood showed only a trace. Perhaps she had a bottle in her hand and it spilled in the fall?"

"Nonsense, the coroner's a fool. He made a mistake. Everyone knew that Martha Marie drank to excess. I'm sorry you have to hear this, Ben. She was your mother after all. Sheriff, I'll thank you to be more discreet under the circumstances."

Ike watched Winslow out of the corner of his eye. He didn't look offended at all. Puzzled, but not offended. "I am sorry." Winslow waved off the apology. "We also have a witness who says you and your daughter were arguing at the time."

"A witness you say? Ah, yes, we had a disagreement. Over what we would serve for dinner, if memory serves. I was standing at the foot of the stairs, Martha Marie, bless her soul, at the top. Well the liquor and…everything. She just toppled over."

Ike had seen some liars in his day. Most of them were convincing, their stories plausible. But this old man took the cake. He lied through his teeth.

"I see. Just one more thing. Were you aware your daughter used cocaine?"

"Sheriff, this is outrageous. I won't have it."

"I'll take that as a no. I have nothing more for you here. The body has been sent to Unger's Funeral Home. We're sorry for your loss."

The two men stood and headed for the door. As they stepped out into the front office, Ike said, "Oh, there is one last thing. The coroner said there was slight bruising on your daughter's back. It could have been made by a hand. Four small marks and a larger, less defined one below, like fingers and the heel of a hand."

Lydell blanched. "She must have hit the newel post."

"Yes, that's probably it. Thank you for your patience."

Winslow stopped dead in his tracks. "The newel post is as big and round as a bowling ball. It wouldn't make bruises like that."

"No? I'm sure there's an explanation. We'll find it." Ike sat in his chair and swiveled around so that his back was to the two men. Interview ended.

Chapter Thirty-seven

Ike slouched back in his oak swivel chair and put his feet on his desk, in the only clear spot left on it. He pulled the phone toward him and tapped the hand set with his index finger while he contemplated which number he would dial first. He picked up and called Ruth. Agnes answered and put him through.

"Ike? Is that you?"

"I am tempted to make what you would term a smart-ass answer but I will refrain. It is I. I tried to call yesterday but you were tied up in meetings. Any news on the merger front?"

"I've managed to get them in a holding pattern while I wait for the U.S. Cavalry to arrive."

"In the person of…"

"Can't say just yet, but we live in hope. What have you been up to? I just realized, I have been so caught up with meetings and strategy sessions, I have no idea what's going on in your corner of the world. I heard about something happening at the State Park. Was that you?"

"My people, not me. Listen, I could use some help if you can tear yourself away from your meetings, duties, and obligations."

"You want my help?"

"I need a listener. You are good at that. How about dinner?"

"Dinner is good. Where?"

"Your choice."

"Take me to that restaurant up in the mountains…what's its name?"

"*Le Chateau.*"

"That's the place. Pick me up at six. Anything else I can help you with, Sheriff? And please don't reach for the obvious lascivious remark."

"Right. Do you know a numismatist?"

"You've been at your word builder again, haven't you?"

"Actually, that one I knew. I had a roommate at college who obsessed over coins."

"It's none of my business, but what do you need a numismatician for?"

"Is that a word?"

"It is now."

"I have some coins taken in evidence. I need a rough idea what they are worth."

"Evidence? What, not the business at the park? What did happen out there anyway?"

"Nothing to do with the park. I have a murder on my hands—a very difficult murder. The coins may or may not have something to do with it. Now, who is your resident numismatician? Are you sure it's a word. I'm going to look it up."

"Your friend, Leon Weitz. He collects coins. He can help. Six o'clock. What kind of murder?"

"Tell you at dinner."

Ties were not Ike's favorite item of apparel but *Le Chateau* had a dress code that could not be negotiated. He'd seen a state senator refused a table for wearing a bolo with his pinstripe suit. Ike always wondered if it was the bolo alone or the combination that got him the heave-ho. If the senator had worn cowboy boots, a Stetson, and linen suit might he have been seated? Ike wasn't in the mood to take chances so he'd dug out one of the three ties he owned and put it on. Karl's call came in the middle of his second attempt at a Windsor knot.

"I'm reinstated, Ike."

"I hope you are not surprised."

"I am, a little. I told you about the old boy network and—"

"It wasn't true."

"No, actually it was, but not like I thought. My old boss got what I told you he would, early retirement and a slap on the wrist. Then they turned around and put a letter of commendation in his file for his years of service or some kind of crap like that."

"And that affects you how?"

"No way, I guess, but it still frosts my—"

"You'll get over it. Now you have choices to make."

"What kind of choices? Are you going to ask me to stay on as a deputy?"

"Lots of choices. That's just one."

"You are offering me a job. I didn't think you would, not after the talk we had."

"The talk was about you as a person, not you as a cop, and…rats." Ike's knot turned into a huge snarl of rep fabric. "Do you know how to tie a Windsor knot?"

"Not over the phone, I don't. What are you doing tying a big knot like that? Stick with a four-in-hand."

"FBI send you to fashion school?"

"Part of the image. So you think I can function as a deputy in Picketsville?"

"I've seen you work, two of your colleagues owe their lives to you, and the folks love you."

"By folks, you mean the diner people."

"I mean the good people of this town. Don't keep on being obtuse, Karl. I have this clip-on thing. Maybe I should surrender and wear it."

"Trust me, if this is, like, a romantic thing, you don't want to be guilty of clip-ons. I'm not being obtuse, just…I don't know…cautious. Growing up black makes you careful about sudden new friendships with white folks."

"I'll do the four-in-hand then. Okay, I understand. You'll have to wait and see, I guess. Are you interested?" The line went silent. Ike finally pulled the long end of his tie through the knot, discovered that if he kept his jacket closed he would be more or less presentable. "You still there, Karl?"

"I'm here. This is the thing, Ike. All my life, FBI is what I wanted. It's my dream. I love working with you and the gang down there. You are as smart and quick as anybody I've ever met, in the Bureau or out. But I have my job back here. What I don't know is whether I have my career back. You know, I made some of these dudes angry and there may be career consequences. I might end up at a desk in Dubuque in charge of lost cats. But I have to find that out. It's the same problem you pointed out before. If I go with you, I'll never know what might have been."

"You're right. Take some time. We aren't going anywhere. You'd always be welcome. Have you told Sam?"

"Just that I was reinstated. The rest isn't something I should deal with on the phone."

"I've gotta go, Karl. We'll talk more in the morning."

It was probably a mistake to put LeBrun in the cell next to his cousin Daryll. George was on the thin edge of methamphetamine withdrawal. He had friends and his cell had a window. It also had bars, a mesh covering, and was easily eight feet off the ground. Whether the window had anything to do with what ensued remains unclear. But somehow he managed to obtain a ten inch spike, lure his cousin over to the bars that separated their cells and drive the spike straight into his heart. Charlie Picket and Billy Sutherlin managed to disarm LeBrun, but in the melee that followed, he suffered another broken bone in his other wrist and a sizable knot on his head. By the time the EMTs arrived, his cousin's life had ebbed away. Charlie needed an ice pack and Billy had a nasty bruise under his cheek bone. The EMTs glanced at LeBrun's injuries and handed him an ACE bandage and some gauze, through the bars, and left. He was taken in shackles to the prison ward of the hospital, stitched up, put in a second cast, sedated and returned, still in shackles, to the jail, now with a first degree murder charge added to his list of felonies.

Chapter Thirty-eight

Sam, disconsolate, listened for the sound of Karl pulling into the driveway which they shared with the older couple who occupied the first floor apartment. Her phone lay beside her on the sofa where she'd dropped it after he called. She'd heard all she needed from the tone of his voice. She didn't want to hear it again, didn't want to have any uncertainty removed, or have the thin sliver of hope she harbored destroyed. She stood and moved restlessly around the room that served as both a sitting and dining area. The windows were closed against the cool night air. She felt stifled and threw open the one with the cardboard taped across it, where the rock had come through. Fresh air flowed over the sill and puddled on the floor. The television needed dusting. She retrieved a cloth and absently swiped it across the set and the few pieces of furniture in the room. She wracked her brains to come up with an argument that would dissuade Karl from leaving. But she knew him and she knew that nothing she said would make him change his mind.

There were other options, of course. They could resume their weekend commuter romance, one in DC, one in Picketsville. Or, she could follow him to Washington, give up her job as deputy, and take her chances with the job market in the city. She could…she didn't want to think about the others. She didn't want to cry.

◇◇◇

Ruth stood on the porch that wrapped around the President's manse. The sun had disappeared behind the college's main building. She shivered and pulled her shawl closer around her shoulders. Ike drove up in an unmarked car. Ruth did not recognize it or him. He tapped the horn and stepped out to open the passenger side door.

"Whose car are we driving tonight? I appreciate your not wheeling up here in that hideous black and white thing and I'm more than happy not to have to ride in that drafty Jeep of yours, so thank you, but where?"

"It's new, it's the department's, it's unmarked, and it's a perk. I am the sheriff, after all."

"So now, instead of that wreck of a black and white cruiser you hide behind the azaleas where only a blind man couldn't see it, you'll park this shiny black job with its umpteen antennae sticking up from its roof instead? It won't fool anybody."

"It's a step in the right direction."

"No, it really isn't, Ike. We need to talk about our arrangements."

"We have nearly an hour's drive to the restaurant. We can talk on the way."

Ike helped her in the passenger's seat, closed the door, and took his place behind the wheel.

"Don't you just love that new car smell?" he said, and started the motor.

"It's great. Speaking of which, I happen to know you are not hurting for money. Has it ever occurred to you that you might just retire that broken down Jeep of yours and buy a car of your own?"

"Buy a car?" The idea had never occurred to Ike. When he took the job of sheriff there was no reason to purchase a vehicle. He had his Jeep and otherwise he drove one of the department's cars. There was no Ruth in his life, no connections to anybody, really, except his family, no need to own and operate a car. "I guess I could do that. How about I get one of those big SUVs like you see TV cops driving around Miami?"

"Oh that would be a real jump forward. Instead of a black but obvious police car lurking behind my azaleas, you want to park a three ton truck. What color did you have in mind…red?"

"Ochre, I think…earth colors are so in, don't you think?"

"You are skating on thin ice here, Lover. Shape up or I'll order a meal that will set you back four months' pay and that's not including a forty dollar bottle of wine."

"I'll have it done in camo, Shenandoah Valley camouflage. It'll look like dogwoods and broadleaf evergreens, absolutely invisible."

"A fifty dollar bottle of wine."

"Betsy Blessing knows a guy with an '85 Yugo for sale. Will that suit? I can probably get it for what you're planning to spend on dinner."

"You never quit, do you, Bubba."

"We both need to lighten up. You've been swimming with sharks. I've had a double attempted murder…" Ike's cell phone twirped. "Sorry, always on call, *toujours prêt,* that's me…hello, Schwartz." His face fell.

"Trouble?"

Ike snapped the cover shut and grimaced. "Our bad guy, the attempted double murderer, kidnapper, and dope dealer, just stabbed his cousin to death while in our custody. This is not going to play well."

"Do you have to go back?" Ike could hear the disappointment in her voice.

"No, it's under control. The benefit, if there is one, is we now have an absolute lock on putting this guy away forever. One more off the streets. Two actually. His cousin was no treat either."

"That's cold, Ike."

"That's police work, Ruth. It's what we do that allows good citizens to sleep at night. Folks sometimes don't want to hear it. They want to worry about whether a monster on crystal meth is being treated with the proper amount of respect. The fact he nearly killed two of my two cops, sells dope to children in our schools, and just spiked his cousin doesn't seem to register."

"Whoa. I'm your best friend, remember."

"Sorry. Make it a fifty dollar bottle of wine."

"Let's just have a nice quiet dinner. We can talk about the state of the world someday when it doesn't seem so dark."

"It isn't necessary, you know? You don't have to go and spend money on a ring. Why not just get a nice wedding band. Someday when we're rich, we can get a big old diamond, Billy."

"You only get hitched up once, Essie. I want to do it right."

"Well then, I guess I like that one." Essie pointed to the one-half carat solitaire on black velvet.

"You don't want the one with all them little diamonds around the big one?"

"How'd it look, Billy? It's me, Essie. I live in a rented trailer at the mobile home park. I dispatch for the police. You live with your Ma. That ring is over the top for us."

"You don't like it." Billy looked crestfallen.

"I love it, Billy. A year ago, a week ago, I would have said, go for it. But that was then, this is now. We need to be, like, practical. Marriage, maybe kids, a real house. Stuff like that. I want a life with you and…well, we got to be sensible now."

"You're not going all serious on me now, are you?"

Essie gave him her patented wicked smile. "You just wait until I get you home and I'll show you some serious."

Sam stared past Karl at a picture of roses in a bowl. She looked straight at it but didn't see it.

"I know how you feel," Karl murmured. He sat slumped forward in what might have been the last bean-bag chair in captivity. His hands dangled between his knees. "But you have to understand—"

"I do understand. That's the problem. You've told me. The Bureau has been your dream since you were a kid. I know. It's like this job that Ike gave me. It's the same thing. Look at me. I'm a gawky, nearsighted geek. I don't qualify, couldn't pass a physical probably, for a law enforcement job anywhere except here. Doing this has been *my* dream. I understand, Karl, I do, but…"

Karl sank deeper in the cushion. There didn't seem to be any way out of this. He had to go back to the Bureau, and he couldn't ask her to leave Picketsville. Not and give up her job and certainly not on a maybe, with respect to where their relationship might go.

"Listen, Sam, I might end up in a dead end, career-wise. That could happen. Like I told Ike, I might have a job, but not a career. I need to find out. Ike said the offer was open-ended. I need some time to find out."

Sam shifted her eyes to focus on Karl. Time. A lot could happen in six months or so. She could make things happen. She brightened a little. "We both need some time. When do you go back to DC?"

"Three weeks."

"Then, we still have three weeks. We have work to do and…we'll see."

"You're okay?"

"I don't have a choice, do I?"

Karl had no answer for her. No, she didn't have any good choices.

"Good," Sam bounced to her feet. "I'm beat. I need a shower and bed. Tomorrow, first thing, I want to show you what I found out about the Grotz thing."

Chapter Thirty-nine

Morning in Picketsville, the promise of a new day, a new start, fresh air, clean and crisp, and even discernible over the pervasive cooking aromas emanating from The Crossroads Diner. Ike slipped through its glass doors, popped an antacid, and headed across the street to his office. He'd had his breakfast, no extras, and could start his day. The bus from the county jail would arrive in a few minutes to take LeBrun to a max-security facility—one with an infirmary. They would have done so the day before except for a SNAFU in scheduling. A minor mix-up that cost Daryll Jenkins his life. Essie was back at her desk and everything seemed to be returning to normal. Ike paused to look at his dispatcher. She held her left hand awkwardly in the air. He couldn't see how she could use the phone that way. Then he saw the ring and smiled.

"Tell Billy I must pay him too much, Essie. That's a nice stone."

She turned and grinned and wagged her hand at him. He settled in his antique oak chair and shifted through the papers on his desk. The dinner at *Le Chateau* with Ruth had been pleasant. He'd filled her in on his locked room dilemma. She brought him up to date on the merger business. Neither had much in the way of advice for the other. Time, Toronto, and possible future scenarios, were carefully avoided.

Karl and Sam burst into the office and stood before him as excited as a pair of kids who've just discovered roller-coasters.

"Ike, you need to hear this." Karl pushed Sam forward like a shy schoolgirl who had just recited the entire Gettysburg Address without flaw. "Tell him, Sam."

"Well…"

"Go on. Ike, she's figured it all out."

"Not all. Just the why. And it's circumstantial."

"It will hold. People have been put away for less. Tell him."

Ike held up both hands. "Whoa. Slow down. What will put who away?"

Sam took a deep breath. "See, I spent the other morning with Leon Weitz. Did you know he was writing a book about the intelligence activities on both sides of the Civil War?"

"No, I can't say that I did. This is about the Grotz business, isn't it?"

"Well, sure. See, in that war the whole business of spying was, like, a new thing. I mean there weren't many real professionals, and the women were treated differently than the men. The majority of the books written are about the women like Wild Rose Greenhow and…that probably wasn't right…the different treatment, I mean. Were women treated differently when you were a CIA agent, Ike?"

"How differently? Wait, is this going anywhere? What are you talking about? Who's a spy?" Ike stood and cracked the window to let in some fresh air.

"No, listen to Sam." Karl said, "She's got it wrapped up."

Ike slouched back in his chair and scratched his head. "I'm trying to, but I can't find the thread. Sam, just the bare bones. Relative changes in social attitudes can wait for another day."

Sam dropped into a chair, put her hands on her knees and screwed up her face in concentration.

"Wuff. Okay, here goes. I said before, I thought the two murders were connected. Now I'm sure. We have to start with the one in 1864." She handed round copies of the *Staunton Spectator*. "You read this, right? The first thing that caught my eye…well, maybe not the first thing but early on…was the line about no luggage."

"You're straying, Sam," Ike said, his eyes focused on the newspaper piece, "what about the luggage?"

"Okay. I was looking at the crime scene pictures and there's a travel trunk in that room."

"I thought you said we had to start with the first murder."

"We are. Just let me do this, Ike. You'll see."

"Okay, okay, shoot."

"At the outbreak of the Civil War...I know, I know...The War of Northern Aggression, The War of Southern Independence, The War Between the States, Mr. Lincoln's War, The Late Unpleasantness, The Whatever War, That war. At its outbreak, families were divided. The nation was divided, and so on. There were two brothers, Quincy and Franklin Brian, from Trenton, New Jersey. They were southern sympathizers. At the start of the war, they went south to Richmond to enlist in the Confederate Army. They were on their way to an artillery unit when they met Major William Norris of the Confederate Signal Bureau."

"The what?"

"Let her tell it, Ike."

"Sorry, go on, Sam."

"The Confederate Signal Bureau was the home of the semaphore troops. They would signal across the battle field relaying messages and troop deployments, things like that. The regulars called them flag-floppers...So, okay, the Confederate Signal Bureau also served as a cover for the South's organized spy network. The Brians were brought in and enrolled as agents.

"According to Weitz's research, they were assigned to spy on Northern troop movements in the New York area, sabotage supply trains, and procure materiel for the south. I didn't know this, but some of the north's biggest names, industrialists and politicians, were war profiteers. They supported the north, but under the table, sold arms, shoes, gunpowder, and so on, to southern agents who would ship them south. The lines between the two warring parties in this area were like Swiss cheese. Franklin Brian specialized in the procurement and shipment of goods. Quincy, his brother, spent his time in sabotage. He was involved, they think, in the unsuccessful attempt to burn parts of New York in 1864. That could have had a major impact—"

"Sam!"

"Right. So this Franklin Brian would ship to Hagerstown or Frederick, Maryland, tip off the troops in the Shenandoah Valley, which in turn would make one of their raids north, grab the goods, and head south. Sometimes, he could just load wagons and take the stuff to Winchester by a back road himself. He had a pass that let him through the southern lines and cleared him with Colonel Moseby's Raiders if they happened by."

Ike sat forward in his chair and noisily plunked his elbows on the desk.

"I know, I know, I'm getting to it. See, he would also talk to people. Ladies were leaving their farms and plantations to stay with families in the cities. Their men were off fighting and they, naively, thought their slaves would stay put. But they mostly headed north. So he'd talk to them and to valley residents and so on, and he began to hear stories about someone acting as a turncoat. Too many bivouacs were attacked and raids broken up by northern cavalry. It was like someone was tipping them off. It took him a year and a half, but it seems he found out who the traitor was. Now this is where the documents from Passaic come in. Brian wrote letters to his brother and sent messages to the Confederate Signal Bureau. He made copies for his own records. Some of them were in a kind of code. Not encrypted, just word substitution and initials for names.

"Now, listen to this." Sam pulled a copy of an old letter from the manila folder in her lap. "'Quincy,' he writes to his brother, who was arrested and hung about the same time as this letter so he may not have received it, 'Quincy, I'm heading south to "The prettier place"'...that would be Bellmore plantation. Get it? Bell—More, Prettier—"

"I got it."

"Right. 'I will proceed to...blah, blah...And take care of J. L. of the Home Guard.'...J. L., that's Jonathan Lydell—the first one—he was a captain in the home guard."

"And this leads us where?"

"For crying out loud, Ike read the story. *Captain Jonathan Lydell, Commander of the Home Guard, reports that a traveler resting for the night in his stranger room was found robbed and foully murdered...The traveler is reported to have been a Mister Franklin Brian...He had no baggage and no apparent reason to be in the Valley...*

"Franklin Brian...Captain Lydell...no baggage...There's a travel trunk in that stranger room with the initials F. B. engraved on a plate. It's in the picture. I enlarged it, and it's as plain as day. He was there. He must have confronted Lydell but before he could 'take care of J. L.' Lydell got the drop on him and killed him."

"And the locked room?"

"Distraction. People then, and today, too, are so caught up in the mystery of the how it got done they don't see the obvious."

"Which is?"

"The only person who could have shot Brian was Lydell. But the war was winding down, Sheridan will roar into the valley the next year, Appomattox after that, and everyone forgot. They had more important things on their minds then."

"So you allege that Jonathan Lydell, the original, shot this Brian character to keep from being exposed as a traitor?"

"Yes."

"You know it is not prosecutable? How does that relate to Grotz?"

"This is where it gets good. Guess what Grotz had in his possession, or looked at, in Passaic, New Jersey?"

"Brian's letters."

"Right. His letters, his brother Quincy's letters, and documents from several collections from all over the south. Some are missing, and I'm guessing he had them with him when he came to Bolton to see Lydell."

"He came down here to confront Lydell, the current one?"

"Confront? I don't know. Maybe he was writing a New Jersey in the Civil War book, and wanted to interview Lydell."

"And misjudged him. Lydell would do anything to keep that story under wraps. He has made a career of promoting his family as heroic and foremost in patriotism—Southern style. That revelation would destroy him. But murder?"

Karl, who had heard it all before, snapped his fingers. "Grotz wasn't writing a history. His wife said he had a 'big one.' History books about the Civil War are a dime a dozen, your friend Dr. Weitz's scholarly efforts notwithstanding. His writing is part of the academic routine, but there's no real money in one more book about an obscure spy and a murder. I doubt if a publisher would touch it, maybe an academic press, maybe he'd have to self-publish like Lydell. No, the big one Grotz had in mind was blackmail."

Ike nodded and pulled a sheaf of papers from a pile on his desk. "According to his bank statements, Lydell is nearly broke. Grotz puts the squeeze on him. He can't pay, not without selling off Bellmore. He's between a rock and a hard place. Grotz foolishly reminds him of the locked room business and, bingo, it all falls into place. He shoots Grotz with that old Webley and locks him up. *Res ipsa loquitur.* We could indict, but probably not convict."

"Because we don't know how he did it?" Sam said.

"How either of them did it. But Lydell knew. And he didn't make that up on the spur of the moment. His ancestor must have left notes, a clue, something."

"We could get another search warrant."

"We could, but not now. I think we'll sweat him for a while first."

Chapter Forty

Benjamin Harrison Winslow stubbed his cigarette out in the remains of his fried egg, and contemplated his grandfather across a littered breakfast table. When he visited Bellmore as a child, he'd thought of this man as god-like. There didn't seem to be anything he didn't know. Young boys, to their parents' occasional annoyance, make their grandfathers into superheroes. But at some point either senility sets in, or the boys develop discernment. In either case, their opinion undergoes a gentle or a radical adjustment. Ben's view of his grandfather had slipped remarkably of late. He resented the humiliation forced on his mother. He resented the snide dismissal of his law practice. His reading in the field had caused him to question his grandfather's knowledge of history. Since the old man announced his plans to restore Bellmore and turn it into a tourist attraction, like some financially destitute English nobleman, he thought the old man might have slipped a cog or two. All of this mattered to him only marginally until he heard what the sheriff had to say about his mother's accident. Something did not sound right.

"Tell me about mother's fall again."

"You heard it all. What's the use of rehashing a tragedy?"

"I need to hear you tell it. Indulge me. It's the lawyer speaking."

Lydell snorted. His opinion of lawyers in general, and his grandson in particular, had been the core of numerous noisy discussions in the past. He exhaled and gazed at him in what, Ben supposed, his grandfather believed to be a baleful look.

"Your mother drank to excess. She was very drunk that day. She fell down the stairs. End of story."

"The coroner said she wasn't drunk."

"The coroner is a fool. The whole police establishment in this town is run by fools. In my day—"

"It's not your day anymore, Grandfather."

"What? Not my day? Well, of course, it isn't. If I were in a position to rearrange things here, that sheriff and his people would be running a haberdashery and sweeping floors. Certainly they would not be holding positions of influence and…" Lydell slapped the table, sloshing half of his coffee from his cup. "They wouldn't be allowed—"

"To exist in your aristocratic world. I know. But they do and they ask questions and they make people think."

"Think," Lydell exploded, "think about what, may I ask? A man was murdered right here in this house and they have no idea how it was done. What kind of thinking is that?"

"You said how it was done, not who did it."

"Oh for heaven's sake, Ben, it's the same thing."

"As your attorney, I'm telling you, it's not the same thing."

"My attorney? Since when did I engage you as my attorney?"

Winslow studied his grandfather; took in the aging face and the lie in his eyes. He refilled his grandfather's coffee cup. "You haven't, but if I read that sheriff correctly, you will, and very soon."

"That sheriff will never…" Lydell brought himself up short.

"Will never what, Grandfather?"

"Nothing. Nothing. I don't need another cup of coffee."

"Tell me about the bruise on Mother's back."

Lydell leaned back in his chair so forcibly he almost tumbled over backward. "Your mother tumbled down a flight of stairs. Of course, she was bruised. I'm amazed there weren't more."

"What about the cocaine?"

"More nonsense. Don't you see what that man is doing? Typical of his race. He's planting seeds of suspicion. He's in over his head on this. He's grasping at straws. I have a good mind to call my friend, Colonel Scarlett, at the State Police."

"No cocaine?"

"No."

"No bruise?"

"No."

"And she was drunk?"

"Absolutely."

Lydell rose. Dropped his napkin on the table and stalked from the room. Apparently, he assumed Winslow would clear away the dishes. The number of them stacked in the sink and on the side board signaled he'd not accommodated to the loss of both his daughter and his cleaning lady. Winslow piled the latest next to the others, rinsed and refilled his coffee cup, and stepped out on the porch. A woman across the street at the bed and breakfast waved to him. He waved back.

Ike had made an appointment with Leon Weitz to look at the pennies. After hearing Sam's analysis, he thought he might cancel. The pennies were a minor and inconsequential concern, but in the end, he decided to keep it. He needed some time to process what he'd heard. Weitz would be a useful distraction. The fact that a trip up to the college would also put him in Ruth's orbit at lunchtime held some attraction for him as well.

Weitz spread the coins across his desk and screwed an old-fashioned loupe into one eye.

"You said these were in a tree stump? How long?"

"No telling, for years maybe."

"They're in pretty good shape considering. I'm guessing they had a dark patina on them before they were hidden. That helped."

"How?"

"If they had been shiny and then left out, the copper would probably have corroded quickly. That might have ruined their value, but the dark formed over the years, hundreds of fingers depositing oil, dirt and so on, made a sort of barrier. In the end, they would have gone but...I'm guessing they weren't in there for more than five years. Does that help in any way?"

"Sorry, no. What are they worth?"

"You have one collector's item here, a 1905. It's in pretty good shape. It could bring three or four hundred dollars. It appears the rest are all in the two to three dollar range. There are forty coins here. For the lot maybe you could raise something under five hundred dollars. Are they for sale? I'll buy them."

"Not yet, but I'll let you know if and when. Would iron corrode the same way, do you think?"

"I'm no expert, but iron oxide comes in two varieties. One is what you see on guns when they're blued. The iron oxide there is saturated, no more oxidation can take place, theoretically, FeO_4—black oxide—something like that. So gun barrels are protected from rust. Red oxide is FeO_3, I think. Apparently there's room for more oxygen or something. Iron can also be pre-rusted like you see on highway structures. Only they aren't blue. They're rust red. Same principle. Don't ask me about the chemistry—haven't the foggiest. Old iron that rusts slowly seems to protect it from sudden exposure to water and oxygen, the way these pennies were."

"Bright red rust then means that the iron was recently exposed, having little or no rust up to that time."

"I would guess so."

"Leon, for your help you gave Sam on the documents and for this, I should make you an honorary deputy."

"Not necessary. Just give me a shot at the pennies."

A stranger sat at Agnes' desk when Ike stepped into the President's outer office. He gave his name and the young woman, whom he guessed to be one of Callend's scholarship students, spoke to Ruth on the intercom.

"You may go in, Mr. Schwartz." Very cool, very formal.

Ruth swiveled around to greet him.

"What happened to Agnes?"

"She asked for a long weekend. She's going to quilt camp."

"To what?"

"A bunch of quilters get together and quilt or something. Like band camp only with needles. She's never had a vacation since we got here."

"Neither have you, Madam President."

"No, nor you. So are we type A or what?"

"Just stupid, I think. I'm going to take one this summer."

"Where?"

"Cop camp. You want to go with me."

"I'll take a pass. Tempt me with the beach or the mountains or Tuscany. Who's going to watch the store when you are gallivanting around...where are you really gallivanting to, anyway?"

"Not sure on the gallivanting locale. Since Whaite died, I've been stuck here for want of a reliable second in command."

"What about the tall guy you have on loan from the FBI?"

"He's not on loan anymore. He's a possibility but I'm working on something else, just in case."

"Leon helpful with your coin problem?"

Ike settled in one of the wingback chairs that faced Ruth's desk. "Very. Did you know he's writing a book about Civil War spies?"

"I suppose I should, but no. With all the machinations going on about this merger business, I'm out of touch with my faculty. Is that important?"

"The book? Only peripherally. We have a motive for, not one, but two murders."

"Who? Are you going to arrest somebody?"

"Can't say. Libel law, professional discretion, all that—and besides, if we can't put the guy in the locked room, we don't have much of a case."

"What will you do?"

"Sweat him. How about we get some lunch in your delightful cafeteria?"

"I brought a sandwich. I'll share." Ruth produced a brown paper bag from a drawer in her desk and peered inside.

"It's not one of those chick concoctions, is it?"

"A chick what?"

"Like chick-lit, chick flicks, quilt camp, like that."

"There are chick foods?"

"Oh, absolutely. Cream of broccoli soup, for example."

"I have a banana and this," she held aloft something wrapped in foil, "is cream cheese and olive on a bagel."

"Thanks for sharing, I'll take a miss." Ike turned to leave. Ruth repacked her lunch and cocked her head.

"Dirty copper."

"Excuse me. What did you say?"

"I was thinking about your pennies. That was an old joke when I was a kid. Question…How's a penny like Officer O'Hara? Answer…they're both dirty coppers. Get it?"

"Goodbye. One more like that and I'd have to run you in."

"Would that involve handcuffs? Because if it did, I might be persuaded to take the afternoon off…"

"I wish. But no, I need to call on a local aristocrat today. I'll check back with you about your arrest later."

"You'll never take me alive, Copper."

Chapter Forty-one

Ike found Sam in her office playing computer solitaire on one of the several screens arrayed across her desk.

"The black four can go on the red five at the far end," he said.

Sam jumped. "You startled me, Ike. Don't do that."

Ike recalled Karl's description of Sam when the rock came through their window and glanced at her hip. No holster, no Glock. "Sorry. I didn't mean to. Aren't you supposed to be in a car on patrol?"

Sam's jaw dropped. "What time is it?"

Ike told her.

"I lost track of the time. I haven't even had lunch."

"Neither have I. In any case, I need you to go with me to interview Jonathan Lydell. We'll stop at a deli and pick up something to eat on the way."

"You're going to accuse Lydell?"

"Maybe, maybe not. His grandson, the lawyer, is visiting and we may not be able to do much, but I want him worrying about what we might know."

They sat in the car, shaded by hundred-year-old oak trees, and studied Lydell's house a hundred yards away and across the street. Sam finished her Boca burger and diet soda and waited, her hands folded in her lap. Ike wiped the last bit of mayonnaise from his lips, crumpled the sandwich wrapper and said, "You ready?"

"Yes, as ready as I'll ever be. I've never had to do this before."

"Just stay cool and detached. Whatever you do, don't let him know you're rattled or intimidated—even if you are. Remember, we're the police. We are the authorities. He is under investigation. We don't need to explain anything to him. He has to explain everything to us."

"Until he lawyers up."

"Let's hope that doesn't happen too soon."

Sam put the car in gear and they glided to Lydell's front door, parked, and stepped out. Ike reached into the backseat and grabbed a fat folder.

"Remember, Sam, you're in reserve. I'm going to push him on the daughter thing. I don't want him to know everything and then have him go legal on us. I have a hunch we may peel his grandson, the lawyer, loose if we play this right."

Lydell answered their knock. The annoyed expression on his face made it clear he wasn't expecting them or anyone else.

"Sheriff," he said, and peered around the door jamb as if expecting more deputies to appear. "What can I do for you? This is quite unexpected. I'm in the midst of arranging my daughter's funeral. I have called the Governor's office. He's a busy man and may not be able to...why are you here?"

"Actually, we have a few questions that just can't be answered from the reports and your previous statements. About your daughter's accident—"

"You never quit, do you, Sheriff?"

"Do you mind if we come in? Perhaps your grandson should be here."

"My grandson? You think I need a lawyer?"

"No, no, certainly not, but it does concern his mother, after all."

Ike stepped around Lydell and found a place on an overstuffed settee. Sam, following his lead, chose a comb-back Hitchcock chair and perched on its edge. Lydell seemed taken aback by Ike, and retreated into the room. He found a place behind his desk, called his grandson who entered from the back of the house, and the four, arranged in a rough circle, stared at one another, waiting.

"Mr. Lydell, here is the problem…" Ike paused and shuffled some papers he'd removed from the manila folder he'd brought. He sighed and shook his head sadly.

"Problem? Problem? See here, Sheriff, I am tired of this constant harassment. I have told you, repeatedly, what happened. It is unconscionable that at this time…in the midst of my making funeral arrangements, you barge into my house just as you please and start in on this…this…witch hunt."

"I am sorry to bother you at this time but, as your grandson will tell you, loose ends are a policeman's bane. We hate them, and I don't want to be the one to hold up the funeral over a detail that surely you can explain."

"What loose ends? What detail," Lydell nearly shouted. "There are no loose ends. She fell. That's it."

Ike ignored Lydell and pulled one sheet of paper from the stack on his lap. "We have your statement that you were at the foot of the stairs and your daughter was at the top—"

"Yes, yes, where is this going?"

"We have a witness, the same that heard you arguing, who says you and your daughter were both at the top of the stairs at the time. Upstairs, you understand."

"He's mistaken."

Ben Winslow had been lounging on a sofa. At Ike's words, he sat bolt upright. "Say that again."

"The witness who heard the argument between your mother and your grandfather, places them both at the top of the stairs, and will also testify that while he did not hear the full content of the dispute, it most certainly was not about the evening's dinner menu."

"I won't have any more of this." Lydell's face had gone from pasty gray to scarlet. "You barge in here and say these awful things. Who is this witness, anyway? It's probably that idiot Henry Sutherlin. That whole family is dimwitted."

Sam watched this exchange with growing amazement. Ike brushed aside this last outburst.

"I just wondered if you'd like to amend your statement."

Winslow stared unblinking at his grandfather. Sam thought, if looks could kill, they'd have another homicide on their hands.

Lydell caught his grandson's look and began to sputter. "I...I..."

"We'll let you think about that for a moment. There is one other thing."

Lydell slumped back in his chair and fiddled with his watch chain. Sam wondered about his dress. How many people wore vests and riding jodhpurs around the house?

"We have been tracking the murdered man, Grotz. You said, when we talked..." Ike pulled another sheet of paper free from his folder and read, "'There's nothing to tell. I never met the man before, had nothing to say to him. He collected his key and went to his room.' And I asked, 'That's it?' And you replied, 'He was from up north somewhere, I think he said.' Is that the substance of your statement?"

"I said it. I do not equivocate, Sheriff."

"Sam, fill Mr. Lydell in on what you discovered about Mr. Grotz's reading habits." Sam hesitated. Ike shook his head fractionally. "Just Mr. Grotz's reading habits," Ike emphasized, "that's all."

He did not ask for the whole story, just enough to make Lydell wonder what they really knew. She collected her thoughts and then outlined the information they'd gleaned from the various sources in New Jersey. Nothing specific, just suggestive. Ike nodded as she recited her brief version of the story. When she finished, he turned back to Lydell.

"Apparently, he'd been studying your books and he was more than eager to switch places with another traveler to use your stranger room. It seems unlikely he wouldn't try to strike up a conversation with you. Wouldn't you say? I mean it would seem like he was a fan of yours. He didn't mention your books?"

Lydell squirmed in his chair. "Now that you mention it, he may have. I don't remember."

"May have." Ike scribbled something on the paper in his hand. "I see. He also had some documents pertaining to a Mr. Brian in his possession, we think. He didn't mention, by any chance, them to you, did he?"

Winslow held up his hand. "I think that's all, Sheriff. You are fishing. If you have a specific charge you wish to place against my grandfather, please do so. Otherwise, this interview is over."

Lydell recovered enough to rise and add, "And you are in this house against my wishes. You will leave and not come back."

Ike stood and motioned for Sam to do the same. "We will leave, but I promise you we will be back and with a search warrant. And when we do, we will tear this house apart. Good day, Mr. Lydell, Counselor."

He led Sam out the door, down the steps to the car. When they had driven for five minutes Ike turned to Sam. "You write up what you told us this morning and go to the judge for a warrant. I want that bastard."

Chapter Forty-two

Winslow watched the two police officers leave. He waited until their car turned the corner and headed back toward Picketsville and then turned on his grandfather.

"What did you do?"

"I don't know what you're talking about and I don't appreciate your tone of voice."

"I don't give a damn whether you like my tone of voice or not, old man. That sheriff knows something—"

"He doesn't know anything. Why he's just a—"

"He knows a whole lot more than he's letting on. What did you do?"

"A man like that. What can he know? I mean this is Picketsville. He's a hack politician's son."

"I looked him up, Grandfather. He's a graduate of Harvard undergrad and Yale law. He served in the CIA, I think. The record is a little vague on that. He is tough and smart. You can believe what you want to about Jews, country folk, and Black Americans, and all the other people who don't measure up to your social standard. I don't care. But you underestimate that man at your peril. I'll ask you one last time, what did you do?"

"Your mother falling down the stairs was an accident, I swear it."

Winslow paced the living room. A piece of carpeting placed near the coffee table, apparently to cover an old stain, snagged his toe and he almost tripped. He kicked at the carpet. "You are going to need a good lawyer, grandfather."

"You're my lawyer. You said so this morning."

"I try civil cases. Criminal law is out of my area."

"Criminal? I am not a criminal."

"Aren't you?"

"You shouldn't listen to those people, they—"

"Shut up! I am weary of hearing you go on about 'those people.' You may be the last of the Bellmore Lydells. I may be your blood, but I will not buy into your bigotry. And I will not defend you in court."

"Court? There will be no court. They can't prove anything. The man was found dead in a locked room. How can I be going to court?"

"That sheriff is smart enough to put together a *prima facie* case and he will take it to a grand jury and get an indictment. What happens after that is problematical, but everyone is going to hear what he has to say and, prosecution or no, you can kiss your connections at the statehouse and any of the friends, organizations, and honorifics you hold so dear, goodbye. Do you understand?"

"This is nonsense. I am Jonathan Lydell. I am not some share cropper, some janitor's son. They wouldn't dare."

"They will dare, and happily. I will get you the best lawyer I can find locally. You are still family and that's the least I can do. And then I'm going back to Richmond. I don't know what happened between you and mother. The possibilities suggested by Schwartz scare the hell out of me. So, I don't want to know. You talk to your lawyer. Come up with something. And you're right. The locked room protects you if, in fact, you need protection."

"You can't leave."

"They will be back here soon with a search warrant. I am constrained by professional ethics from saying this, so we will pretend I didn't, but a word to the wise, get rid of anything that might even suggest you had anything to do with anything. Burn it, shred it, bury it under a ton of manure, but get rid of it."

Winslow retreated upstairs. When he came down he had his bag in his hand.

"I called a firm in Winchester. They are very good at criminal law. They will call on you tomorrow."

"But your mother's funeral—"

"Start without me."

Essie huddled in the corner like a kitten confronted by pit bulls. The dogs in question were leaning across the booking counter. Ike had no idea what they'd said to her before he entered, but it apparently frightened Essie. The men turned as Sam and Ike entered. Randy LeBrun he knew. A stockier and shorter version of his brother, he had the same malevolent look and posture. The nondescript man next to him, he didn't know. He seemed merely scruffy. Ike gestured toward the men.

"Sam, you know Randy Lebrun and…" he turned to LeBrun's companion, "excuse me, I'm afraid I don't know your name."

"Oscar Benoit."

"…and his friend, Oscar." Sam took the two men in with a nod. "What can I do for you, Randy?"

"I came to settle a few things."

"That wouldn't include threatening my dispatcher, I hope."

"She sold George out. He's in the slammer because of her."

"He's in the slammer where he won't ever come out for kidnapping, possession, and for ramming a ten inch spike into your cousin, not to mention threatening to kill two of my deputies and my dispatcher."

"None of it would have happened but for little Missy there."

Ike turned to Sam while LeBrun spoke and muttered something in her ear. She frowned. "Probable cause," he said, and turned back to Randy LeBrun. Sam grabbed Charlie Picket by the arm and left.

"How do you figure that?"

"George, he was just a little shaky from the meth. He didn't mean nothing. Murder ain't in his nature."

"Tell that to Daryll's mother."

"Daryll had no business talking out of turn. He musta' really riled George to bring that on himself."

"I must say, Randy, you have a unique take on personal responsibility. Next thing you're going to tell me is you want to file a wrongful death suit against the department."

"I maybe might just do that."

"In that case you should probably check out the scene of the crime, as we say." Ike led him and Oscar Benoit to the cell once occupied by George LeBrun. The two men stepped in and Ike slammed to door closed.

"Hey, what's going on?" Randy yelled.

"Your cousin Daryll sang like a bird. One whole chorus was about you, Randy, and Oscar, thank you for identifying yourself. You had a verse or two as well. We're holding you on suspicion of drug trafficking. My deputies are turning your tractor inside out as we speak. What do you want to bet they will find drugs in the compartment under the seat?"

"You can't do this, Cop."

"I can. I am."

Sam and Charlie returned with a block of what could be uncut cocaine and several blocks of weed.

"There's more," Sam said. "This is just the start."

"It looks like you are going to be guests of the township for a while, gentlemen. Make yourself comfortable. You will be booked on as many charges as I can dream up, and that includes assault on Miss Falco. You each get a phone call."

"Assault? We never touched her."

"That would be battery. Assault is the crap you threatened her with before I came in. You and your brother are going to be spending some time together soon. Family reunion, you might say. Oh, and by the way, since your rig was where we found the stuff, it now belongs to the government. Have a nice day."

Ike turned his back and a deaf ear to the cursing coming from the cell. He gave a thumbs up to Sam and Charlie. Essie seemed calmer now that the men were behind bars.

"Ike, how much time you think he'll get?" she asked.

"Hard to say. But we're not done with him. If we can show he had anything to do with Daryll Jenkins' murder, and I think we can, he'll be in for accessory at least and that could be stretched to murder one. Either way, he's in for a long time. You'll be a grandmother before he's sprung."

Essie looked relieved. Ike hoped what he'd said to her was true. But, he knew the vagaries of the judicial system and nothing was a lock anymore.

He went to his office and pulled the evidence bag containing the tree stump materials from his desk drawer where he'd dumped them in the morning. He needed to look at the key once more.

Chapter Forty-three

Ruth's office door stood ajar. Agnes nodded to Ike and stood. She gathered her purse and a quilted bag Ike guessed had contained her lunch and started to leave. It would take a while to get used to an amicable Agnes. He waited for the next shoe to drop.

"How was quilt camp?"

Agnes beamed. "Wonderful. President Harris, I mean, Ruth, says you may be taking a vacation soon."

"It's a possibility, Agnes. Are you off somewhere?"

"It's nearly five, Sheriff."

Ike glanced at his watch. It was. He smiled Agnes out and peered around the lintel of the inner office door. Ruth, her back to him, finished a phone call.

"So where are we, or more accurately, where are you, Madam President?"

Ruth started and spun her chair around. "Holy cow, you scared the hell out of me, Ike. What are you doing here this late in the day?"

"Checking up on my woman."

"Excuse me, on your what?"

"Sorry. Grossly incorrect. Um…I'm following up on the state of affairs with my significant other. Better?"

"What is it with you, Schwartz? Why can't we have a simple conversation, using normal figures of speech and conversational gambits? Why do you need to push my buttons all the time?"

Ike flopped down in his accustomed chair. "I do more than push them, I'm happy to say."

"If you want to keep that occupation current, you'll show some respect around here."

"You are up to form, I see. Good news on the merger front?"

"Great news on the merger front. It's fixed."

"How, fixed?"

Ruth leaned back in her chair and began swinging it from side to side. "I took your advice and called in a business honcho to work on the details of the deal."

"Who did you call?"

"The big Kahuna himself, M. Armand Dillon."

"Ah. In that case, I would guess you got a good deal, or failing that, a fantastic severance package."

"Better than that."

"Wow, how better?"

"He said he did some 'due diligence'—"

"Which meant he made some phone calls."

"Exactly, and discovered that Carter Union College has its endowments locked up in unbreakable trusts. They can't flip them into the kind of dollars they need to stop the money hemorrhage from their bank accounts. With no room to expand, a fixed student body and, except for the business school, no other area of excellence in place or in the offing, they are the beggars, not us."

"So he bought the school and gave it to you for a wedding present."

"Wrong on both counts. Sorry…about the wedding part, anyway. No, he negotiated the deal so that Callend stays intact. I stay on as its president, and all those delicious endowments and the business school move here. We will add the Carter Union College of Business, complete with an MBA tract, to our liberal arts college and, thereby, become a university. Callend University. Tah Dah! And it all happened on my watch. So, what do you think?"

Ike had lifted himself from the wing chair and had begun pacing while she spoke. He was unsure where this would lead and uncertain whether he wanted to hear it all, either.

"I think it is a huge coup for you, for Picketsville, for education in general, and maybe the world. I'm not too sure about that last one, though. You have managed to slither Callend into coeducation without an upheaval to your school or its character, as well as gain some much needed dollars, and hang on to your job all at the same time. Nicely done."

Ike had his back to her when he finished.

"Ike...are you okay? Am I hearing real stuff or are you being ironic. Hey, look at me when I'm talking." Ike turned toward her.

"Me? Ironic? My, my, how you do go on."

"Okay, enough already. The deal will be done in a month or so, after the semester ends in May. I have my work cut out for me for the rest of the summer and the major part of next year. We have to reassign dormitories, integrate their male students, and figure out what to do with the redundant faculty. I will be up to my rear end in this business. You do remember that part of me?"

"How could I ever forget? Still no tattoo, I assume."

"None. If it would make you happy I can arrange one."

"Not necessary. I'll bring a magic marker next time. More fun, less expense."

"Yeah, yeah, dream on. Look, I thought the whole thing through, not just the Callend thing—the you and me thing—and, Lord knows I probably won't get a better offer—but right now, I just don't see how—"

"It's not our time, is it?"

"Can we just stay the same for a while?" Ike had stopped his pacing in front of the mantelpiece. He stared at the clock. "I'm sorry you went to all that trouble to buy a clock, too. I guess I do need more time, and maybe, that will remind me that it's ticking away, but for now..." Ike had opened the clock case and pulled the winder from it. "...you're not looking at me again."

"Right, sorry. It's something about the clock..."

"The clock? I love my new clock but I'm afraid you spent a lot of money…"

"No, no, that's not what I mean." He continued to inspect the clock's face. "You know, Ruth, we've only known each other for less than a year. You have a huge challenge facing you and I will only be a distraction in any case. We'll plateau. Is that about what you had in mind?"

"Plateau. Yes, that's a good way to put it. But…"

"But what?"

"It's about your car and parking…and, well…"

"We need to use my A-frame more often. Stick to weekends, normalize this business—stop acting like a pair of hormone driven teenagers. I've got the unmarked car, but I don't see that helping too much, so I'm going to spring for a used, nondescript Chevy…silver or gray, I think."

"It's a start. We'll think of something. Ike…?"

Ike had stopped listening again. He pulled the winder from the clock face and turned it over in his hands, fitted it back onto one of the winding stems and turned it, at first slowly then, more rapidly. He withdrew the winder and absently dropped it into his pocket.

"Buying this clock was not a waste, Ruth. It was a stroke of…what?…"

"Midnight?"

"Serendipity." He turned and smiled. "Would you be terribly angry if I said I am okay with maintaining the status quo? The truth is, I like pushing your buttons and a shift in our…relationship from courtship to, well…doesn't that sound just too…quotidian?"

"Will you please stop with the word builder? I mean…maybe you're right at that, too ordinary, everyday?"

"Not quite, but close, I guess. Anyway, we are not kids and we are not designed to go through life as Nick and Nora. You know what I disliked most about that series, the movies, I mean?"

"What series. What movies. Is this more of your classic movie channel trivia?"

"I'll explain later, but it was the appearance of the kid. Cute kid in a uniform—it just never worked."

"You've lost me. You're not upset?"

"Not really." He squinted at the clock once more. "As for the clock…by God, now I know how he did it, that slick old sonovabitch!"

"You've lost me. What slick old sonovabitch are you talking about?"

Ike gathered his jacket he'd tossed over the back of the chair and headed to the door. "I'll call you. Dinner tonight…your choice of restaurant…no wait, tomorrow night. I'll explain everything then. But right now I have to visit a judge, pick up a search warrant, and then see about arresting Jonathan Lydell for murder."

Chapter Forty-four

Ike gathered his deputies for a quick briefing. He'd asked three of the night shift to hang around and watch the office while he, Charlie Picket, Sam, Billy, and Karl went to confront Lydell. He glanced at his watch. It had taken longer to pry the search warrant loose from the judge than he'd expected. It was nearly ten in the morning. He'd spent the night going over the materials Sam had put together, the key from the tree stump, and two coroner's reports. Charlie Picket came into the office and waited, shifting his weight from one foot to another.

"Problem, Charlie?"

"It's my mother."

"Something wrong with your mother? Not sick, I hope."

"No sir. But she tol' me to tell you she had something important for you. She said that on the same day deputy Sutherlin and Miss Falco come near to getting shot, and I forgot. She is pretty short with me this morning and I promised to tell you."

"What did she want me to know?"

"You know my momma. Could be anything or nothing." Charlie handed Ike his cell phone. "She's on the line."

Ike chuckled and took the phone. "Hey there, Miz Picket, how you doing?" He listened and slowly his grin faded. "Be more specific...third floor...turn right. It's the first bedroom and I should check the bedding...yes ma'am, I think it might be very important. Thank you." He hung up and shook his head at Charlie. "Didn't you learn anything growing up, Charlie? You should always listen to your mother." He stepped into the outer office and called his group together. They had a busy morning ahead of them.

◇◇◇

A large black Mercedes blocked most of the space in front of Bellmore when Ike and the others arrived.

"Who's that?" Sam asked. "Undertaker?"

"I don't think Siegfried Unger owns anything that fancy. Possible though."

"Ike, shouldn't Lydell have a lawyer?"

"Last I heard, his grandson was staying with him. He's lawyer enough to keep him out of trouble. Besides, that is his worry, not ours."

When all of the deputies had parked, Ike signaled them over. "Billy, you and Charlie start in the basement, Karl and Sam, the third floor and attic. You are looking for papers, documents, diaries, things like that, and something that looks like this only bigger." He held up Ruth's clock winder. "You begin on my signal. Now, let's have a chat with Mr. Jonathan Lydell."

A fat man, with a bad comb-over and a shiny suit, answered the knock at the door. Ike could see into the room. Lydell and a third man, the precise opposite of the one at the door, were standing within. *Laurel and Hardy*, he thought.

"Yes?" Hardy said.

"I am Ike Schwartz of the Picketsville Sheriff's Department. I have two warrants to serve on Jonathan Lydell. May I come in?"

"What sort of warrants?" Laurel said from inside.

"Okay, I have had enough. Please step aside and tell me who you are and what business you have with Lydell."

The fat man did not budge. "I am Harvey Hergenroder and this," he jerked his thumb over his shoulder, "is my partner, Silas Mumpford. Perhaps you have heard or Hergenroder, Hergenroder, and Mumpford, LLC?"

Ike had. "You are his lawyers. What happened to the grand-son, Winslow?"

"He is not here. He engaged us yesterday and we are here to interview Mr. Lydell although I am not sure about what. He can't seem to elucidate any recent wrongdoing."

Ike handed two blue-covered folders to Hergenroder. "Warrants—one to search premises and property, a second for the arrest of Mr. Jonathan Lydell." He turned and called to Billy and Charlie who remained on the street. "Okay, you can start now." Karl and Sam followed him into the room. "Upstairs. You know what we're after. Top of the stairs on the third floor, turn right, first bedroom, turn the bedding inside out."

Lydell leaped to his feet. "This is outrageous. Tell them to stop."

Hergenroder held up his hand, read the warrants, and peered over his reading glasses at Lydell. "These are all in order, I'm afraid, Jonathan. They may search at will."

"I'll call the Governor. He'll have something to say about this."

"Sit down, Lydell," Ike snapped. "I've had all the hot air I can take from you. Mr. Hergenroder, please inform your client I will require his full cooperation. I will Mirandize him and then you can advise him how best to respond. We can, if he decides to be uncooperative, take him to our jail and continue there, but in view of his age and the seriousness of the charges, I believe here would be best."

Hergenroder nodded his agreement and Mumpford placed a hand on Lydell's arm to lead him to a chair. Lydell jerked free from Mumpford and positioned himself at his desk. Ike read him his rights. Lydell sniffed.

"You said murder, Sheriff. Can you be more specific?" Hergenroder was all business.

"Two counts of at least murder two. I think at the end of the day, it may end as two counts of murder one."

"Mr. Lydell," Mumpford said, "do you understand the charges?"

"You think I'm an idiot? Of course, I understand. This man has a mess on his hands and he wants to accuse me of crimes he can't possibly prove I did and..."

Mumpford and Hergenroder exchanged glances. Almost in unison, they cautioned him to say no more.

"Sheriff, you want to spell out what you think our client did?"

Ike settled on the same settee he'd occupied before and opened his folder, now much fatter than previously. "Certainly. The first charge is that he killed his daughter."

"Hergenroder," Lydell exploded, "this is what I was telling you about. My daughter fell down the stairs. It was an accident but this man—"

"It wasn't an accident. Your client insists, in the face of evidence to the contrary, that his daughter was drunk and fell. The coroner's report says she was not even marginally incapacitated."

"The coroner's a fool. Nobody will believe that quack. I said it before and—"

"The coroner has served in his official capacity for years. He is certified by the usual boards and commissions. He will be believed. Secondly, your client stated on numerous occasions that he was at the foot of the stairs when a witness places him at the top, with his daughter, at the time of the fall."

"The witness is the village idiot. His brother works for this man. It's all nonsense, a conspiracy."

Ike ignored him. "Here is what we think happened. Lydell, you were arguing about something, missing documents, I think, and maybe she taunted you, I don't know. She turned her back to you and in a fit of anger, you gave her a shove. The bruises on her back are most certainly those made by a hand forcibly pushing at her."

Hergenroder broke in. "Assuming you are correct in this allegation, and we are not accepting that, you understand, could it not be reasonably argued that his prior statements were clouded by the enormity of the tragedy?"

"Of course."

"And could it not also be argued that this alleged incident was done in the heat of the moment and certainly not an instance of murder?"

"It could. There is one more problem, however. Mr. Lydell, do you recognize this picture?" Ike handed him a photo of his daughter at the foot of the stairs. He glanced at it and turned away. His lower lip began to quiver.

"Yes, of course, I do."

"There is a pillow under her head. How did that get there?"

"I placed it there. I don't know. She looked so…uncomfortable."

"You called nine-one-one and fetched a pillow from the other room, and then knelt beside her and cushioned her head with a pillow?"

"That's what I said."

"Here's the problem. The coroner's report does mention a fractured neck but—"

"Precisely. She fell and broke her neck."

"No. That's not quite all of it. She fell, broke her neck but did not die. She was alive when you came down stairs. What did she do, plead with you, promise not to tell what she'd discovered about you? You went to this room, picked up the pillow and a bottle of bourbon. You held the pillow to her face until she suffocated. The coroner's report lists petechial hemorrhages on her neck, face, and perhaps in her eyes. You get those when you suffocate, not from a fractured neck. Then to make your drunkenness story work, you poured the whiskey in her mouth. It spilled on her clothes as well. Finally, after all that, you called for help and put the pillow under her head."

"You can't prove any of this." Lydell slouched back in his desk chair.

"Once again, Mr. Lydell, I caution you to say nothing." Hergenroder looked worried.

"You don't think a jury is going to buy this story from the only Jewish sheriff in the Commonwealth, do you? I'm Jonathan

Lydell. My ancestors were carving a civilization from the wilderness when his were still in Poland sewing shirts for the Tsar."

Hergenroder frowned at Lydell. "Petechiae can be produced a number of ways as you must know, Sheriff."

"Really?"

"Goodness yes, Rocky Mountain spotted fever, for example."

"I hardly think—"

"Chronic substance abuse, alcoholism, a subdural hemorrhage. Mrs. Winslow suffered a great deal of trauma in her tumble—a broken neck, who knows what else. Does your report have liver scans, a neurological assessment, brain studies, anything?"

Ike knew it didn't. Everyone accepted it was an accident at the time. The focus was on the locked room business and that had pushed common sense aside. The coroner had been asked to expedite the autopsy—by him, ironically—and he'd skipped over some of the finer points. Hergenroder was good. Hanging this on Lydell was going to be a challenge. He doubted the County DA would even try.

"Reasonable doubt, Sheriff...*ipse dixit*...and what were my client and his daughter arguing about that was so important that it could have resulted in this alleged scenario?"

A smiling Sam entered the room with a stack of papers.

"Unless I miss my guess, we'll know in a minute."

Chapter Forty-five

"Documents, Mr. Hergenroder. Documents that we believe Mrs. Winslow discovered, read, and after discerning their meaning, became the substance of the argument that led to her death."

"Give me those." Lydell rose from his chair. He stepped forward into the room and reached for the papers. "They belong to me. You have no right to them."

Ike took the papers from Sam. Mumpford had to forcibly restrain his client. He eased him over to the sofa and sat him down. Ike collected his folder, the papers, and took Lydell's place behind the desk where he could spread them out.

"They were obtained with a duly executed search warrant. We can take them. As it happens, Mr. Lydell, these are not your property. Several are clearly marked as the property of the Passaic, New Jersey Historical Society. They were removed from that facility by Mr. Anton Grotz, whom you murdered and locked in your stranger room."

"That's nonsense. I never met the man...I..."

"Then you will need to explain how these papers came into your possession."

Lydell slumped back in the sofa's cushions. He looked at one of them, pulled it aside, and held it up as if reading a book, and dropped it on the floor.

"Martha Marie," he mumbled.

"This is far too complicated for me," Hergenroder said. "Can you shorten this interview a bit? And then you will need to formally charge my client or leave the premises."

"I will try, Counselor, but I repeat. If we cannot deal with this here, we will go to the lock-up and do it there. You have the arrest warrant. The charges listed in it, stand. Is there a problem?"

"No, no, go on."

"Very well. Sam, tell these gentlemen what we discovered, in our attempt to understand why Anton Grotz was in Bolton in the first place."

Sam slowly and painstakingly walked the men through the scenario she'd laid out for Ike previously. As she spoke, Ike removed and displayed the appropriate document copies they'd received and, then the ones found in the upstairs bedroom. When she finished, Hergenroder scratched his head and fixed her with his best defense attorney stare.

"This is all speculation, is it not?"

"Not quite," Ike answered for her. He was not going to have his deputy harassed by a slick defense attorney.

"If I understand you correctly, you allege my client, when confronted with the story, only a story, mind you, of a potential blot on the family escutcheon, so to speak, pulled out an antique pistol, shot the poor man, and somehow managed to secrete him in a room which was, by your own admission, securely locked from the inside, correct?"

"Nicely put, Counselor, yes that is what we allege. Grotz was a mediocre freelance writer. His wife said he had stumbled on the 'big one' as she put it. He might have been writing a book about the Civil War, but that would hardly constitute the 'big one.' He had blackmail in mind, and your client is nearly broke. His only real asset is this house and what's left of the original acreage. His whole life has revolved around his family's history. A revelation like the one Grotz threatened to make would ruin him, emotionally, financially, and socially. There was no way he was going to let that happen."

"And so he murdered the blackmailer?"

"Not right away, I don't think, he had to prepare first."

"Prepare?"

Billy entered the room arms extended, palms up, and shrugged a *sorry*.

Ike nodded, paused, and pulled open the desk's drawers. On the third one, he smiled.

"Yes, prepare. The problem with killing Grotz? He would be the prime, no, the only suspect. Except for his daughter, there was no one else here who could have done it, you see? And she was, according to her father and our interview, dead to the world upstairs. What is the only reason someone would go to all the trouble of arranging something as complicated as a locked room mystery?"

"No idea. I've never run across one except in works of fiction."

"Exactly. Why indeed? The only reason would be to distract us from the obvious. The only person with a motive, and we have demonstrated that absolutely, and opportunity, is your client. He needed to divert us. Thus, the locked room."

"Very well, assuming that to be the case, and I am not as convinced you have the case you think you have, how did he do it?"

"That's the interesting part. Grotz's death is the second locked room murder to have occurred in this house, in that stranger room."

"Yes, so your deputy said."

"The first occurred in 1864. Mr. Lydell's ancestor, the first Jonathan Lydell, killed Franklin Brian, the southern agent working out of New Jersey, for much the same reason as the current Lydell killed Anton Grotz. These papers," Ike held up a handful of documents, "contain the letters from Brian to his brother. Lydell the first, if you will, the traitor, had informed Union Troops of the location and movements of General Early's units operating in the Valley. Brian felt he needed to take care of that Lydell. He, in turn, tumbled on what Brian had in mind, killed him first and then locked him up."

"You've already alleged that. You have a problem, Sheriff. You cannot prove the first murder, even if you wanted to, and the same holds for the current one. Once again—how?"

"Your client told me that his family members were packrats. Somewhere along the way he found a diary, a document…something, describing how the first lock-up was accomplished. Before he dispatched Grotz, he found it, collected the things he needed to pull it off, and then killed our victim."

"You have this alleged document?"

Lydell's rheumy gaze slid to the fireplace. A thin smile crossed his face. Ike followed his line of sight to the fireplace.

"I hope you had the foresight to stir those ashes around, Mr. Lydell. Otherwise we could reconstruct most of that paper."

"I don't know what you're talking about, Schwartz," he croaked. Smug did not do justice to the expression on his face.

"No matter. The how was easy enough to figure out, once I understood about the keys."

"You have no way of…a man of your background could not possibly have…" Lydell's face turned ashen.

"Keys?" Hergenroder stood and peered at his client.

Billy, who had been watching Lydell closely, stepped up to Ike and murmured in his ear. "He don't look too good, Ike."

Ike faced around, glanced at Lydell, whose complexion had turned gray-green, and said, "I think it would be a good idea to get an ambulance over here."

To Hergenroder he said, "Yes, keys. Door keys, clock keys, keys hidden in a tree stump—keys."

"Not possible," Lydell said in a gravelly voice and slid further into the cushions on the sofa.

"Very possible, simple, in fact. So simple, a descendent of the shirt maker to the Tsar could figure it out. When I asked Lydell to identify his pistol and anything else found in the stump, he hesitated. He had to acknowledge the pistol and the ammunition. He'd reported them stolen, after all. But he was stuck on the other objects. There was also a key and a box of Indianhead pennies. The pennies had some value and he wanted very much to claim them but if he did, he'd have to take the key, too. And he couldn't do that or, as they say, the cat would be out of the bag."

"I am not following you."

"Before we arrived, but after the door was forced, Lydell switched one of the keys. Later he hid his pistol, some ammunition, and the key in the tree stump. He didn't count on a trespasser finding them and ultimately their coming into our hands."

"Again, I'm lost here."

"You are, but Mr. Lydell knows exactly what I'm talking about." Ike removed the key, obtained from the tree stump, and laid it on the table. "Look at that key. Do you notice anything special?"

"Besides the fact it's rusty, no."

"It's old, handmade probably in the 1860s, and different from these others." Ike pulled out two keys from the desk drawer.

"You can't know." Lydell said in a weak voice. His face had shifted to gray-blue.

"How about that ambulance, Billy."

"On its way, Ike. I know CPR, I'll watch him."

"The cross-sectional area at the end, Mr. Hergenroder. This key was made from square stock, the others from round. Does that suggest anything?"

"Sorry. I'm a lawyer, Sheriff, not a locksmith."

"Would you like a demonstration?"

"No!" Jonathan Lydell slid off the sofa and landed on the floor like a bag of laundry. "Martha Marie, I'm sorry," he said, his voice barely a whisper. His eyes rolled up, he coughed one last time, his jaw snapped shut, and he went limp.

Billy leapt to his side and took a carotid pulse. He looked up at Ike and shook his head.

"Try," Ike said. Billy began CPR. In the background a siren wailed as their ambulance drew closer.

Too late.

Chapter Forty-six

By the time the last of the gawkers cleared the area and the Picketsville fire department, ambulance, and crews pulled away, lights flashing but sirens muted, it was mid-afternoon. The sun had already started its descent westward and shadows crept across the roadway. Ike, his four deputies, and Lydell's attorneys stood on the porch and watched as the vehicles turned the corner and headed for Stonewall Jackson Memorial Hospital in Lexington. Lydell's stay there would last only long enough for an official death certificate to be generated and then he would join his daughter at Unger's funeral establishment in Picketsville. Smoke from a chimney drifted down the street scenting the air with burning softwood, apple, Ike guessed. A little early but it would turn chilly in a few hours.

Silas Mumpford, who had had little to say throughout the morning's interview, shook his head and clucked, "Terrible way to go."

"I'm not sure. Quick, apparently painless, and better than dying in jail," Ike said.

"I don't think he would have gone there, do you?"

"Yes, I think so."

"You really think you could get a conviction?"

"Not for me to say. It would depend on the DA, but for my money, if I were prosecuting the cases, that old man would be locked up for the rest of whatever remained of his life. How many men will kill a child of theirs to preserve their reputations?"

Hergenroder cleared his throat. "You don't know that he did. Your take on what happened on that stairway is, at best, an untested assumption. I could get him off. Except for the petechial hemorrhages, the case against him for the daughter's death is purely circumstantial. And, as I said before, there are too many other possible explanations for the hemorrhages. The poor man would sit there in court looking ancient, weak, and broken. Reasonable doubt, Sheriff. No jury would ever convict him on a charge of murder two."

"Maybe, maybe not. DA's call."

"And the locked room business. I would hammer away at that. And the rest of your case, elaborate as it is, is also entirely circumstantial. Maybe it was blackmail…maybe not. Fingerprints on his own gun that he's reported stolen…an unemployed writer he didn't know—couldn't have known…Sheriff, your chances of a conviction would be slim to none. Again, picture the poor old man who just lost his daughter in a tragic accident, sick, tired—you get the picture. He walks. If you can't put him in that room with the body, your case is toast."

"But I *can* put him in that room—him and his namesake ancestor as well, for that matter."

"You mean you weren't bluffing about knowing the method just to get Lydell to crack? You really do know?"

"No, I wasn't bluffing and, yes, I can show you how it was done."

"I'm glad to hear it. If I thought you had pretended to know the secret and the old man had a heart attack because he believed you, I would have been pretty upset, more than upset, in fact. I might have brought charges against you. You really weren't bluffing?"

"Not at all. Would you like to see how he did it?"

Hergenroder hesitated. He glanced at his wrist watch and seemed about to leave. Mumpford broke in, "I would. Yes, indeed, I would very much like to see how it was done."

Ike retrieved the keys from the parlor. "Okay. Again, please look at these three keys. They are all similar except in one important way."

The two attorneys and four deputies crowded around and studied the keys.

"You told us that the rusty one was square in its cross sectional area but I don't get the significance. The other two are identical except one seems longer than the others."

Ike led them to the stranger room door. He unlocked it with the longer key. Then as they watched he demonstrated that each of the three could lock and unlock the door from the inside.

"Three keys," he lectured. "It's important. All three will throw this bolt. Now watch."

He inserted each of the shorter keys in the lock from the outside and demonstrated that they were not long enough to throw the bolt.

"Now then, Lydell claimed this key was in the lock on the inside and prevented the longer key from working." He held up one of the shorter keys. "But in fact it was this key." He held out the rusty one. "See, with either of the shorter keys in the lock from the inside, and slightly off-center, the bolt cannot be moved from the outside."

"So, the door had to be locked from the inside. How?" Mumpford asked.

Hergenroder held one key up. "Someone could have used pliers to grab the end of the key and turn it from the outside,"

"I thought of that—very thin needle nosed pliers, perhaps. But the distance from the outer key hole to the tip of the key in the lock is just too great—maybe two and a half inches. Even if you could reach in that far, you couldn't open the pliers' jaws, grip the tip and then turn it, and especially a rounded one like this."

"You'd need a special tool, then."

"Not special in the sense you mean, but yes, special. Look, let's assume Lydell used the rusty key, the one he put in the tree stump."

"Back up. What has happened up to this point?"

"Right. First he shoots Grotz in the back. As with his daughter, Grotz isn't dead. He steps over and shoots him once more in the forehead. I think he did this in the parlor next door."

"Why?"

"The carpet that Grotz was lying on did not go with this room. Whatever else Lydell may have been, you can see from the way this house is decorated, he had a sense of style and color. That carpet came from next door. I'd bet on it. In fact, when we're done here, I'm going to shift the rug under the coffee table, in there, and see if we can't dig out one slug and turn up some trace blood stains."

"All right. So, next, he drags Grotz in here and then what?"

"Then he puts the rusty key in the lock like this," Ike slipped the key in the lock from the inside. "And then he uses this." He produced a clock winder from his pocket.

Hergenroder squinted at the object and said, "What the Hell is that? It looks like a crank."

"Clock winder," Mumpford answered, "judging from the length of the stem, it must be from a pretty big cabinet clock."

"Correct. Look at the end. The shaft had a square cavity in it designed to fit over a clock winding stem—a square winding stem, you see?" Enlightenment appeared on their faces. "I'm sure it was this one, there is still something that smells like bee's wax in the end. I expect he put that there to make it sticky. Anyway, as Mr. Mumpford has noted, this winder has a very long shaft. It's the special tool you imagined, Mr. Hergenroder. Watch. I slip this winder in the lock from the outside, fit it onto the square end of the key that is already in the lock, pull the door to, and use it like a crank to throw the bolt. Once done, I pull it out but I leave the inner key off center. Try to unlock this door."

Hergenroder took the larger key from Ike and tried to insert it in the lock and failed. "I'll be damned, the room is locked from the inside."

"Precisely."

"And in the excitement of discovering the body—"

"He switched the keys, just in case."

"But he didn't count on a descendant of the Tsar's shirt maker to figure it out."

"Or that a kid, named Tommy, would raid the tree stump after he cached the pistol, ammo, and the key."

"How did you figure it out, anyway?"

"Routine police work. Any of these deputies could have done it."

The four in question looked dubious.

"Okay, I was standing in front of an antique clock trying to follow a conversation that I really did not want to hear, and there it was right in front of me. The clock had a winder like this one. I used it to wind the clock and I remembered the rusty key and…" Ike spread his hands.

At a signal from Ike, Billy reentered the parlor. The remaining six stood quietly staring at the door. Hergenroder exhaled and turned to Ike.

"Can I ask you a personal question, Sheriff? What do you intend to do with all this?"

"All this…what?"

"My client is dead. Are you planning to make this whole business public? After all, you solved a locked room mystery, possibly two locked room murders, involving this area's most prominent citizens. That is not something someone does everyday. It could create a great deal of very positive publicity for you."

"Not my thing, Counselor. As you said, the man is dead. I can't see dragging him through the mud now. No, I'll write a report and file it. That'll be the end of it."

"The locked room, though…" Mumpford said.

"I'll give the details to Dr. Leon Weitz at the college. He's writing a book about spies and the Civil War. He'll be happy to have it. It ties up a loose end. Hardly anybody reads those academic tomes and, if they do, they will not care much one way or the other about your client. This house and family are probably going to end up as a chapter."

"Thank you, Sheriff. I was afraid you might be one of those publicity seeking, political animals like your…"

"Like my father?"

"I didn't want to say it, but yes."

"No problem. I love my father and normally I would take offense, but not today."

"No offense intended."

"Bullshit. Billy, what did you find under the coffee table?"

"Dug out the slug like you guessed."

"Mr. Hergenroder, do you have any more reasonable doubts?"

"We're done here, Sheriff. Perhaps we'll cross swords again some time."

"Let's hope not."

Chapter Forty-seven

The sun hovered over the mountains to the west, poised to make its daily plunge beyond the valley's western horizon. Thin cirrus clouds drifted across the sky promising a spectacular sunset. Ike had the grill lighted and generous burgers wrapped in waxed paper ready on the counter when Ruth drove up. She struggled up the steps of the A-frame dragging a heavy suitcase.

"You planning on moving in?"

"Would you object if I did?"

"Nope, but that isn't just an overnight bag, I think."

"Very observant, Ike. That's why you're such a good cop."

"Thank you, I think." He reached out and took the handle and lifted the case to the landing. "What's in here, your rock collection?"

"You must be getting weak in your old age, Hon. I carried this down a flight of stairs, across a parking lot, and put it in my car."

"Hon? Where did that come from?"

"I spent an hour on the phone with a distant cousin from Baltimore."

"Gotcha. So the case is...?"

"We said we'd try to be discreet, remember. No more sneaking around the President's house, my house, in the middle of the night and so on. You remember, we had a conversation—"

"I remember. The case...what's in the case?"

"Okay, so here is the place we meet from now on, weekends, whenever possible. But that's it. I brought some casual clothes, toothbrush, that sort of thing. I'm going to leave them here."

"Good thinking. I like it."

"Be careful, it's a serious move, Ike, a step toward permanency, a foot in the door, the…"

"Camel's nose in the tent?"

"Whatever. Are you sure you are okay with that?"

"I bought a car yesterday."

"Good move. A Chevy?"

"Even more unobtrusive, a five-year-old Buick."

"A retirement community special. I'm impressed." Ruth dragged her case across the floor. "I can't remember…you do have closets around here, right?"

"Closets, dresser drawers, you name it. Just move my stuff aside if you need to."

Ruth looked through the glass sliders at the deck that faced the down slope at the rear of the house. "I'm going to do something about this winter pallor this weekend. I'm going to lie out on that deck and…what did we used to say…catch some rays."

"You brought a bathing suit?"

"I don't need one."

"You don't need…oh…umm. I'll start cooking now. Be five minutes."

"Make it ten, I want to shed this power suit and get into something comfortable."

Twenty minutes later Ruth reappeared in an acid-washed tee with a picture of Natural Bridge across the front, worn jeans, and Birkenstocks. She'd scrubbed her face and gathered her hair back in a ponytail.

"Nice," Ike said.

"You like? Consider this, Lover, this could be what you'd be looking at over the breakfast table someday."

"What a person may or may not look like over toast and eggs is not the test you want to make, if you're thinking of getting serious."

"No? What is the test?"

"What will she or he look like when you are trundled into an ambulance during a heart attack, or when you're diagnosed with cancer, or when you are rendered helpless by a stroke? Who the hell cares about style and grace then?"

Ruth gazed at Ike with something close to tears in her eyes. "You are a 'keeper,' Schwartz." She looked at the dinner on the table. "And you can cook, too."

"Burgers from the frozen food section, salad in a bag, and I nuked the potatoes. If you call that cooking, you really are easy."

"No dessert?"

"For you, mocha latte ice cream. For me—you."

"You're on. So, have you decided on your vacation?"

Ike tonged salad into two wooden bowls, plopped the burgers into buns, and hot fingered the potatoes onto plates. "Sour cream is in that little plastic tub. I'm thinking beach. Do you want to come?"

"Catsup? Who'll watch the store when you're gone? Is Karl Hedrick going to stay?"

"Here," Ike shoved the catsup bottle across the table. "Karl needs to find out if his indiscretion cost him a career so, no, at least not for now. If he returns it won't be for six months or more."

"Who then? Not the cowboy."

"Billy? No, but you're close—his brother Frank. What almost happened to Billy upset his mother enormously so Frank decided to transfer from the State Police to the Picketsville Sheriff's Department. It allows him to be closer to home."

"Very convenient. How's it going to be with two Sutherlins working for you?"

"Three Sutherlins. Billy is marrying Essie Falco. He'll be moving out of the house and Frank isn't married and will move in, so that works out fine. I figure in three months or so, he can take over temporarily."

"What's the wine?"

"Tuscarora Red, from that place out near Raphine where Agnes got the ice wine."

"It's good. Four months from now will be too late for the beach."

"The beach is best after Labor Day, off season, quiet, and peaceful. Only you and Frank will know my phone number. Would you be interested in finishing your tan in September at the beach?"

"No way. I will be up to my you-know-what then. Maybe I'll catch up on a weekend, but don't count on it. Holy cow, look at that sunset!"

The moon, at full, lighted the loft and painted their bodies silver. Ike rolled over on his side to admire the view, that is to say, Ruth, and that's when he saw it. He did a double take and peered closer. It was small but unmistakable, between her breasts.

"You have a tattoo." He looked again. "Good Lord, it's a tattoo of Tweety Bird."

Ruth began to giggle, one of those throaty ones that seem to bubble up from somewhere down deep. "I bought a whole book of transfers at the drug store. I saved all the Sylvester the Cats for you." She propped herself up on one elbow, faced him and punched him on the arm. "I taught I taw a puddy tat!…"

Ike flopped back on his pillow with a hoot.

"Now that was a classic movie."

To receive a free catalog of Poisoned Pen Press titles, please contact us in one of the following ways:

Phone: 1-800-421-3976
Facsimile: 1-480-949-1707
Email: info@poisonedpenpress.com
Website: www.poisonedpenpress.com

Poisoned Pen Press
6962 E. First Ave. Ste. 103
Scottsdale, AZ 85251